"I had come to know silence well during those months after my mother died. When you sit in silence long enough, you learn that silence has a motion. It glides over you without shape or form, but with weight, exactly like water."

Magda's mother always said the world was full of strange and beautiful secrets only the two of them could see. But now she's gone and Magda's world is flooded with anxiety and loneliness—and maybe, madness. As an imaginary family of bickering fish begins to torment her, Magda's only outlet is starting beautiful but destructive fires in the marshes near her house.

The Shape of Water is a darkly lyrical and surprising tapestry of the mundane and the surreal, in which Magda begins to untangle her family's secrets and search for a stable place in the world.

• • •

This book, as all else I do, is dedicated to my children:

Christopher, Philip, and Emma

the shape of water

anne spollen

flux
™
Woodbury, Minnesota

First Edition
First Printing, 2008

Book design by Steffani Sawyer
Cover design by Lisa Novak
Cover image © 2008 Ken Wong
Fish graphic © 2008 Ken Wong

Flux, an imprint of Llewellyn Publications

The Cataloging-in-Publication Data for *The Shape of Water* is on file at the Library of Congress.
ISBN-13: 978-0-7387-1101-0

Flux
Llewellyn Publications
A Division of Llewellyn Worldwide, Ltd.
2143 Wooddale Drive, Dept. 978-0-7387-1101-0
Woodbury, MN 55125-2989, U.S.A.
www.fluxnow.com

Printed in the United States of America

chapter

one

I discovered windows one afternoon and after that, nothing was ever the same. They had always been there, of
course, glass panes shimmering in the color of rain, but that
spring, for the first time, I was able to open the windows in
my room. The locks had been painted shut for years, but
during that winter the heat from the radiator finally steamed
enough paint off the metal wings, and the locks could be
twirled open. Knowing that I could open the windows
attracted me to them, and I began sitting under them, staring through the glass at the sky. From that position, on a
chair in my room, the sky did not seem real; it seemed a
place I was making up, so I watched it.

The white wood of the windowpanes acted as frames, so the sky came to me slowly and the huge openness of its space did not touch me. All the window glass in our old house had waves and bubbles inside it, so at times the clouds moved by like water, melting and blurring until they passed outside of the warp. But after a few afternoons of sitting, the heavens seemed too quiet to keep watching, so instead I began watching a small patch of woods next to our yard that housed little more than trees and a scatter of bony, mean-looking rabbits.

I started gazing at the sky and the woods in March when the branches were still wet, and it was then, with nothing outside my windows but trees and rain, that I noticed a shine inside darkness, colors glimmering within the darkness of the wood. I watched birds come and go, I watched rain nipple down from buds to the grass. The water dripping from branch edges and leaves created optical tricks; I could see that as I watched leaves melt.

Then one day I ventured into the space outside. I did not think about doing this much beforehand. I simply opened a window and dropped to the ground below, uncertain as to why this should be a so much more satisfying exit than simply using the door; my father worked until seven o'clock and I could do whatever I wanted until then. But I liked the solid sound my legs made when I landed. Leaving via a five-foot drop seemed so much more a *decision* than just using a door. The sense of escape made my heart pound, though all I escaped was the soundless spread of moss-colored light inside my house, and the silence.

I had come to know silence well during those months

after my mother died. When you sit in silence long enough, you learn that silence has a motion. It glides over you without shape or form, but with weight, exactly like water. Its color is silver. And silence has a sound you hear only after hours of wading inside it. The sound is soft, like flute notes rising up, like the words of glass speaking. Then there comes a point when you must shatter the silence, when you must shatter the blindness of its words, the blindness of its light.

I did this by going into the yard. Once I stood there, in the grass next to the trees I had been watching, I found silence outside as well. But I was happier outside than I had been in the house, so I stayed for a bit. I stood beneath my bedroom windows for a few minutes, looking up at the branches and the crooked pieces of sky colliding between the branches. I believed I could identify the scent of the sky as I stood there, a blue menthol fragrance similar to the scent of seawater that sprayed into my face when I first dove into the ocean. That initial scent was much more subtle than the ocean's heavy, fishy aroma; it was a whiff of salt and mint, just as I approached the water on a dive, that warned that a more powerful scent would soon enter my nose. It was the scent I dreamed in. And it was the scent of that spring sky as I stood in my yard.

I repeated this act of leaving through the window each day until the middle of April, when I decided to leave the yard as well. I had never been drawn to the outdoors in the way some people are, always gardening or jaunting off to the beach or the park. The first time I ventured outside, I stood in the yard for a few minutes listening to the silence concuss. The silence outdoors differed from the silence inside the house. Here, I stood inside a cavity with no borders, with no limits, a place as terrifying and infinite as the ocean, as space. At least inside the house, I could believe the silence ended, that it was finite, that once I stepped out of the house I would find the rest of life continuing. The silence outdoors stunned, and the first few times I stood in the yard, I could not move. So I had to will myself to leave the yard, a task that some days I could not carry out, and on those days when I could not leave, I retreated back inside the house, the sharp taste of failure filling my mouth.

When I finally left the yard, boredom helped me grow bolder. Each day I walked farther until I began walking through the woods to adjacent blocks. Our neighborhood spread about a mile up from Raritan Bay, through a simmer of marshes to dry woodland. Nothing was balanced about this section of Staten Island. Houses in our neighborhood were separated by large thatches of woods, or they were so close together that someone doing dishes in one house could glance up from the sink to see the family next door doing their dishes. Bungalows abutted glassy, modern homes, duplexes shadowed the backyards of older homes. In this jumble of buildings and residences, a bait shop might be directly next door to a family house; a family house might have a side yard where cars were painted or boat engines were stored.

At the top of our streets ran a four-lane boulevard, a seam separating where we lived, in the older, beachier part, from the newer houses. If our neighborhood lacked symmetry, this neighborhood defined it. All the houses above the boulevard were new and resembled one another, candies in a box. They each had the same size yard, the same number of windows, the same placement of doors and driveways, as though the streets served as a board game and the houses were the playing pieces. The windows were positioned on either side of the door so that each house had the appearance of a face looking out over a long, rectangular nose. The only trees were short shrubs planted by the owners, all in the same spots so that the shrubs resembled nothing more than a green collar framing the glassy faces of the houses.

Near us, veins of tree branches twisted, vacant bungalows, uninhabited for years, listed, emitting the same haunted damp as caves. Marshes harbored milky plants that grew pods and sharp-beaked Halloween birds gackled about. Walking our streets, surfaces changed without warning from asphalt to woods to sand. Up there, in the miles of new housing, the streets stretched predictably in the way I imagined the days lived inside them to stretch, shaped by routine, each day dissolving perfectly into the next.

On one of those streets lived my closest friend, Julia Hallon. I thought of her house each time I looked to the boulevard, the way her mother had planted circles of flowers around each sapling, the way she had placed frothy curtains so each window appeared iced and festive as a cake.

Life proceeded differently inside those houses, that much I knew. Those houses existed in the same safe pocket

I slipped inside each time I went to school or watched television, a pocket stitched in such a way that dream and error could not enter. I had been allowed enough glimpses into that pocket, where those lives were kept, that I had begun to recognize the smooth contours of their fabric. On Julia's last birthday, we went ice skating with our mothers and two of Julia's cousins. My mother skimmed the ice with the fluid grace of falling snow. When she saw Julia clutching the edge of the rink, my mother took her hand.

"It's really no different from swimming, Julia. You just have to lose your land legs and open to the ice."

Julia shook her head. "I can't. I'll fall."

Mrs. Hallon had looked on, her mouth tightening with the realization that her surprise party might be failing.

"If you predict you'll fall, then you probably will. Let's predict that you'll make it to the circle over there." My mother pointed to a circle about ten yards from where she stood with Julia. "I'm telling you, Julia, it really is like swimming. You just have to give a few things up. And the first one is your assurance of gravity."

"Give up gravity," Julia repeated, a little stunned by my mother's phrasing. But she took my mother's hand and managed to skate to the circle. Mrs. Hallon's face brightened and her admiration for my mother was as obvious as the lighting of a neon sign. The party went on, the birthday was celebrated, plans proceeded according to Mrs. Hallon's schedule.

Back at Julia's house for the cake and ice cream, her mother turned to me.

"Maggie, your mom really saved the day. I'm not sure

what would have happened if she hadn't been there. I guess I thought Julia was more athletic than she is."

I nodded and murmured something vague and gauzy to match the party mood. I wanted to tell Mrs. Hallon that nothing would have happened, at least if it had been me who had feared the ice. My mother would not have held the party; she would have changed plans entirely and taken me to a movie instead, or out to watch birds land on a pond. We lived a life that moved more with the plans and motions of water. Julia's life had walls and dams, places of prediction and intent. Julia's life, unlike mine, would never collapse. I thought this while looking outside at the solid roofs of the houses surrounding her house, at the endless rows of fencing.

Our neighborhood had no such geography, and at times the whole area did not seem real, with ocean fog and smoke from beach fires left to smolder. People coming out to retrieve the morning paper or relieve their dogs could look like ghosts in the haze, their bodies moving in an edgeless way so that if I looked too quickly, I believed spirits had come up from the beach—drowning victims or lost sea captains, come to reclaim what they had not finished during their time on earth. Then I realized it was only the old, retired tugboat captain who hollered nonsense out his windows, or the always-drunk lady out to check the mail that had piled in her box for days. I could not imagine these people or these acts occurring in Julia's neighborhood, or anywhere above the boulevard. We lived in one of life's basins, a place where whatever or whoever could seek refuge.

I asked my mother about our neighborhood once, why

it was so open, so irregular. She explained that we lived closer to the wind, to the water, where ancient dreams still spirited the air. My mother wanted me to like where we lived, to like the susurrus of the sea and the way wind rose from the ocean year-round, to like our house, which was dark and old and sprouted lozenges of mold under the eaves. Because she had wanted me to like it, I said I did.

But even back then, before my mother began having headaches that blackened her vision with their force, I thought of the homes above the boulevard, over us, as permanent, as a place where no raw examples of life or death lay on the surface as they did on our beach. Up there the only moving life, other than human, was an occasional well-mannered dog or a yard cat.

On our beach, my mother and I found starfish adhering to logs; we watched crabs scurry back to the water; we found eels and fish inside logs and barrels. Many of them were dead, their flesh and veins open to the salt air or the birds who pecked at their stilled forms. Swimmers walked past the bodies, or swam and floated around the ones that were washing ashore, as if the water served as a margin between life and death, a place where boundaries vanished.

The houses above us were quietly contained places, and as I began school and met children mostly from the new houses, I separated the two places in my mind: I gave them names. The houses above us were "the standard," and where we lived was "the drift"—a place that changed, a place more prone to oddities and the random, shaping forces of wind, of water, a place of motion. The standard had stillness. I told my mother what I thought of the two places and she said, "But who would want to live in stillness? Here, we have treasures, surprises." I knew what she meant and because I did, we lived apart from most other people, or we did until she died. Then I was alone.

I feared the standard, feared that I had lived too long in the drift to ever leave its silent strangeness. I feared that the drift had formed me, and wherever I went its influence would be evident, setting me apart as people noticed a certain peculiarity to my thoughts, to my behaviors. And I could not stay in the drift much longer. It was too lonesome, and far too terrifying a place to inhabit alone; my mind was growing in strange directions inside all the silence. I tried to explain some of this to Julia one day during gym.

"You are so weird," she had laughed after I whispered to her how ever since my mother died, I saw creatures and heard sounds I never knew existed before. "You probably just need to get more sleep. Or stop reading so much. Maggie, all that reading is making you think this way."

I laughed with her, but her response warned me that I could not approach her again. Not only did I lack the knowledge of how to exist in the standard world, I lacked the tools to obtain that knowledge as well. Julia would have phrased her awareness in a way that would have been interesting; I could imagine being curious about her new-found abilities. I spoke more in the freighted tone of public confession. And I certainly could not tell her about the fish that had begun swimming in and out of my thoughts, their scales glittering like patches of sun in a cloudy sky.

I had to get better control of my mind. My thoughts existed much like the chaos below the ocean's surface, seemingly quiet while an entire universe scurried about beneath shining glosses of water. It was the same with my brain, with my mind, with the oddness of thoughts that were only all right with my mother, or alone at the beach. To see me at school, behaving and acting normally, nodding and walking like everyone around me, was to see my shining gloss. The rest of me, most of me, was hidden like the secret of undertow. And I could no longer remain inside the undertow; I was alone there with silence and memory and gazing. Each of these activities had begun speaking to me in the slow, weighted vocabulary of loss. I would have to think of a way to leave.

Leaving my room was a beginning. Once my feet had landed so solidly on the ground outside, I knew I could never return to sitting by the window, to the solitude of that place that moved like a dream unfolding backwards. I would have to leave the silence that waited to swallow me in a waterless drowning.

The idea of the buses came to me one day as I looked up to the boulevard while standing on the sidewalk by my house. I could see the buses stuttering along, boxy vehicles slow and lumbering as elephants, yet they offered containment within the vastness of the outdoors. To reach the nearest bus stop, I had to wait in front of a strip of stores that were as random as the contents of a tide. A pet store stood apart from a bakery that led into a tavern, a shoe repair shop shared a roof with both a deli and a notions store. I never saw people inside any of these places and the whole mess seemed ghosted.

The junk shop especially terrified me. It looked entirely constructed of dust, and its sepia-toned window held items that had no reason to be together: vacuum bags shouldered typewriter ribbons and dolls, spools of thread tumbled around drill bits, tins of candy towered in one corner. Under the eaves of the notions store, a string of Christmas lights had rusted into place. The wire dipped just below the overhang and the few remaining bulbs had all broken, resulting in a jagged hobo's grin. I could not imagine whoever shopped in such a place. While waiting for the bus, I brought a book with me to avoid glancing at the stores. It was while standing there, in the middle of the day right on the boulevard with cars and trucks and bicyclists whirring around me and the ghostly notions shop behind me, in the middle of that day where everything was running as normal as water, that thoughts of fires would not leave my mind.

I did not want to think of fire, to think of the girl who had set the fire. I could not get my mind to obey. I wondered if the junk shop pressed the memory of fire on me, pressed on me with the weight of two hands resting on my shoulders. The building's air of defeat, of failure and disuse, would stir dark thoughts in anyone.

I pushed the image of the fire from my mind. I stared into my book. I knew my mother would walk away to the next bus stop. She believed places influenced us, she believed in spirits and premonitions, in the ability of wind to prompt vivid dreams, even fevers. I refused these beliefs but as I stood in front of the store, my face steady in front of the open book, the words I read began to whisper:

Did you just walk through the woods on those days? Maybe you heard the hissing of the fields and the trees. Maybe you sat down in a hidden spot. You start with a ring of stone. You make a circle, like the commencement of a witch's ritual, a circle of stone. Nothing can be in the shape of a wing. You collect sticks from the floor of the woods, dry, small pieces not much bigger than straw, but dry. That is the most important: dryness. Then you place those pieces tenderly inside the stone, the permanent with the fragile. One match. While the straw burns, you look for larger wood about one foot long. After you find just the right amount of wood, you place the larger pieces, one by one, on top of the fire. You listen for a while. Slow popping, cracking sounds. You've created a hot wind. Pieces from the ground rise into the sky, swirling like water you've made in the air, connecting sky and sea. When a large piece of wood begins to smoke, move the stones. Leave a path of wood, stacked lightly on each other to allow air and flames, but securely enough so the fire gathers strength. Once the larger pieces begin to smolder, you can be sure the fire will spread. Be sure you have left nothing and leave. When you get

home, remember to wash your hands, your face,
maybe change your clothes. Listen for sirens.

I closed the book. Rain had begun falling and I knew that today fire would not be possible. Fire would not be possible for hours after rain; I had learned this much, that the ground had to be dry as shadow if the fire was to travel and amount to anything. The bus came just as large spatters began blooming against the dry pavement. I found a seat in the back, away from the driver, away from the other passengers who sat reading newspapers or dozing while saliva iced their chins.

I had a window seat and I knew, once I looked out at the moving world beyond, that the windows of my bedroom would never again be enough. These windows, moving as they did, offered the perfect membrane for me to watch people, to watch motion, without having to touch any of it, without having to participate in any of it. With the soot, pedestrians and houses took on the surrealistic look of one of those foreign films that my mother and I went to on nights when my father worked late. I had complained to my mother that I did not understand these movies, that the scenes moved forward, disconnected from one another, pairing incongruous items like trains and potatoes. She told me I understood more than I realized, that I should just sit back and let the story speak. After a while, I learned to do this and my mother had been right; the films transported me.

The bus moved at just the right speed to seem like a film, and through the haze of soot the world tumbled by like those scenes in Paris or Warsaw, appearing edgeless and mutable, a place made of dream and water rather than anything of substance. If I closed my eyes, even slightly, the outside world moved from the simple distortion of the dirty window to modern art. Frame after frame of canvas sped by, a dot, a square, a fade of blue into silver, nothing real or solid, just impressions and whispers.

I could do this without my usual fear of being outdoors. After all, I was connected to a tidy world of schedules and stops, driven by a person who knew routes and directions; I felt safe and untroubled, unable to be reached, the way I often felt while reading or watching a movie. I knew I would take the bus again.

The next morning in school, I told Julia about my new discovery, hoping one afternoon she would take the bus with me. She was looking at me the way a fish looks up through a tank. "What's wrong?" I asked her. "We can go for free. Our bus passes are valid until six o'clock."

"Listen, Maggie, I have terrible news." Her face rumpled before she continued. "Do you remember that boy we met in the park a couple of weeks ago?"

I did. I had been envious of Julia's ease with the boy, of her breezy style. I had stood there gracelessly, solid and mute as a landed barge, unable to speak. I could not figure out how Julia could continue to think of things to say, as I knew her mind moved more slowly than mine did.

"He came over to my house last night and my mother caught me with…" Julia looked around quickly. "If I tell you, are you going to hate me?"

"I hope not," I answered.

"Listen, Maggie. I don't know why I did this, but we

started, you know…kissing. I let him take my shirt off and my mother walked in and found us."

"Take your shirt off? Then what happened?" Stones fell between us, large, black stones with a mineral shine, stones that had traveled soundlessly through space.

They fell one after the other from the school ceiling. The floor filled with them.

"Everything. Tomorrow is my last day in public school. She's switching me to Our Lady Queen of Peace."

Something inside me collapsed. I could not imagine school without Julia. Not one day of it.

"Maggie, it's not like we can't still do things. I mean it will just have to be on the weekends now is all."

I put my hand on Julia's shoulder. We stood there until the bell rang and the hall monitor came up to us, hollering, "Ladies, that was the late bell. Are you deaf? Move along."

I walked through the stones to first period math, my mind filling with gas. First my mother gone, now Julia. My only connection to the standard gone; my only connection to the drift gone. I saw myself entering a new world, diving into the deep sea with only a mask and no compass or chart, my assignment to draw a map of water. Only I would not be given equipment. For the rest of the day I sat inside invisible gas, inside a drifting substance lighter than smoke. I copied from the board, I went to my locker, I took the bus home without any kind of mooring to my surroundings.

I walked inside my house to find Hannah mopping the kitchen floor. She would never be reading a glossy magazine or baking a cake: Hannah would be mopping the kitchen floor, scrubbing out a toilet, soaking a stain in the sink.

"Hello, Magdalena," she said without looking up from the lop-shoop rhythm of her mopping. "Nice to see you."

No one, with the exception of my father's half sister, Hannah Leppter, called me by my birth name. Everyone else called me Magda or Maggie.

Hannah came to clean and cook on Friday afternoons with a palpable sense of duty evident in her every movement, as though my father and I were natives of a remote island nation she had been sent to vaccinate.

"I thought you would be here tomorrow," I said.

"I'm doing a novena tomorrow." She said this with surprise, as though I should be up on her prayer schedule. "I won't have time."

"Oh." I could not imagine Hannah ever being busy. Ever. I resisted any agreement with the idea that Hannah suffered from overwork. That suggestion had begun long ago, when my mother first began leaving.

> You will have to help Hannah more, Magda, especially now, your father had said.
>
> You were looking over the edge of the Staten Island Ferry while your mother sat on a bench, alone, in the glassed-in section. Wind sliced through your coat. You were looking at the agate-blue water,

at the color your mother said looked like pul-
verized jewels. (Winter water, your mother had
just commented, is never the same color as sum-
mer water. Summer water is clearer.) Now things
are different and you will have to help me more,
Magda, your father's voice said, but you were still
trying to see if your mother's belief in the water
color difference was right or not. Your father's voice
was an interruption of your thoughts. Magda, he
went on, you will have to help Aunt Hannah more,
do you understand?

Yes, you had said, I will help more. You were
holding your mother's hand in the elevator inside
the sand-colored building in Manhattan, and you
pretended not to know what he meant. You wanted
the trip into Manhattan to end, you wanted your
mother's parched stare to end.

Looking down at your mother's wrists on the
elevator and thinking how white they were, lam-
bent as patches of snow or moon, and those tiny
rivers of blue pulsing through them.

A man came into the waiting room to take
your mother inside, then she disappeared until
after the New Year. She came back and spent entire
days staring at dust, and you knew the hospital
had turned her into a fossil. She sat on the sofa, the
light gone from her eyes, her face dark and feature-
less as shadowed stone.

She had already begun her leaving.

"I made a stew," Hannah said.

I wanted to say, of course you made a stew. You only make stews or casseroles involving canned fish and peas. None of your food is happy or light, it is food born of duty and obligation, food meant for utility. Never would you think of making a pie or adding slices of fruit to a dish, never would you purchase a tin of cookies, never would you indulge in spices. Even though my father gave her money to purchase groceries, she was prudent in her use of money and she did not purchase good cuts of meat; she had never, not once, splurged or surprised us in any way. She did not even use salt in her cooking and the result was food that tasted like steam. But Hannah did not know how to make anything connected to happiness as my mother had. My father told me I should have sympathy for her, that she only wanted to help. But I saw her help as veiled contempt, a phrase one of my teachers used to describe manifest destiny. Hannah had learned to cook in the convent, where a great sorrow (or a great disgrace, I could never be sure which, or if they were the same since everyone simply referred to "Hannah's time" in a hushed, sorrowful tone) had doomed her back to secular life, and, eventually, to my father and me.

Whatever had happened, her life was now so spare and bleak that looking directly into Hannah's eyes depleted you.

When I complained to my father about her being inside the house so often, he told me, "There, there, Magda, Hannah's your aunt. We have to welcome family. She helps us now. She has always helped us. You can't expect me to do all the work in the house. And Hannah loves doing it for us; she loves the fact that she can help."

"Then why do you pay her?"

My father looked stricken when I asked this, as though I had just hurled thorns at him.

"I pay her because I value her services." Then he had turned away, done with my complaint.

Even that day I looked at the pale blue envelope on the counter holding Hannah's check.

"You look like you've seen the Holy Ghost," Hannah observed. "Are you feeling all right?"

"Yes, thank you," I said.

"You better lie down."

"Maybe I better," I agreed. Feigning sleep with a pillow hiding my eyes, I watched Julia through the gas, her small breasts exposed and tender looking, her nipples large as bulbs while the hands of the boy from the park raked over them, his fingers in the shape of lobster claws.

"I brought you this," Julia said the next day during the last few minutes of school. She held a small box out to me. "I want you to wear it always."

Inside was a twist of gold on a chain.

"I hope you like it. The shape wasn't definite and I thought you would like that, Maggie."

"See," she said, lifting the chain from the box and allowing the charm to dangle, "it's either a harp or a bird, and I remember how much your mother liked harp music. We always listened to harp music at your house. Remember my mother was so amazed? She said she didn't think anyone still played the harp." Julia clasped the chain around my neck. "Whenever I hear the harp, I will think of you and your mother, of all those times we went swimming at the beach at the bottom of your street."

I touched the chain around my neck. Students walked past, pausing to watch as we stood together.

"And I'll remember how much you like birds," I said, my voice slipping.

"I was hoping you would think that. Will you wear it?"

I held Julia's hand to my neck for a moment. I listened to the stones fall. I wanted to believe I would still see her, that it was the boy Julia's mother hoped to take her from, but I knew Julia's mother suspected me of setting the last fire. I had ridden my bike over to Julia's house moments before the fire trucks arrived.

"Why do you smell like smoke?" her mother had asked, and not nicely, while I waited for Julia to come outside and see the fire trucks. "Is it your hair that smells smoky?"

"I must have been standing too close to the fire," I answered, regretting that I had showered but not taken the time to wash my hair. "This fire is a big one."

"Yes, yes it is," she murmured, her eyes falling on me like the eyes of God on Judgment Day.

She knew. I could see that in her slow assessment, and because she knew, I feared I would not be seeing as much of Julia. Her mother's eyes had burned into my back as Julia and I rode our bikes over to the woods to watch the firemen. That fire had been two weeks ago, before Julia had met the boy her mother discovered in her room. Now Julia was leaving. We let go the embrace.

I held the gold chain with the harp or the bird on it while watching Julia get into her mother's car. A bunch of us stood waving at the window. I turned away from the sunny window, knowing that afternoon I would go into the woods. The ground would be dry as salt.

I had set several fires before, the first few small and unimaginative, some spiky flames that sputtered out before they went anywhere. The fourth time I learned how to make the fire travel, how to lead it away from the source to gain strength. One fire truck had come for that one and as I watched the truck flash down our street, I knew one truck would never again be enough.

Three fire trucks had come for my last fire, as the brush in the woods had, unexpectedly, ignited. That is how I approached this fire, the one I wanted to show Julia, though I had no plans to tell her I would be setting the fire. I only wanted her to witness the excitement.

I had not set a fire since the big one, as my father, a fire dispatcher, had told me the police were going to "keep an eye" on the woods. That was enough to scare me. And there was the new problem of Julia's mother. I still walked the woods surrounding our house, prospecting spots for possible fires, but I did nothing. I imagined eyes watching me from between branches, neighbors coming to their windows the minute I set foot in the woods, Julia's mother stepping out from behind the ferny silence of the trees with a snapping camera. But I would find a way around all that.

This fire would be in honor of Julia. It had to be perfect.

I smiled, knowing I would set it this afternoon, on the last day of her attendance at our school. After watching the windows all day, I knew the day had been a warm and gusty one. On the bus ride home, I saw lines full of washing. That was always a good sign.

I checked the inside of the house to make sure Hannah was off doing her novena; she was. The house was so much darker inside than the bright day that, for a few moments, I could not make out the tables and chairs; my eyes were full of greenish lights as though I had just dived beneath the surface of water and lost the sun as navigation. No sound rang from anywhere in the house, and for a moment I stood, weightless as a swimmer, unable to move in the unfamiliar atmosphere. Then I saw the porcelain teapot where Hannah kept matches to rekindle the stove's pilot light. Everything came back to me as I dipped my hand inside the teapot; I knew exactly what I needed to do.

I walked roundabout into the woods, my seemingly loopy route tightening in concentric ovals while I kept watch. Seeing no one, hearing no one, my heart began to pound: the woods were mine, these dry woods, with a strong wind blowing from the bay. I fingered the matches in my pants pocket, feeling the nearly full pack push out the fabric of my jeans. No matter how much wind welled up from the bay, each match was one more chance.

On days when I had fire tasks, I moved with a certain swiftness. Browsing the area for future fire sites or inspecting branches for dryness dispelled my usual fears that I would drown in the fray and commotion and infiniteness of the outside. My senses opened; I heard light whisper; I tasted the yeast of rain. Muscles over the exterior of my ribs, in my flank region, tightened as I walked. I thought of nothing else while tending my fires; nothing except the flame and the crackling pops and snaps of my fire. Fire, like silence, had a language I could not speak, but I could translate. I listened to the pops and snaps growing louder as they grew closer together, and the voice of the fire warned me when to leave.

I walked rapidly through the woods, past the field where old cars were dumped, and spotted a clearing inside a sky of trees. About twenty yards from where I stood, an old mattress had been dumped in the middle of the clearing. The stained atrocity sprawled there like the carcass of an animal and when I looked at that mattress, at its improbable appearance in the middle of these woods where rabbits scampered and squirrels chittered, at these woods so close to people's homes, anger rose inside my brain. I could imagine the purpose of the mattress, dragged there by boys I probably knew, and I wanted it gone, destroyed, and I wanted to be the one to do it.

The mattress had to center the fire, so I rapidly gathered sticks and leaves (only the ones from the top of the piles, as the rest were still wet; I had become something of an expert at inspecting the properties of kindling). I blanketed kindling on the mattress until its fabric could no longer be detected. The mattress blended in with the surrounding woods, a rise, a bank full of sticks and dry leaves. For a moment I was tempted to leave the thing, to leave it and walk away. But as I turned to a nearby stump to consider this idea, a hollow log caught my eye. It proved light enough to be dragged over, a prize conduit for spreading flames. Never had I been so lucky.

I wondered, briefly, if my mother had intervened for such luck, but I quickly pushed thoughts of my mother out of my mind while I worked. She had no business here.

Artfully, I used the log as a bridge between the mattress and the dry field bordering the woods. I stood back, admiring my work for several minutes, admiring the artistry of the pile, the varying shapes and colors of the connected heap.

Then I struck the match.

Obediently, the leaves and twigs on the mattress leapt up with a soft ripping sound, a quiet, contented sound as if they had been waiting there all day to be destroyed. I sat on the stump watching the flames swallow progressively larger and larger sticks, growing close to the log. Flames shot up from the sticks and I could see them, clear and yellow at the same time, in the way that urine is clear and yellow at the same time. I could not understand, watching the flames grow to a fire, why our English teacher insisted that water was a symbol for the soul.

"For damp British souls maybe," I had written in a note to Julia, who had nodded. She never wrote notes and I saw now how she would do well with nuns and a focus on cursive writing instead of thinking.

Watching fire always cleared my thinking.

Fire should be the symbol for the soul, I thought, watching the fire move with no definite pattern or prediction, shaped by the wind. That was a soul, right there in front of me. These were the kind of thoughts I could share with my mother, and I missed her now with a longing that made me shudder. I did not want to convulse like that in the middle of this warm spring day with the heat of the blaze on my face, yet I did.

A large cracking sound splintered the air. The log had caught and I could see how the wind, which had increased its force as the afternoon grew later, would tunnel the flames through the interior of the log to the field of brush. It was time to leave. I took one last appraisal of my fire, and satisfied, I ran through the woods. The woods wheeled by in patches of green and brown. By the time I sat down inside the moss-colored silence of my house, I heard sirens and long yanks of horn; I heard neighbors out on the street calling their children inside.

I changed my clothes. I showered. Then I sauntered outside as though the disturbance had interrupted my afternoon of reading.

"What's going on?" I said to Mrs. Langley, our next door neighbor. She was leaning on her car watching the commotion. She turned to face me and as she did, two of her chins followed.

"Oh, jeez. Those teenagers again, this is what, the third time in a month they did this."

"Did what?"

"I hate even tellin' you," Mrs. Langley sighed. "You bein' so emotional and all."

"You mean the fire."

"When they catch those kids, there'll be trouble." Mrs. Langley swung her head back and forth. "There'll be trouble all right. The cops have been down here every day. Your dad is lucky you're such a good kid the way you stay in the house and do so good in school and stay away from trouble."

"Hmm," I murmured. I was scanning the crowd to see if Julia and her mother were there. I saw no sign of them.

People ran everywhere, talking, pointing to the gray clouds of smoke rising from the woods. I stood in the street by Mrs. Langley, removed from the crowd, thinking, I have brought this neighborhood together, I have created this storm in the sky, this scent of ash that rides over us. I have changed the day, shuffling around the calmness of the afternoon, opening the houses, the people inside them: I have made a window.

I remembered the fire, the great splintering sound as the log ate the flames, and I saw what I had done as happy, creating a leaping force full of light and warmth that lit the darkness that spread inside all the houses around us. I brought light to a place where there had been only darkness, in the exact manner of a redeemer.

two

My father lived underwater. My mother would say this to me, crossing her legs and laughing as we talked on her bed. She had a heart-shaped face and when she smiled, her entire face smiled, her cheeks rounded and her eyes slit to crescents. You had to smile, looking at her. "I have to tell him how he feels," she would tell me. "He doesn't know sometimes and I can look at him and read his face as easily as a book. I say, 'Michael, you're so angry or Michael, why are you worried?' He looks at me, astonished. He thinks I'm a witch."

"When you play your harp records, he says witch's brew is in the air."

My mother smiled. "He likes harp music, too. He just doesn't remember. I remember. That's my job, to remember it all." She put her arm around me. "I want you to stop worrying. There's dark water in your soul, Lena, and you can't keep letting the dark water blot out the light." She rubbed my shoulders.

We were talking about my breasts.

"Only you would think such a thing. Cancer. Imagine." She shook her head.

A tender, swollen knob had lodged in the center of my right breast. I woke up that morning and instinctively put my hand to my breast. At breakfast I asked my mother to make an appointment for me. I knew cancer grew lumps. I had seen a poster of the seven warning signs while riding the Staten Island Ferry.

"Let me see," she said after I told her what I had found. She looked carefully. "This is not cancer. This is development. You're at that age now, nearly thirteen. Your cells are going berserk, that's all."

To calm me down, we sat on her bed with the door shut, eating ice cream. It was a Saturday and my father had gone to Manhattan with Hannah to help her buy a sofa, so we didn't have to explain our indulgence. It was kind of a celebration, but one that would only be understood by me and my mother: we were celebrating that I didn't have cancer when there had been no threat. If we explained ourselves, my father would smile, but I knew Hannah would give my mother the same glare as moon reflecting on ice: a glare of ancient coldness, without any chance of warmth.

We sat on her bed with Hitchins, our cat, eating ice

cream at eight o'clock in the morning, letting Hitchins lick out the bowls. (Hitchins vanished a week after my mother died. I still waited for him.)

"Tell me," my mother said in her secret voice, "what kind of couch do you think Aunt Hannah will buy?"

"I don't know," I said thoughtfully. "I can't even picture her in a store." The image of Hannah in one of her cloth hats with the elliptical brim came to me. Whenever Hannah donned a hat, it was gray, the color of a thunderhead, and when she walked, it seemed a storm front was moving toward you. I saw her moving around a furniture warehouse, her thunder-gray hat on, moving slowly, checking the prices. "She won't buy a couch with wisteria on it." My mother laughed. Our couch bloomed wisteria on a pale mint background. Hannah had made the comment that it didn't look substantial enough to sit on, with all those purple dots.

My mother looked down at Hitchins, who was moving the bowl with the force of his tongue. "It will have to be a solid color, maybe brick red or silvery steel. It will have to endure."

"Yes, it will have to endure," I agreed. We smiled.

I only wish we had known that two years later my mother would get sick, that she would not endure. I only wish I had known.

My father came home early the night of Julia's fire. I was lying on the couch reading *Jane Eyre*, a book my English teacher got worked up about. I was changing my opinion about Jane. She was stronger than she seemed.

"What a day," he said. He sat in the chair across from me, rubbing his forehead.

"What's wrong?"

"Just one thing after the next," he said. "And they're no closer to finding the arsonist in this area than we were a month ago. The leads have gone nowhere."

"How do they know it's arson? You said fires in the woods were caused by cigarettes mostly."

"Not these. These are as deliberately set as a campfire. I'll never understand what would get into a person to start a fire. What is it…do they just get up from the chair, walk over to the window, look out and say, 'Looks like it's time for some arson?' Do you think that's it?"

My father had said these same sentences in the same tone ever since I was small. He looked over at me and I think, for a second, he had thought he was speaking to my mother. "It's good to see how much you like to read, Magda. Your mother always read."

"You look tired," I said.

"I am. I think I'll put Hannah's stew on, then call it an early night."

I went back to Jane. She had just arrived at Mr. Rochester's house to take the governess position and she was gazing up at the stairs leading to Bertha's tower as the housekeeper showed her around. At that moment, just as Jane looked up the stairs toward the unknown, the fish moved into my head.

I had been trying to ignore these creatures since the beginning of spring, the same creatures I had tried to tell Julia about and she told me were just part of a dream. These fish were no dream; they were clearly taking up residence inside my brain. At first they were shadowy figures, nothing more than flickers of rain or shadow darting inside my head. And these fish had no basis in my life; they simply appeared, blocking out the world around me. I had always been able to ignore them, but this time they meant business. I put the book down.

Mrs. Fish stood at a sink, washing out a series of crinkled conch shells. Around her stood jumbles of boxes and bubble wrap. She took dishes from one box and wore an apron that was scalloped at the top and the bottom; on her head, at an angle, was one of those tiny, fluted cups used to serve tartar sauce. It acted as her paper hat, inverted on her head so that the open part of the cup was closest to her head. She had lipstick on in the manner of a cartoon figure, a red heart covering what I presumed to be lips and a mouth. Then her mouth opened; I saw that I was right.

"If I ever get these dishes done and put away in this place, and if you ever finish with that paperwork, then maybe I'll understand because right now, I really don't know, I just can't tell you. Why don't you ask him when you see him? It's not like he doesn't owe us a huge favor. After all we've done for him, you'd think…"

"Oh, don't start that now," Mr. Fish interrupted. He sat at a round stone table looking at a series of papers scattered in front of him. "You can't go thinking that the only reason we do things is for repayment. We've been over and over this, and it doesn't change. There's one lesson here, and only one: you can't trust eels. It comes down to that basic and simple truth. You just can't trust them. I wish it weren't so, I wish it were not the case, but I can't change what is." Mr. Fish stacked a pile of his papers with his fins. "Maybe I can be looked at and people can say how it's awful that I don't trust an entire species, but over and over, the eels disappoint. They bring it on themselves. In all my dealings with them, they've either cheated or…I don't even want to say." He wagged his head back and forth and returned to his papers.

His eyes were shaped exactly like lightbulbs placed at forty-five-degree angles to his temples, tiny at the corners then opening to a large circular bulb of silvery amber.

Mrs. Fish shook out a large conch shell. "You're right, honey," she said, turning to Mr. Fish. "So right. There is just no dealing with eels. They have hearts just like their caves, dark and full of venom. I was just hoping that this one time, this one eel would surprise us. Actually, you surprised me when you told me you were negotiating with an eel in the first place."

"You act like I can control everything," Mr. Fish exclaimed, raising both fins upward in a gesture of helplessness.

Mrs. Fish walked over to the table. This was accomplished by rocking back and forth on her bottom fin. She sat down across from Mr. Fish. "I'll never understand why you even go there. I mean, they're not like family. With family you might have to put up with certain things, but to go to the eels . . . " She pursed her generous lips. "You just have to stop this. It's one thing to feel sorry for eels. That's understandable. But at this point, you need to end your association with them. They're really no more than a bad habit."

"I suppose," Mr. Fish agreed.

"Who are you?" I whispered. Mr. and Mrs. Fish exchanged glances then blinked up at me. They sat in a translucent green substance that looked like water, only nothing around them was wet. The substance shone with unnatural brightness; it was as though they moved only within shafts of sun.

"It just seems the older I get, the less..." As Mrs. Fish said this, Baby Fish tumbled by. She leaned down and scooped him up with one stubby fin and deposited him in a small, roofless pen. "We're going to have to solve this problem, no matter what," she continued.

"I have an idea. You're not going to like it, but it's the only way I can see out of this right now," Mr. Fish said with ponderous slowness. "Just give me a chance to talk. Please. Just hear me out."

"How can you even say that?" Mrs. Fish exclaimed, alarm in her voice. "That I wouldn't hear you out? How can you even say such a thing to me?" She turned her eyes toward me. They shone, their hazel irises igniting in the sun, their lashes as long and curled as a llama's. "I will hear anyone out, anyone. Though I have to tell you before we even start, that I see no solution to this problem other than . . . well, ending the relationship. Total termination."

"We have to visit the grave tomorrow," my father called to me from the kitchen. The fish vanished at the sound of his voice and I sat up on my bed, trying to pull the world back into some kind of order.

"Why on a Saturday? Don't we usually go after Mass?"

"Magda, I'm surprised at you. You're usually right on top of these things."

"I don't know. Can you tell me, please?"

"It's your mother's birthday. She would have been thirty-nine, God rest her soul."

I heard my father leave. The fish did not come back. I woke to the sound of rain at dawn and then it rained all that morning. My father said we could wait until the afternoon when the weather cleared up a bit, but the sky remained zinc-colored and laden, cold for spring with raw scrapes of wind.

"It's too late to go now," I complained when he knocked on the door to my room at three o'clock.

"Your mother's on eternal time now, honey. She won't mind."

I had to go, though I did not kneel when my father did; I stood next to him, not looking at my mother's grave or at him, but out over the rows and rows of tombstones. I waited in the car while he prayed. As we drove back home, I asked him if we could skip our usual movie and ice cream. I couldn't face sitting there with my father while my classmates writhed in booths around us like banished spirits of fornication in an Old Testament painting.

This request surprised my father. "Not feeling well?"

"A little tired."

I went into my room and tried to will the fish back. I thought of how my mother and I once swam beneath the pier with goggles on. We went to the bottom and watched the fish float toward us, drifting soundlessly as angels, their fins delicately thin and fragile as eyelids in all that green dark. They fluttered past us with the grace of brides.

"They're like souls," my mother had told me as we dried off on the pier. "The way they float."

Her sentence had scared me and I did not know why. Now I knew why. She knew things, things she did not share with me, and that sentence had hinted at her unspoken knowledge.

I thought of my mother, I thought of the fish, but nothing came to me until I fell asleep. Then my mother stood before me, calling me into a place where things rolled and floated, free of boundaries like gravity or physics, a place similar to space, though we could breathe and speak. We walked like astronauts across a spongy surface, bouncing along in long steps.

"Where have you been?" I asked her. "You've been gone since August."

"I'm back now, I'm here now, Magda," she said, rubbing circles into my palm. "I'm right here. I never meant to leave you, you have to know that. I never meant to leave you and have you end up like this." She kept rubbing my palm. "Magda, listen to me. You cannot go on like this, with only silence and memories."

"But I don't want anything else."

"I know, I do know, we all want only silence sometimes. But it's not all you can or should have. Promise me you'll find a way out of the silence."

"I can't promise that. I can only try. You never taught me how to enter…"

My mother looked at me. She smiled, cupping my cheek in her hand. Then I woke. I sat up in bed, my nightgown soaked through as if I had been caught in rain. I had dreamed of my mother: I saw her, heard the sounds of her drowning, and I watched her hair flower in the water, her breasts trembling beneath the water, her arms moving like light. She had touched me.

"Are you there?" I whispered. "Have you come?"

I listened to long vowels of wind rush by and turned my head to the pillow. I could feel the place she had inhabited inside me, and I could feel that space, gone hollow now, spin within me.

Loss. Grief. The words people had said to me after she died. Short words, easy to say.

I thought of all the space that had been my mother's life and I wanted a larger word, a grander word that did not fall from my tongue like water.

I dreamed my mother's face all night. Her skin and her features remained in my mind, steady and bright as the moon. A sense of falling woke me and when I opened my eyes, Hannah sat on the edge of my bed causing the mattress to slope. For a moment, I could not translate Hannah's pinched features into anything I understood; seeing her face after my mother's was the same as watching an angel fish turn toward you only to reveal the face of a Gila monster.

"I wanted you to know I'm leaving for church." Her voice landed on me like a hoof.

"Okay," I said. "I'll be fine." We both waited inside the ticking silence. Hannah studied my face, her small black eyes looking down on me from hooded lids. The effect of the darkness against Hannah's moon-skin made her pupils appear distinct from the jelly of her eye, as though they could move independently of one another like lizard eyes. She continued looking at me and I realized how strongly she resembled George Washington, had he worn a wig of close-cropped, ash-brown curls and given off a vaguely amphibious air.

"Where's Dad?" I pulled the blankets closer, up over my shoulders.

"He's gone to early Mass with a group from our church."

"Who?"

"A group of people in a similar situation." She patted the blankets by my leg. "I take it you're not coming to Mass with me then."

I shook my head. "I'll just pray here."

"Well, say a good Act of Contrition. That's the most important part, a good Act of Contrition. Let Him know you're sorry."

"Right."

Hannah stood and put on a worn straw hat that looked as though it had been lifted directly from the head of the old mare in the barn. She leaned over, brushing my face with her dry cheek.

Then the silence returned. I could not imagine where my father had gone. Hannah knew.

Of that, I was sure. She knew things.

Just like when you went to visit your mother in the hospital, and Hannah waited calmly in the lobby, pretending to scan the pages of a cooking maga-

zine, her face as composed as if your mother had gone in for gall bladder surgery. Only your mother did not look up at you, not one time.

Then you realized this wasn't the regular hospital where your teachers went to have babies or kids went to get their tonsils removed. This hospital had a solarium where you met the patient, double locks on the doors; they did not allow bags, packages of any kind inside. Patients shuffled along the hallway in pajamas, which was not unusual, except these patients cried. Men, women, all of them, in only two states: tears or trance.

You knew then that this was not any kind of hospital that cured, but a hospital that held, that kept their patients away from the rest of the world, a kind of ark that floated along full of life, but not participating in life. These people had been plucked from the warm ocean of life and placed on this ark like salvage that had to be stored in order to keep the water moving for the boats and swimmers. These people no longer made progress.

You thought all this, then instead of admitting what you knew, instead of bearing the truth, you went home and took a scissors to your hair, cutting off all of its length, a punishment for something you did not do, a punishment for your mother not acknowledging your presence.

Amber light began filling the windows. I watched the light pool onto my bedspread, bright obelisks swimming across the purple wisteria sprigs. As I watched the moving light, a restlessness seized me with such vigor that I could no longer stay in bed. I got up and dressed, then I did something I had never done before: I left the house on a Sunday morning and walked through the woods inside a canyon of white daylight, straight to the clearing where the mattress had been. I wanted to see the burnt scar in the earth where the mattress had once rested; I wanted the scent of its sear to fill my mouth.

To my horror, the mattress was still there, or pieces of it that had been axed and doused, rendering it unable to be used for sex. But I had wanted the thing gone, not just mutilated.

As I stood in the woods, I heard a snapping sound distinct as a bell. I turned to see a man, an adult, watching me.

"Oh," he said. "We thought maybe we had him."

"Had who?" I asked. The man's eyes pecked about the woods, done with me and already moving on to other concerns.

"The pyro. You better not hang around here. They usually come back to inspect their handiwork. That's why this area is being patrolled." He coughed and turned to leave. "Run along now, honey. You don't want anything to happen to you out here."

"Right. I was just on my way to the beach, anyway."

Afraid the man might be keeping track, I walked the familiar path to the beach. I waved to a group of fishermen sitting outside the Chum Bucket, a double-wide trailer that served as a diner for bay workers. The fishermen and bay workers seemed to be one family of men all connected by their weathered faces, and long, thin bodies. Benny sat with them, gazing off into the water while the men around him joked and laughed. He had once been a decorated detective in Manhattan, but now spent his days combing the beach with a metal detector and an AM radio. Even my mother, who lived inside her own form of isolation, told me Benny was a lost soul.

A lost soul. I had never thought much about that expression, but as I sat on a tarry log apart from the beach-goers, the words made perfect sense. Perfect. Everything around me was lost, or on its way to losing its path.

That afternoon, after my father came back from Mass with his church group, I told him about the man who had been watching the woods. We had just finished the lunch dishes when I brought it up.

"Why were you in the woods alone?" my father asked, as I knew he would.

"Just went for a walk."

"Well, I'm going to have to ask you to stay out of the woods until this matter passes. The woods are not safe right now for young ladies."

"Are they guarding the woods constantly?"

"I only know what I hear at the dispatch office, but I think they have shifts coming in pretty regularly. Probably not in the wee hours, as there have never been fires there at that time. It's best to avoid the woods for the next few weeks. Anyone could be lurking in there. You know, anything could happen in those woods when there's...well, when there's someone loose like this."

"You're right."

"Are you feeling better?"

"What?"

"Are you feeling up to your ice cream?"

"It's all right, Dad. We can skip it this week."

Since my mother died, my father had begun a Saturday ritual of movies followed by ice cream. We watched whatever was showing without the slightest discrimination. We sat through westerns and mysteries and love stories and did not speak later of the plots or the characters or anything we had just experienced, which was, after all, how we lived our lives.

"You weren't up to it last night, so I thought if we wouldn't be seeing the movie, at least we could have some ice cream." He smiled so hopefully that I could not turn him down.

"You're right. Ice cream is never a bad idea."

We went to the Flavor Galaxy, a place that irritated me with its wobbly circles representing the planets all over the walls and its plastic stars glued to the center of each table.

The motif seemed bizarrely childish, especially when I glanced into the back booths (my father and I sat at a table in the front) and kids my age were making out like mad, their hands riding up and down each other's backs with the urgent motions of a tide running in to shore. Not once, in all our visits to the Flavor Galaxy, had my father glanced toward the back to see what kids my age were up to.

"How is school going this year, Magda?"

I opened my eyes very wide. It was nearly May. "The same as always," I answered.

"You're very lucky to get such grades. You know, Mrs. Dillon called me at the office the other day. She's going to be sending home some papers for scholarship application."

"For college? I'm only fifteen."

"She thinks you might qualify for early admission." My father dabbed at his ice cream. "I always thought Saint Anastasia was a good choice for a girl."

"Dad, I'm not interested in elementary education. We've been through this before."

My father looked at me. I blinked back, feeling the transformation beginning to occur.

I had always struggled with an odd affliction, one I had never heard of before: during times of stress, particularly social stress when I had to interact with other people, everyone around me, including myself, turned into an animal. I had been fighting this disorder ever since I could remember. I could not help what I saw before me any more than I could help exhaling. And once the process began, I was powerless to stop it.

The worst was my own transformation. Whenever my father pinned me in conversation, or whenever anyone scrutinized me in any manner, I slowly transformed into a giraffe, my neck growing impossibly long, my eyes bulging, each eyelid slow to blink, my movements precisely gawky in the manner of a giraffe. This was not the type of behavior that would help me enter the standard world. I could be sure this affliction did not plague Julia.

"It's a strange thing for a young girl to be so addled by small children."

"But I am," I replied flatly, in giraffe-speech. "I'd rather be buried with pythons than put in front of a group of six-year-olds." I thought of the small children who toddled at the edge of the water on our beach, their mothers, alert as eagles, cooing about them. I would look at the child and feel only a vague panic, as if being presented with a creature whose needs and whims were as impossible to translate as an ancient language encrypted on a sphinx.

"Well then." He wiped his mouth with a Mars napkin. "How about secondary education? French or geography?"

"I don't want to teach. Period. Besides, I take Spanish."

"Your uncle in Boston is a lawyer. Do you remember your mother's brother, Alex?"

"A little," I replied, recalling a vaguely effeminate man who visited one Christmas, patted my head once, and never looked at me again.

"So should I tell Alex if there's any thought of law school?"

The thought of the Constitution made my mouth go numb.

"No. No law."

"I guess you have time."

I wanted to say, people like me always have time; we're too odd to have friends. As I thought this, a girl from my high school bounced past. A cloud of blonde silk floated to her shoulders and she wore a necklace of tiny gold hoops;

the shimmer of the hoops matched her hair. I did not know how such girls were made.

My own hair was short and spiky, its color the subdued bronze of old pennies, the kind you find on the floor of a car or in the bottom of a purse. Whenever I put jewelry on, I took on the artificial look of a pirate draping plunder onto flesh unaccustomed to decoration. Her jewelry seemed as much a part of her as her hair and eyes.

She and I could not be from the same species, despite what my science book proposed.

Somewhere along the line, two sets of monkeys had bred on that savanna. I knew this. My primate ancestors had sat dourly behind a gloss of banana leaves, peering out between the fronds at the social monkeys frolicking in the primordial sun. We had evolved along entirely different lines.

"We'd better be going," my father said.

"Yes, before this whole place turns into Africa."

"What's that?" My father looked so baffled at that moment that I reached over and touched his wrist.

"Nothing, Dad. I was mumbling."

I sat in English one Monday, about a month after Julia had left. I sat inside the same gas that had overtaken me when Julia told me she would be changing schools. I wondered if the rest of my life might be like this: a pattern of loss and silence. Even Hannah had hinted yesterday at Sunday dinner that she no longer wanted my father to pick her up and bring her to Mass; she had found new friends from her parish group who attended an earlier Mass.

"It's not that I don't appreciate all the years you've taken me, Michael," she told my father. "It's just that sometimes I'd like to go with the girls."

I looked at her. The girls. Her hands were folded in her lap, coarse and red as ground meat.

"We're already planning a trip to Atlantic City this summer, the whole group of us." She smiled broadly, exposing the crookedness of her lower teeth.

"I don't want to keep you down on the farm," my father joked. I could tell she had hurt him. My father made smarmy jokes whenever he was hurt.

"Oh, I'll still come with you two from time to time," she went on. "It's just that I'm an early bird and I really like the idea of dawn service. Takes me back."

"That's fine, Hannah. How about you give us a call when you want to attend with us?"

We all knew she would never go to church with us again. Hannah had moved on.

I wished I could tell Julia how Hannah had looked when she talked to us, about her hands and the way she referred to herself and her friends as girls. I did not even know how to listen to Mrs. Keith in English without Julia next to me, smiling and nodding and communicating in all the little ways we had developed over the past five years.

Mrs. Keith was talking about the rise of the novel in Britain and I sat there, watching clouds crash into one another without any ability to navigate themselves, with only wind and current pushing them along. One cloud in particular caught my attention: it had a rounded shape and a smaller tail, and it drifted all by itself in the sky like a roaming chalice. As I watched the chalice migrate across the sky, it occurred to me that Julia may have wanted to go to the Catholic school, that she could have steered her mother in a different direction, that she could have put up much more of a struggle to stay than she had. Boys would still find their way to a girl as attractive and flirtatious as Julia. Did Julia want to get away from me?

I could see Julia sitting on her bed, listening to her mother, nodding in agreement with whatever she said. It seemed that after that day of the fire, when her mother had stood looking at me from the front door, I had seen less and less of Julia, that she had begun dissolving in that way people do just before they step out of your life, not really listening or answering, just showing up and staying with you for a time, like weather. Weather never touches you or lets you touch it, it's just there.

Perhaps her mother knew other things.

You were never naked, not entirely. The first fire, the one that fizzled out, you sat in front of its flames and unbuttoned your blouse. You didn't know why you did this, you simply did it as though you were in a trance. It seemed right.

The next time, you took your shirt off, slipped your pants down, and you sat there in the warmth, your back to the woods, letting the heat of the flames touch your skin.

Only once did you take all your clothes off and that was the fire for Julia, the one where you got dressed again after just a few minutes. So you were never naked for very long. And her mother could never have known any of that. You did not touch yourself, you did not touch the ground. You simply sat by the fire, letting the heat you made warm your skin. So you would not be cold, so you would not shudder anymore.

"Maggie Sorrin," Mrs. Keith said. "Can you explain this metaphor?"

I pulled myself up toward the cooler surface of day again, away from the fire. "The metaphor." I said this plainly, flatly, the awareness of my classmates' eyes on me causing my neck to lengthen, my flank to twitch, my eyelashes to grow curled and long while my hooves stilled in the dry jungle heat.

Mrs. Keith stood far away from me, on the other side of the desks, squarely in the middle of the standard. I heard her dishwasher going, the paper boy wheeling his bike up the driveway. She came through French doors, revealing a glimpse of pies cooling behind her on a green metal baker's rack. Then Mrs. Keith came into focus: the classroom, the blackboard behind her, the dull rows of desk and chair. "Yes, Maggie, the metaphor that you wrote here, this one that you later changed to a simile."

I looked up to see a page of my work on the overhead. I was not at all sure how we had gone from the rise of the novel to looking at student writing samples, but I cleared my throat. I had to say something: school was my window into glimpsing the standard now, with Julia gone.

"I guess...metaphor is a stronger statement than simile," I said in a slow voice. I had no idea Mrs. Keith was going to make our attempts at poetry public. "The word 'like' weakens the comparison, at least I think so."

"So, here," Mrs. Keith said, looking back to the class, "'Silence falls like cold stars' is changed to 'Silence falls in cold stars.' Do you agree with Maggie, that metaphor is stronger? Or is it just more direct?" Mrs. Keith waited. "Or is stronger simply a word for more direct?"

"I don't get it," one boy said, a new boy I knew only vaguely. "I mean, aren't all stars cold? Wouldn't everything in space be cold? It's like freezing there."

Mrs. Keith sighed. "I suppose, yes, technically, but sometimes, Mitchell, you have to see things symbolically rather than literally. Most of us think of stars as brightness, as a kind of symbolic heat."

Mitchell looked over at me, his head turning with the slow rotation of a turtle. He opened his mouth to speak directly to me. At that moment, the bell rang and I was saved.

About a week later, Mitchell, the boy who did not understand the warmth of starlight, asked me for a date. When it happened, I was eating lunch with Carrie, a pale sigh of a girl who asked nothing of me, not even conversation. We ate in monkish silence each day while our classmates shrieked and chattered around us.

"So, Maggie," Mitchell said, sliding a chair in next to me as though he had permission, "you talk to Julia lately?"

I raised my head from my book, but I did not look at him. "Not lately."

A lunch monitor blew a whistle and moved her head frenetically, gesturing to two boys. One held the other in a headlock while they threw stunted punches toward one another. Mitchell's eyes followed my gaze. "Lunch time at Raritan High."

"No different from lunch time at the open-air asylum."

He laughed. He had nice teeth; I counted fourteen of them before he closed his lips again.

"Sort of, it is. But I never would have thought of putting it that way." He looked at me. I met his gaze. Mitchell looked at me with expectancy. My stomach tightened. He wanted something.

"So," I said abruptly while gathering my books, "I better get up to the library."

Carrie looked up, blinked, then looked back down at her math page.

"Maggie," Mitchell said, standing as I did, "do you go to the CoRecs here?"

"The CoRecs." My mind sifted through names. "You mean the school dances here?"

He nodded, still smiling.

"Never. I never go. I don't dance," I said, turning from him. "In fact, I don't even hum." I walked past him, past the fighting boys and the lunch monitor, past the cafeteria and up into the silence of the library. I stood in the middle of the room staring outside at the colors of the sky, at the sharp brightness of the clouds that had faded from only a few moments before in the cafeteria. It was as if Mitchell's conversation with me had caused my vision to dim.

The dimness stayed. I even stopped dreaming of my mother. Days went by where I stayed in the house, lying across my bed thinking no thoughts. The fish did not come. My mother's face did not come. I did not leave the house or go near the woods. In the space of my mind where thoughts had once been, I held only moving static.

For almost two weeks, I fell through holes during the warm afternoons. The holes rose, one after the other, a series of connected holes with no sides or bottoms or brightness; I fell through the lightless holes in dives that turned into tumbles, a fall through dry water. I kept falling through the holes every time I got up off the bed; I fell through them when I stayed on the bed.

In school, I moved automatically, not letting anything in or out.

"So what's with you?" Mitchell said one lunch period as I sat going through papers in my locker. "What does it take to get a conversation with you?"

You're not an imaginary fish, I wanted to tell him. And you're not dead.

"Really, Maggie, what does it take? Ever since Julia changed schools, it's like you're not even here, it's like you're vacant."

"I'm simple-minded." I shrugged and returned to placing my papers in stacks.

"No, that's just it," he insisted. "You're not simple-minded. You just deliberately choose to be silent. And I asked about you, I asked some of the girls. They said you used to talk a lot more than you do now. I didn't know you then, before I came to this school, but they said you used to be a lot more outgoing."

"Huh," I answered, still not looking at him, "you've been spying on me."

"No, I just wondered what was up with you."

"I'm at that age, Mitchell," I said. "That age our teachers refer to all the time."

He smiled. I smiled back and turned from him. He still didn't get it. I was a closed membrane who walked through school, only to return home to sag across the bed. I stayed in the bed, the blankets cocooned around me, listening to birds land on the windowsill in a place where time moved slower than sleep. And I fell through the holes. How could I tell Mitchell all this?

"What is it that you like to do, Maggie?"

"Fall through holes," I answered, truthfully.

I was doing just this when Hannah came in to speak to me, a sudden slap of lightning across an inky, arctic sky. It was Saturday, not her usual day at our house, but my father had gone out and his usual habit was to call Hannah when he went out. He had not told me where he was going. "Be back later," he called into my room. Then I heard the door shut, the car start. I did not know Hannah had entered the house and begun prowling in our kitchen.

"Is everything all right with you, Magdalena?" Hannah stood in the doorway, her mouth small and worried, a tiny minnow darting up and down in a forced smile made of obligation.

Obviously, my father, the dispatcher, had dispatched Hannah to find out what was wrong with me, to find out why I lay across my bed for hours like a moored barge.

"Yeah, everything's fine."

"When I was your age, I would sometimes get..." Hannah's face reddened. "Stomach troubles once a month."

"No, it's not that," I said very quickly. "I've just been really busy in school. A lot of tests."

"Oh. I see. So you're tired then. Busy and growing."

I nodded.

She stood in the doorway a few more seconds, rubbing the finger of one hand across the knuckles of the other. "Magdalena, I just want you to know...actually, I was speaking to your father and we would like you to know that if you need to talk about anything, really anything at all, we are here to talk with you. All right? We are here to listen."

"Thank you," I said stiffly, shocked by Hannah's suggestion. Then, before the shock wore off, suspicion set in.

What was going on that would prompt Hannah to offer such an idea?

Something was going on and Hannah would not tell me. It had to do with my father's sudden absence; beyond that I could only guess. I hoped he wasn't ill. That was my most abiding fear: that my father would grow ill and I would be left with Hannah, eating pea soup inside the motel-blankness of her apartment while listening to the evangelical station on the radio. It was an image that terrified. Hannah had full knowledge of what was going on with my father, but she would never tell me. Never.

"You might have questions," Hannah pressed on, "about...any number of things."

"Mom explained a lot of that stuff to me," I said without meeting Hannah's eyes.

"Well, you could still have questions. Those kinds of...well, the stuff you refer to, that stuff can be confusing. You might have questions. If you don't want to ask directly, there are a number of excellent books..."

"I'll keep that in mind, the books. Thanks."

"Girls your age go through any number of changes and you should know that these changes can cause very specific moods. It has nothing to do with you, it all has to do with your glands."

As she spoke the word "glands," I saw in my mind's eye a puddle-shaped mass of grayness, exactly like a clam's shining, lobed innards. The word stayed between us for a few seconds, visceral as rain.

"Your father will be back later on."

"Where is he?"

"Out with the parish." Hannah raised two fingers to her lips briefly, then dropped her hand as though she wanted no more words to escape. "I'll be in the kitchen, finishing a few things up."

"All right." Hannah and I looked at each other for a long moment. "I'm going to work on some drawings," I told her. "Maybe finish up my homework."

"I'll be in the kitchen then," Hannah repeated. "If you need anything, you just let me know."

I watched her turn from my bedroom door.

As I flopped across my bed, Mrs. Fish stomped squarely into my brain. She held open a book of some kind. "You have to do what it says here, in the book." I could not see anyone else with her. She wore a plain black dress, square-collared and cut severely as a Pilgrim's frock. White cotton gloves covered both her fins. She sat on a gigantic white mushroom veined in vermilion threads. Then I saw Mr. Fish, as though a stage light had just been switched on above him. He was dressed in a dark suit and a tie, a pair of black-framed glasses over his bulbous eyes. The glasses were gigantic.

"Are you two going to the opera?" I asked.

Mr. Fish cleared his throat. "You found the rules, I see," he said to Mrs. Fish. "I've been keeping them safe for quite some time now. They're quite valuable. Quite."

"I did find the rules," Mrs. Fish said. "All the rules. Only…" and here Mrs. Fish grinned, keeping her heart-shaped lips together, "none of them apply to you. Not one."

"Who do you mean?" I whispered. "They don't apply to Mr. Fish or to me?"

As I said this, both of them shot up through water, leaving behind a squall of inky black.

"Do you mean the rules for entering the standard? Is that what you found? Please, let me see them. I can't stay here any longer."

"See them?" Mrs. Fish winked at Mr. Fish.

"Wait," I implored telepathically, "are you speaking to me or Mr. Fish? Can I see them?"

"Alice, why are you displaying them like that?" Mr. Fish moved one of his fins upward. "Keeping them where they can be seen, where they can be *measured*. Don't you know those rules can never be measured in any way? You know that, I am sure of it. Here, let me help you put them back."

"Hold on," I said, "just show them to me."

I waited a few minutes for them to return, and when they didn't, I stayed on my bed and finished *Jane Eyre*. Late in the afternoon, I heard the door open. I heard the splintering glass of Hannah's laugh, I heard dishes being taken from the cupboard, the sounds of greeting and reunion.

"Come say thank you to Aunt Hannah," my father called through the door. "I'm driving her home now."

"Thank you." I stood at the precipice of my room, not wanting to be invited into the car.

After they left, I ventured into the kitchen. Hannah had attempted Irish soda bread that tasted like salted sand. I spit the piece into the garbage, not even bothering with a napkin. I made tea and waited for my father to come back.

"Well then," my father said, taking off his jacket. "It's a lovely night. Getting warm out there."

"I made tea."

I waited until my father finished stirring. I looked at his face, at the gray curls mixing in with the dark, at the blue of his eyes and I understood that my father was growing unreachable. I saw myself swimming past him, on the surface, while he sat on the ocean's bottom without looking up, a boat left on the bottom of the sea.

"I was wondering," I began softly, "when you think I can be left alone. I mean, if you want to spend the day by yourself, I'm probably okay alone."

"Oh, not yet. You can't rush these things." He took a sip and closed his eyes. "Maybe later this winter, when you turn sixteen. We'll see about things then."

"So." I heard wind rushing outside, a timpani of branches. "Where did you go today?"

My father looked at me, then he looked down into his teacup. "I went with the Catholic Society of Widows and Widowers. After Mass this morning, we took a bus trip to the seashore."

The seashore. Widows and widowers. "Are you dating?"

He laughed. "No, no, I'm just going out." He reached over and touched my hand. "You know, sweetheart, it's not that I don't miss your mother. I'll always miss her. But life has to go on. It has to go on for both of us, you know that, right? So I'm just going out." He looked down into his cup for a moment, then he looked back up at me. "You know, Magda, all I do is work. Work at my job, or around here keeping this old tub of a house running, and we go out once a week. That's no existence for a man." He said this last sentence in the exact tone Hannah would use; I knew then

57

who was responsible for my father's outings. "Life has to go on and from time to time, we all have to venture out."

Going out. Going on. I had never thought of this possibility, of my father looking at any woman other than my mother. What else would be the point of such a group?

"It's only once a month."

"Once a month, that's not so much," I said, thinking how I had not been enough to keep my mother, and now I was not enough to keep my father either.

"Staying light a lot longer now," my father said, pushing Hannah's soda bread into his napkin. "That's always a good sign."

I looked out the kitchen window, watching darkness patch through branches. In the jagged light, with darkness moving over them, the leaves looked exactly like fish slipping beneath water, fish that had come up from land and were now taking over the sky.

It didn't rain for three weeks. Fires burned all over the woods of New York City and my father came home every night exhausted from work. The mayor's office only called it a water emergency, not yet a drought, though everyone at school said a drought was near. People were asked not to water lawns or wash cars or fill pools.

Since there had been no fires in our woods for a while and they needed every man, the fire department dispensed with the guarding of our woods. I began roaming the sandy terrain again, remembering how much I liked the beach at this time of year, at the first flourish of summer. More boats had begun nodding in and out of the bay. The bungalow colony, a zigzagged scatter of small rental houses nearly identical in structure and each painted a pastel shade, filled with summer families who milled about on the flat marsh fields that served as their yards. Sailboat regattas billowed across the bay on Saturday mornings followed by the more ominously purring charter boats that departed the bay to fish the cold depth of the Atlantic.

People waved and smiled, glad for the brightening of the days. I waved back, then entered the darker, stiller woods, thinking of what I could create inside all this greening quiet.

Just thinking of flames, of their white heat and the way they swallowed all that lay in their path, just thinking of how flames multiplied one another so rapidly and effortlessly, how they grew from sparks to a force formidable as a tsunami, a delicious sense of secret knowledge thrilled through me. I walked rapidly through the woods. Then I found the mattress.

Of course it would still be there. I had been foolish to think otherwise. Broken, charred, and axed, but still there. Why the sight of broken cloth and springs could enrage me so I did not understand, yet tears sprang to my eyes when I saw the ragged corpse of the thing. I had assumed the fire department would have taken the mess with them by now, burned it into oblivion, but they had not; the husk lay there like an excised tumor. Without bothering to look around, I kicked the remains into a pile, then walked home.

I walked back slowly, noting how the woods had changed since my last fire. The treeless areas had grown brighter, with stronger sun, and the shady areas were murkier, with leaf growth. Heat trapped in the shady beds held webs of dankly humid air that made me think of capture. Quickly, I moved to the edge of the woods, back into the sun.

Beer bottles and cigarette packs littered the ground, and rusting cars lay abandoned all around the perimeter. The wind carried blooms of music. As the days grew brighter, more people would be using the beach and walking through the woods; I would have to be careful.

The guards might be gone, but teenagers lurked in the area all the time.

I came out of the woods and looked at my house, but I walked past, unable to face the mossy light inside. I could not bear the silence or the solitude right then. Just thinking of lying across my bed made my skin feel taut and wet, as though a slow-spreading, cold, blue gel were sliding up my body. I turned to walk to the boulevard, knowing what I would do: I would take the bus to Julia's block. That would make me feel better.

A police car sailed up our street, slow-moving and watchful as a bear. The officer inside the car waved to me, and I wondered if he had any suspicion of what I did with my time in the woods. I waved back and continued on to the bus stop.

The bus came right away, before the notions store had a chance to affect me. I took my usual seat in the back. We traveled the same loop, around the edges of Staten Island, then down to the ferry before starting back. This was my ride: once around the island, then back to my neighborhood. I had come to know the stops the bus would make in the same way fishermen knew the tides.

I could see why my father liked ritual; there was comfort in sameness, in predictability, in attending the same Mass, in ordering the same flavor ice cream in the same shop every Saturday night. The ride calmed me, made me think more clearly, and I could feel the gas lifting from my skull as the bus turned away from the ferry terminal and began its crabbed start-stop motion toward the boulevard again. I knew I would get off, finish my homework, and fold the clothes from the dryer. My father would come home, we would take out the bland dinner Hannah had left in the freezer, heat it, and we would talk. We would go on. That was the attraction of ritual: you knew what to expect, you knew you would go on.

My mother had been immune to ritual; each day she undertook different tasks, practicing music or arranging shells in the garden, baking a cake. Perhaps habit was a trick of sorts, a way of anchoring a day, a week, a life. Things could not slip away from you if your days had perimeters, boundaries; they could not bounce out of control.

The day outside burned yellow. I thought of seeing Julia, of how she might be outside on such a brilliant day. I longed to see and speak to Julia. She had not called since beginning her new school last month, and I feared her mother answering the phone if I called. I began watching the scene of reuniting with Julia in my mind. Just as I imagined Julia coming toward me with her arms open in welcome, a voice broke in, catching the edge of my reverie.

"You smell gas?" a woman asked. I had not noticed her sitting across from me. I had been staring out the window in a trance.

For a moment, I thought she meant the gas that had

filled my head all day like helium. Then I realized she meant gas from the engine of the bus. "A little," I answered. "I think it's exhaust."

"Oh. Exhaust." She did not release her gaze. I tried to look away, but found her gaze exerted a subtle gravity on me, almost like an undertow. The sounds and motions of the day dissolved around me as she spoke.

"I always sit in the back," she said. "Then I can keep track of all the people. You know, in case a maniac gets on." She laughed. "Of course, there are those people who might call me a maniac on account of what I do for a living."

I didn't dare ask what she did for a living. The woman had the overall appearance of a bag: her skin and clothing wrinkled, every part of her filled with sag and crease to the point where she seemed boneless as a jellyfish.

"You want to know what I do?"

"Only if you want to tell me." Heat flowered through my body. The woman suddenly seemed far too close, although she hadn't moved her physical spot.

"I do the makeup for the dead. All of it. Hair, nails. One day, all of us will get done by someone like me. Every last one of us. No exceptions." The woman waited. The air between us ticked, a slow, atomic sound.

"Do you like to do that?"

"I can't complain. And they never complain, my clients, never." She waited. I smiled.

Then she leaned forward slightly. "You know, what I do is make them look nice for the family." She crossed her arms in a casual, breezy way, in a way that let me know she was in the mood for a confidential spill. "What I do is ask for a picture of the person and I tell the families the same thing: I want a picture of the deceased before he got sick, in the natural state. Always. I won't even start without one. I work from that. You gotta get the skin tones right, the skin around the eyes. That skin, right under the eyes, looks real different when a body is sick. Get that right, that under-eye skin, all that skin around the eyes and the person looks like death is…well, a cure, like they're well again in some other place. So it's important to see the flesh color, all the tones, in the well person."

The woman rummaged inside a bag that I feared contained a dark version of the kind of things Mary Poppins' bag held: boiled bones or tufts of hair she used for conjuring spells. She pulled her hand up empty, then scanned the bus passengers quickly. "I even remember when my grandmother died," she said in a low-tide voice, "and I'm going back years and years now, honey, when they still used to wake the dead in the houses. Imagine that." She smiled and her teeth were surprisingly white, snow in an August garden. "You're too young, honey, to ever remember that, to even think that, but they used to wake the person right there in the living room. Kind of a nice idea if you think of the spirit staying put for a time. Anyways, they put ice under the body before they had the mortuary sciences and my uncle, this one uncle I had, Lester, he was a real card, always kidding around, always handing out nickels to us kids, but he had you know, a bit of a Scotch problem."

She shook her head from side to side, and I could see she was recalling other anecdotes involving this one uncle and his Scotch. Her eyes dimmed and I thought she had gone underwater, far away, but then she continued. "He put his bottle right under the body, right there under my grand-mother to keep it cold. Imagine. To keep the Scotch cold, he said, and my mother let out this little squeal then nearly fainted dead away when Uncle Lester pulled that bottle out from under the body and took a chug. He said it was blessed now, that this Scotch had touched the other side."

I looked around at the other passengers, trying to pull someone else into the web of this conversation, but none of them looked back.

"'Course, that was in the days when the dead looked like themselves, before they started with all the hiding and changing of the natural features. I remember my grandmother lying there." She paused, blessing herself. "I remember as she lay there, she looked as natural as when she was taking a nap on the porch, and ever since that day that's how I want to make people look after they pass, natural like that."

I deliberately turned my head and looked out the win-dow. Outside, the day filmed on and on, people buying hot dogs from vendors, women pushing babies in carriages, while I sat in the middle of this yellow day with one of the crones from Macbeth. I wondered if I had about me an aura, the way people from the Bible did, a glowing sort of ring that let the world know I was born of the drift, that I was not to be allowed access to the standard, an aura that people like this woman could recognize. Would this woman have approached Julia? Of course, Julia would not be sitting on a city bus in the middle of the afternoon either. People in the standard visited friends or made dinner or watched television crime or game shows in the middle of warm afternoons.

"What do you think?" the woman asked in a louder voice. "In your opinion, should the dead be waked in a public house for the dead or in their own homes alongside their living spirit?"

"I'm not sure," I answered, still looking out the window.

"Seems to me it's just more right to have people waked in their houses. Nowadays you die and you have to share your death with all the departing souls that have lain in state before you, all of you in the same lift-off space, in the same air, same as a NASA launching pad."

I turned back to look at the woman. She was looking at me very intently, and I worried she was picturing how she would do me up in my casket. "How come you're not scared of the dead? I know you're not 'cause you didn't get up and change your seat when I told you what I do. And that's how most folks respond. Just change their seat like I'm old mortality myself come for a call. So how come you didn't get up right away seeing as what I do for a living?"

Because, I wanted to say, I am more afraid of what you would do if I left than if I stayed.

"The dead don't really scare me," I replied. I did not tell her how my mother always told me, "Lena, you have to remember, the dead aren't really dead. No matter what people tell you. They're all around us."

I had been scared when she told me that, imagining tear-shaped ghosts floating around us with moaning O-mouths. When I told my mother she was scaring me, she had bent down to hold my jaw with her hands. "They're around us in the way clouds, oxygen, all the elements are. It's like being afraid of water or air touching you. And there's nothing to be afraid of with souls; they're just souls."

"I was never scared of the dead neither." The woman blinked rapidly, as if fighting a crying jag. Then she brightened. I wondered if she was insane, if she had a job at all, if she had a knife in her bag and planned to kill me, silently slit my throat on the back of the bus and walk away, leaving my still body slumped under the seat until the cleaning man in the bus terminal made the gruesome discovery.

"My license is in cosmetology, mortuary cosmetology. But I am also a parapsychologist. I read tarots down at the beach sometimes. The way I see it, I touch both worlds, the coming world and the gone world, so I'm connected in that funny way. On both sides." She smiled at me, exposing two back teeth that were golden and startling as jewels beneath water. "You should know this, honey. Now don't get scared on account of what I'm about to say, but you've got an undissolved soul around you, right in your central meridian. I study these things and I think you should know you have an undissolved soul, a soul that hasn't, you know, found its lift-off space yet. That's a soul that should move on, should accept that staying here will only be a border, a netherworld. Souls can't live in margins, you understand?"

"I think so," I answered, not sure if she was speaking to me or shooing away the soul that she saw drifting around me. But what she said made sense about the two places and a margin: I thought of the boulevard, how it separated two worlds and how I existed in both. There probably wasn't any soul around me, unless my mother was still hanging around, which I doubted since I was so lonesome. The woman probably said this to anyone who would listen. I did not want to compare myself to this woman, yet I couldn't help it. I was probably crazy, too, or going crazy, and that's what she sensed about me.

"You can come down to the beach sometime; I'm only there in the warm weather. I'll read your cards." She stood up. "Find out your future."

"Sure," I called, watching her walk to the bus door, a close-up fading into the larger picture outside, then vanishing.

I wanted to tell her that I knew my future, that I had seen it. It was gray and blank, moving without making any progress in the exact way static moves, and it was filled with nothing.

A satisfying feeling of calm came over me as soon as I began walking the zipper-straight streets of the above-the-boulevard houses. I had similar sensations in school, where my day was organized for me, plotted clearly and wholesomely as a vitamin dosage chart, in a place where people were taking care of things. Tragedy could never occur in places like these, in places so carefully controlled and run with such regularity.

Walking around our neighborhood, I was guarded, my eyes on stalks, ready for a heron to rush the woods in flight or a disheveled man to stumble from the woods. In our neighborhood, I walked with the inner core of my spine held rigidly as a spike. Here, my stride was languid, my steps loose and flowery. Julia's block was cleaner, drier, safer. It was like entering a television show: everything that happened here would be sane and right, its actions governed by great and benevolent forces. Even the meals at Julia's house were programmed like shows on channels. Julia's mother kept to a schedule, serving three meals at the same time each day.

At Julia's house, no dust accumulated underneath the sofas and beds as it did in our house; glass inside picture frames glistened like hair, bills were stacked in a cubby marked *Bills* on the kitchen wall next to a calendar, stamps, and several pens. Nothing could get lost in the standard, especially not a mother.

Turning the corner to her block, I saw Julia just beyond her yard, straddling her bike. I recognized her immediately: her small jaw, her wide cheekbones, the way her hair curled to her shoulders. Quickly, I moved toward her, anxious to greet her but una ware of the other girl waiting by the hedge. That girl moved suddenly from behind her camouflage of hedge, her mouth open and laughing, pedaling toward Julia. I dove behind a car where I crouched on the curb, stricken, embarrassed.

I should have known Julia would not be alone for long. I listened to their voices curve into the air and I sat, hidden by the car, biting the knee of my jeans while waiting for them to pass. They went by a few yards from where I sat.

Julia called, "We can go down the hill to the boulevard. See if Dave and John are down there by the ATV path."

"And what if they're not? Do we come back up?" the other girl asked.

No, I answered telepathically, continue on down the street, past the boulevard and enter the sinking place with people like me.

"Yeah, just come back up," Julia replied. "Want to?" Julia's voice: easy, light, inviting. Nothing in the standard, not even voices, held the kind of dark weight I carried. I wondered, for a short moment, what would happen if I rose up from behind the parked car and looked directly at Julia and said, "Hey, Julia, remember me? I'll trot along beside your bikes and I'd like to go down and meet Dave and John myself."

Once I heard their bikes wheel past, I ran in the opposite direction to the bus stop, grateful not to be detected. Again, a bus came almost immediately. I sat alone, in the back, my head turned toward the window. The absence of rain had allowed the bus windows to accumulate so much grime that looking outside proved impossible. I could make out only the bluntest of lines and shapes, but still I stared, my eyes averted from the other passengers, my face turned fully away; I did not want to connect with anyone around me. I got off quickly, running down the street, anxious to be indoors.

For an hour, I sat in the familiar silence. I sat in the sun porch of our house, a neglected room where my mother's plants had withered on the sills and an unused sewing machine hulked in one corner. I stared at the window screen, realizing how much this screen had in common with fly wings, the same thin black lines and delicacy of weave. When sun hit the screen, its rays ignited the same iridescent sheen that rose from fly wings.

Then I did something I thought I would never do.

I called Julia's house. I heard the miracle of her voice. I knew right away that the other girl sat on the green stool in Julia's kitchen. I used to sit on the same green stool when I talked to Julia and her mother.

"Hey," I said, though it took me a few seconds. My first impulse was to hang up.

"Hi. Who's this?"

"This is Maggie. Remember me?"

I heard silence, silence infinite as the bottom of the ocean, a silence that sealed.

"Maggie. Of course I remember you. How could I ever forget you?" Her tone rang neutral, simple, an even line of beige.

"I was just wondering how you're doing since I haven't seen you in a…"

"That was sweet of you," she went on in the same tone, only now I heard her moving away, the distance widening from neutral to detachment. "Maggie, I'm fine. Really great. I like my new school. And Mom and I think about you. How are you and your dad doing?"

"We're fine. My dad has joined some kind of church group."

"A church group? That sounds great. He'll have fun there."

"Now you sound like Hannah."

"No, I mean that. A church group would be a good thing for your father. Listen, Maggie, I'll tell my mom you guys are doing well." She wanted to hang up. I decided not to let her.

"So, I thought maybe you'd want to come over or do something this weekend. You know, go to a movie or something."

"A movie. I'm not sure that would be such a great idea. Okay? You know how my mom can be. But, listen. Have a great weekend. Say hello to your dad for us, okay? I have to go, Maggie. I'm not even supposed to be on the phone with you. All right? Sorry, Maggie, but I thought you knew that, the way my mom is so careful with me and all. I mean, sometimes I think she suspects things that aren't even true."

"Does she have to know everything, your mom?"

She coughed. "Maggie, it's not that, it's just...oh, I don't know. The funny thing is, I do really miss you. Sometimes I think about you so much and I can't tell anyone because...It's just my mom, she finds out everything."

"Yeah," I said, "I know. So listen, Julia. Call me sometime. Maybe we could just go for a walk on the beach or something. When your mom isn't around, so you don't get into trouble. Okay? You take care."

"Maggie."

Those two syllables of my name rang in my mind as I walked into the woods, matches in my pocket. An offshore breeze, warm and salted as blood, fanned the trees. Collecting the mattress pieces, I arranged them like stepping stones, exactly like the patio stones I had watched Julia's father shape into a little pathway to their backyard. Between the mattress pieces, I tumbled twigs and brush, ending at the largest part of the mattress. Then I pulled some old tires into a bridge, spanning it from the mattress pieces to some freshly abandoned cars. I worked quickly, precise as a cat in my grace and surety. The world dropped off behind me as I worked: I did not think of Julia or my father, I did not think of my mother or Hannah or of anyone. I did not think of school or holes or drowning; I did not think of my father's recurring, unexplained absences from our house. I thought only of the clean brightness of the fire, how it would cleanse. I lit the match and turned away. Before I got to the edge of the woods, the ripping sound of fire filled my ears.

This time I meant to burn the sky.

The explosion satisfied me. Mrs. Langley panted out to the street, yelling words lost to sirens. The street swam with people, with kids and neighbors from other blocks. From our front steps, I looked out over the scene I had created, a director admiring her dailies. People continued pouring down our street, and I wondered why no one ever admitted they liked fires, they liked to watch them. It wasn't as though they were coming to help; they came to watch, to see what the fire ate. They wanted to see what power looked like when it was not controlled. Only they would not admit that. That was my job: to recognize truth.

The second explosion surprised me, shaking the earth as it did. I looked up at a mushroom filling the sky with its black smoke, a cloud that blackened like the moments before one of my mother's headaches. At least that's how she described it to me when I asked her what one of her migraines felt like, what it looked like.

"The light fails," she told me once while we were lying on her bed. I had gotten her a cloth for her forehead; I had closed the blinds. "It all turns to night just before the nausea."

I used to lie with her for hours, dozing in and out of sleep until she felt better.

She never got those headaches in the hospital, she said. She smiled when she said, "Hannah always comes at the same time on Fridays, carrying the same package with the same thing inside. That's Hannah. That's how some people are." She said this in the sunroom where visitors came. She sat on an orange beanbag chair, smoking, pulling the smoke inside her lungs like a thing on fire, as though she needed the smoke to breathe, to keep on breathing. Everyone there smoked, even the doctors. She smoked and Dad kept patting her leg as though she were a draft animal undergoing difficult labor. Potted rubber plants lined the solarium and she looked up and asked if they actually got rubber from those leaves. He had laughed, quietly, and smiled, sitting inside the smoke that traveled in and out of her lungs.

The next time she didn't smoke. She lay on her bed with the shocked eyes of a fish who had found himself landed squarely on sand.

I watched the sky churn. I heard a man call, "The firemen aren't letting anyone over into the fields since the tires are all burning, and one car's gas tank exploded. It's a real mess."

I wanted to see the mess. I wanted everything a mess.

Smoke spumed from the woods, into the sky, from trees and behind houses as though the world were ending. I walked as close to the field as I could, near the murmur of the crowd. "That's some sky you've made, my friend," I heard a voice rise from the muted whisper of the crowd. This voice was clear and arrant, blue water in a crystal bowl. "Land and sky, you can change, but you'll never touch the sea. Never. Never. Never."

Mrs. Fish rose to the surface of my brain. She wore a miner's hat with the connected light on; she was dressed in denim overalls, her fins covered with thick work gloves. "What do you think when you look at that sky? See the blackness you've put there? See the clouds of darkness you've made? They'll be gone in an hour. No, Magdalena, none of these changes are permanent. Your fires are the most temporary attempt I've come across in quite some time. In quite some time. You think you are effecting change, but you always go back to the same place: your hole of nowhere. Though," she said, reaching up to dim the light on her miner's hat, "you are beginning, in just the tiniest way, to enter more into that place you fear. Magdalena, darling, you have one foot firmly planted in The Sinking, and your other foot is poised on the precipice. You wanted to send Julia's new friend to The Sinking, but she is not our next customer. You are. But of course, you already knew that. You must have because there's nothing newer here than yesterday's rain."

"Why don't you come back later?" I said mentally to Mrs. Fish. I did not want her interfering with my pleasure in watching the fire.

"Oh, I see. Well, I remember a different Magdalena. You used to think the sky was just an extension of the ocean, of that little bay at the bottom of your street, that the sky was water, waiting to empty into the sea. You thought you could get into the sky by crossing a bridge, remember that? Even when it grew dark at night and your mother asked you why water would grow dark, you told her all water grows dark at night. And you thought stars fell to the earth and that was how fish were born. Tell me now, Magdalena, do you think I was once a star?" The light on her miner's cap went dark. My brain went silent.

"Mrs. Fish?"

She was gone. Firemen ran across the field with cumbersome hoses, their faces blackened with soot. A third explosion, then a softer fourth one, just a thud really. I stood on the field's edge, watching the firemen move frantically about, smelling the sharpness of the rubber, the smoke, the brush burning and I knew it was over.

I had set my last fire. I had no desire to set any more. Something about the men's faces caused me to feel sorrow. None of my previous fires had evoked anything inside me, but this time I was hit with pangs of remorse. The desire to create fires left me in the exact manner in which it had come: suddenly, without explanation or provocation, the desire drained from me in the same way I could feel the tide drag from the basin of the bay when I was swimming.

I watched flames rip into the brush as if I were watching a movie. The other fires had ignited me, thrills zigging through my abdomen while witnessing the blaze I had created, as though their heat and power had entered me; I burned inside those fires. This fire did not enter me.

The flashes of terror and excitement that I once felt while standing before my fire did not touch me while watching these men struggle. Perspiration glimmered above their lips; it ran down the sides of their faces to their mouths and jaws. The metal twists of cars charring were as dull and ordinary as fish left to rot on the sand. I drifted off, away from the fire, disinterested in ever creating another one. I turned from the field, empty, and for the first time, ashamed.

Mrs. Langley came over to me, shaking her head. "Oh, Maggie, thank God it's over."

I stared at her. Had she known all along? How could she know it was over? Was she an oracle, a seer? I stared at her. My mother had told me to watch ordinary people, that they were the ones granted gifts of sight, of the stigmata. "The plainest person God can choose to do His work, that is the person He will choose. Not the fancy, beautiful person, but the most humble-looking. They are the ones doing God's work." I had thought at first she was explaining Hannah to me, but then I looked up to see several fishermen leaving the bay under dark skies. Their boat was small and looked as if it were made of twigs. "Those men right there remind me of the Apostles," she had whispered. If those fishermen could be disciples, then Mrs. Langley having sight into the soul was possible.

"How do you know it's over?"

Mrs. Fish had been right. I had begun crossing over to The Sinking. It would begin with my arrest on arson charges, then descend into blackness.

"Finally, one of the neighbors told the police they saw a girl running from the woods."

A girl running from the woods. Ice ran through me. I shivered despite the heat of the day, and turned to see if the police were coming for me.

"Me, personally, I never woulda thought it would be a girl, but they got her, right over there, the detectives got her." She pointed to where Spring Robinson stood, surrounded by four humorless-looking men. Spring moved her arms and her head in short, stabbing motions, an animal snared inside a moving wheel. Spring's mother looked on, her face white and blank as aspirin, black bra straps dipping out beneath her sleeveless blouse. The woman looked annoyed, but not worried.

Once, in seventh grade, a janitor had found urine on the floor and everyone in school whispered that Spring Robinson had done that because the bathrooms were locked during class time. She had been expelled for the act and when she returned to school, she sat alone during lunch, during gym, during assemblies. None of us spoke to her. She walked through the school alone and unnoticed as shadow. The teachers made no attempt to organize her life; they looked at her and then looked away. Only the boys watched her walk down the hall with her narrow waist and full breasts and harp-shaped hips. She wore tight black clothing and lots of makeup, a look she had borrowed from her mother, a mother that Julia's mother told me one day was only fifteen years older than her daughter.

No one had ever seen Spring's father. We only knew that she lived with her mother in one of the bungalows on the side of the beach that always held a stiff, fishy wind, in one of the dilapidated bungalows that fishermen used to rent for the summer, not to live in, but for cleaning fish. They were damp huts, crusted with barnacles, landlocked boats really, not a home fit for anyone except squatters.

"Who saw her running from the woods?" I asked, noticing that we had the same coppery shade of hair cut in a similar way.

"I don't know. One of the people who lives around here has been watching the woods on account of all the fires. Imagine if one of those fires caught on the edge of the wooden frames of my house or your house. You know what would happen?"

I nodded, knowing Mrs. Langley had been the only person watching the woods. She had identified Spring Robinson even if she had seen me running from the woods. No one ever believed honor students capable of anything more than studying.

"Look at that girl. Just look at her, how she's dressed, that attitude. It has to be her."

They put Spring inside a squad car with the light flashing on top. Her mother turned around, glanced pointedly at me, then got in the car with her daughter.

"That should be the last of it," Mrs. Langley said. Her words fell on me like stones. "It's finally over. Thank God in this drought. Can you imagine what could have happened?"

I wanted to tell Mrs. Langley that she was not safe, that none of us were. Lots of things could still happen to her, to any one of us.

"Those fires kept me up at night," she continued, "just thinking what if they came close to our houses. To think that girl lives around here, too. I've seen her, right down on the beach. You think you know a person…well, thank God. It's over now."

"Yes, that should be the last of it," I agreed. "I think she's done now, that girl."

I walked to the bench on the piers and watched until

the crowd and the firemen left. I waited until I was the only person left on the beach. Then I turned to look at the structure of the piers, how they grasped up from the water with their jagged edges like claws. But I knew they were not sea creatures. They were only piers.

Wobbly piers. Gulls overhead; boards thin as membranes serving as dock. Careful where you step. So many holes in the pier, so many sharp-edged openings you could fall through. Always hold hands, never go alone.

So early, oddly early, just as the sun was coming up you decide to go for a walk on the piers, on those piers, alone with no hand to hold, no witness. Then slipping into water that clouds with cold, you enter the cold solidness of the water until your body grows cold as well, the water and your blood running the same temperature, the water and your blood sharing the same place. Slipping further from shore, from what holds you on shore, to a place with a different gravity. How could you relinquish your desire to swim? Especially with a fourteen-year-old daughter sleeping at home, unaware, left behind in the place where her gravity would change as well. And the newspapers said you fell.

chapter
four

"School will be over tomorrow," Mrs. Keith announced during study hall. I sat in her class watching a bank of clouds drift toward the building. I knew that school would be ending, that it was already late June, but I knew this more in the way I sensed I would have to stop and turn when I swam underwater with my eyes shut. To hear Mrs. Keith say the sentence out loud made the knowledge inescapable, like bumping into a submerged seawall with my skull. I looked around at the other kids in my class, at the only area of the standard I had left now that I could not see Julia anymore. I had been hoping to find a new guide into this world, to look at this group I had been with since elementary school and see a new facet to one of the kids, in the way I could sometimes look at a poem or a painting and see something that had previously escaped me.

But I hadn't found one. Most of these kids and I had traveled through all of middle school together, straight from elementary school, a group of us separated from the rest of the student population by our reading ability. (There were similar groups for math and science, but we did not mix with them or even know their names.) This separation served to further keep me from entering the standard: I was accepted here for my silence, for my detachment, for my lack of sociability. Had I been thrown into the general mix, I might have had to venture into conversation and utilize the tools of the standard in a kind of social battlefield promotion. At the least, I would have had to talk. Here, I could sit inside my silence, a spider glinting in her web.

As soon as Mrs. Keith made this pronouncement, kids began buzzing around me, a hive of chatter, speaking of trips to Yellowstone or camps in woodsy states like Vermont or Pennsylvania. My father probably had a couple of trips to my mother's grave planned, but other than that, summer stretched before me, a long, barren drought of silence. I would fall through holes throughout the sunny afternoons, wandering further and further from the people around me.

"Hey, Maggie," Elsa called to me. She sat directly in front of me in Mrs. Keith's study hall and now she screwed herself completely around to speak to me. "What are you doing this summer?"

"Nothing, really." I turned to face Elsa. She was a shiny, happy girl who had called me a few times, asking if I wanted to go shopping with her or to the zoo. When she had invited me, her voice rang with the prudent cheerfulness of a Miss America contestant; I imagined Elsa's mother standing behind her, coaching Elsa into asking me somewhere, into asking the odd girl, Maggie, to do something normal. Her mother would be standing next to Elsa in a bright and clean space, smiling with approval.

My mother had still been alive during those few calls. Our living room was strewn with old magazines and tea cups (my mother drank tea endlessly), and shallow bowls spilling the gray turds of my mother's cigarettes onto end tables and carpets. She rarely opened the drapes fully, so we functioned in cave-light like a couple of moray eels shunning the sun. My mother had looked at me quizzically after I hung up the phone.

"Why didn't you go?" she asked. "You should go out more with your friends."

"I don't really know Elsa that well," I told her. I could not tell my mother that I did not want to leave her, that I feared leaving her alone. I thought she might grow despondent. Never did I think it would be my mother leaving me, falling off a pier and forgetting to breathe in the water.

"What's wrong?" Elsa asked, as I pulled myself away from the memory of my mother's voice. "You have a funny look on your face. Are you sick or something?"

How could I explain to this bright and shimmery girl that I fell into pockets of thought, slid down holes, that I listened to fish that swam and spoke in my head. "Oh, sorry. I'm just not sure what I'm doing this summer. I have to ask my dad I guess."

"Well," Elsa pressed on, "he probably doesn't have plans for every single day. You can call me if you want to go to my pool club this summer. I can bring a guest any Tuesday or Thursday."

"Thanks." Then Elsa turned back to her desk, her duty done.

Something about Elsa's invitation disturbed me; the rest of the day I felt cluttered and lumpish, filled with murky thoughts. I came home and tried to read on my bed, but my mind rambled about like tumbleweed, rummaging through faces of my classmates, faces I had seen in the hallway or on the bus; it dragged up old bits of conversation I had heard and believed I had forgotten. Ordinary sounds from outside, barking, a lawn mower, the jangle of an ice cream truck, fused and amplified into scrambles of noise piercing my brain. I closed the window to my room; I closed the door and opened my book again. The minute I stapled my eyes to the page, the fish showed up.

I had believed they were gone, vanished back into some gray recess in my skull, but here they were, wriggling bright and happy in the middle of my muddy brain.

"Thought you guys had gone back to sea," I said without speaking out loud.

"Who us? No, no, not us," Mr. Fish said, smiling, reading my mind. "We've been here all along. All along, Magda pie pie. Just watching from the fence."

"Fish on a fence," I said mentally. "Yup. Great. Just great."

Mr. Fish smiled widely. He had the smile of a cartoon barracuda, all needle teeth and bulbous snout. "You knew we were here, too. Didn't you, Magda? Didn't you know we were here?"

Then Mr. Fish turned quickly. "Oh, quiet, here she comes. You know how careful we have to be with her. She brooks no nonsense, this one." He rolled his eyes.

I did not see Mrs. Fish coming. I simply saw light. But there Mrs. Fish swayed in a lounge of some type, or a net, hung in the manner of a lawn hammock. Mr. Fish came in holding a platter, which he offered to Mrs. Fish. The same bright green light glowed around them.

"I was thinking we really need to work on Baby Fish's room, add more color." Mrs. Fish yawned, and I saw the same needle teeth inside her mouth as Mr. Fish had, only hers were smaller and more mustardy in color. "Those shells of his have no zip."

"Shhh," Mr. Fish said, "watch what you say; the window is wide open."

"Do you want me here or not?" I thought to Mr. Fish. "You act like you want to speak with me and then in front of Mrs. Fish…"

Mrs. Fish looked up and I felt she was looking not only at my eyes, but through them. "I don't see anything now. Really, Mr. Fish, you are getting so jittery. If you ask me, this has all been brought on by those eels. The whole nervousness. If I never saw another eel in my life, that would be just fine. Just fine."

"I tell you, Mrs. Fish, the window is still open and there is shadow directly in our light." He moved his left fin up. "See right there, in that small rhombus, see the eyes?"

Mrs. Fish squinted. She turned slightly in the hammock and only then did I see Baby Fish snugged in next to her. "Oh, not again. Why doesn't she leave us alone? Shoo, will you?" Mrs. Fish said, moving both her fins at once. "Shoo." Then they disappeared.

My father began disappearing, too. As the days of vacation wore on, I stayed in the house alone. My bus pass was not valid in the summer months and I did not answer the phone the few times it rang. I assumed my father would be around more, but he vanished now for hours and hours, even on the weekends and he no longer mentioned going to the movies or out for ice cream on Saturday nights.

In his absence, I began to view the house as mine, spreading my books and clothes out into the sun porch and walking to the corner deli store (I walked quickly, early in the morning when I was less likely to bump into anyone I might know from school). I bought the kind of easy foods I liked, foods I remembered eating at Julia's house, puddings and crackers and soft cheeses that Hannah would never select. My father gave me more money now, and we both pretended it wasn't because he was rarely home.

I knew he had a girlfriend; I could hear him talking in a low voice that purred through the kitchen wall into my room. It was with her that he disappeared, it was with her that he was widening the hole where our family used to be. I wondered if he wanted me to sink right through the hole his absence made, to move on as he had put it. Maybe to move on, he would have to jettison me. I thought about this for a few hours one afternoon, then I went down to the beach, not really thinking of anything. My mind was strangely loose, as if light had filled the space my thoughts usually occupied, a kind of strange greenish light that reminded me of water or clouds. Anytime a thought began, the light swallowed it, or dissolved it, and I just sat on the beach until I got up and went into the water. No one looked up. I saw some fishermen cleaning hooks on the pier, and the mothers clucking around their small children, the tourists in rowboats and kayaks. Plunging into the water, I sank. I held my breath until my lungs began to burst and the light inside my head filled with blood. Without trying, my body surfaced automatically. A will rose in me that lifted me from the water. When you lost that, you would sink.

That's what had happened to my mother.

The next night the sky filled with lightning bugs just after dusk. My father had come home early and we sat on the front stoop watching the bugs light blades of grass. I thought how attracted we are to fire, that I should say this to my father, how we all want to sit near fireplaces, that people sitting on the beach at night regularly lit fires, that it was a natural human urge to fill voids, to fill darkness, with fire. He would understand this, I reasoned, after working for so many years in the fire dispatch office. We sat there a long while, but I did not say this. We did not speak at all; we only watched the insects sail through the lawn, lighting up the Rose of Sharon tree, diving into the cones of bell flowers. The air was thick and smoky with the scent of fish and beach fires. A mournful, creaking moan of boats pulling at their mooring ropes rose from the bay, a sound like stones stretching.

While I sat in the cobalt dark with my father, kids from my school slipped in and out of the grassy weeds around the marshes, down to the beach where they could find spots for sex. I did not see them, but I knew they were inside the same darkness I was, slipping around me in the same manner eels slipped past me when I swam in the bay. I heard their shouts, their laughter, their silence.

"What are you thinking?" I asked my father, wondering why he had not mentioned my mother's name in so long. I wanted him to say her name. I wanted him to look at me and say, "I am thinking of how much I miss Ellen."

But instead he said only, "I was thinking maybe one night we'll have to go down to the marshes to see these fellas," and he gestured toward the lightning bugs kindling our lawn. Then he patted my shoulder. "Imagine the kind of things you'd see down there at night." He got up. "I'll go and see what Hannah's left us to eat."

"Do you want to go there now?" I asked my father.

"Go where?"

"Down to the marshes."

"Now? Magda, for heaven's sake, we haven't had dinner yet."

"Right. We haven't. I'll eat with you in a couple of minutes."

My mother would never have spoken of the marshes. She would have grabbed my hand and we would just have gone together, taking the old dinghy from the side of the house and launching it soundlessly to watch the lightning bugs.

"Magda?" my father called from behind the screen. "Don't disappear down into those marshes. You stay put in this yard."

"I'll be right here." I didn't tell him that I had not been near the marshes in nearly a year, that the only way I could go there would be with someone else, that I could not face the marshes alone. I had not been there since that day, but I could not say this to my father who did not connect the marshes with my mother.

> *Early August, days before she died, you were watching the marshes, just watching them, remembering how you and your mother would row through the choked veins of the marshes, weeds and skeins of grass adhering to your oars, pulling the oars out of position. The two of you would laugh, making no progress for several minutes, just wheeling in circles with the plants wound around the oars. The oily fur of the marsh animals close enough to touch, the polish of their eyes, bright and flawless as dark jewels. You were watching the marsh and listening to the warmth on your skin, thinking of the punks that grew on the cattails, how your father lit them, pretending to smoke them, the musky smell of those punks, half animal and half plant, how the three of you had sat on the stoop lighting those punks, remembering this and smiling, thinking how your*

*mother had finally gotten out of bed, how the worst
was over of whatever her sickness had been.*

    *And thinking of her, you look up, out over the
water. She is out farther than she should be. All the
still alarms ringing inside you, you call to her, but
her head goes under the water. You run. How you
run. Your rib cage aching, your heart beating in
your teeth, shrieking, shrieking, your throat splinters
and finally, finally you see her head. She turns and
her face is ghosted, her eyes gone blank as spools.
Her gaze turns to you and you feel her eyes are moving like terrible hooks, but they hook into you and
change: they come back. She begins her long strokes
toward you, toward shore, through the opal water
and when she comes to shore, she takes you in her
arms for a long while, her wetness leaking onto you
until you can't separate your tears and her wetness.*

    How you didn't recognize goodbye.

"Why don't you come inside now, Magda?" my father called.
"The bugs must be getting terrible out there by now."

By the middle of July, I could no longer stay indoors. I
began walking more often to the beach, gazing at the couples and families who came there and swam in the water,
water in which my mother had died. I felt I owned the

beach more than they did, seeing as how one of my parents' lives had ended in that water. It was a perverse sense of ownership, but one that I could not seem to shake.

I had always had a problem sharing the beach. During my extreme youth, I wondered how anyone had even heard of "our" beach, the one that my mother and I shared. And on some fanciful level, I believed my mother had created the beach in the same manner in which she brought forth other marvels: birthday cakes sparkling with pink fancies, puppets made of fabric scraps with feathers for hair, flower beds in the space where only sand and pebbles had lain. I thought of her as the woman who made the sea and it never occurred to me that the sea might continue on in any place other than where my gaze stopped. When we came across other swimmers, I viewed them as I viewed the people who stopped to admire my mother's garden: they had come to take pleasure in what my mother could create.

Of course I knew differently now, yet I could not rid myself of all the traces of that fundamental childhood belief. Having more right to the beach than anyone, I walked right through the orbits made by beach visitors. When groups stood talking and laughing with their feet in the shallow water, I banged through their circle without uttering a word. I did not get up from my seat on a log if anyone sat next to me, I did not move out of the way when they stood on the beach with their cameras to take family shots. When they looked at me, I met their eyes, knowing they would leave, knowing they would go back to their lives for three seasons and I would stay here. I would walk here in the fall when the sand grew cold and hard, I would listen to wind scraping the sand all winter, I would be here when sun began to lighten the water come spring.

They would not be. They could get out of my way.

With all the people on the beach, fires burned all day and all night, orderly fires, ringed in stone and checked by the police cars cruising the border streets. No one worried about fire this close to water, and I was grateful that I could walk through the woods with little desire to set fire to anything (although I still noticed the day's dryness, I still calibrated wind direction, I still paused before clearings assessing what type of fire I could create in the spot; these behaviors I could not seem to control). I watched families cooking over flames and sitting around the embers as the sun set and I did not feel the excitement that I once had as I stared into the flames. The flames made me think only of the dull thud of exploding cars, the worried faces of onlookers and the firemen running with hoses. In the actual presence of fire, I felt shame.

I especially felt shame when I thought of Spring Robinson.

The two of them had left town. After my last fire, Spring didn't show up for school. By the end of the week, we all knew she would never be back. I walked over to their bungalow that seemed made of dark water. The door had no lock except for a stone they wedged on the bottom. How easy it would have been for a murderer to find his way to this pair. I pushed the stone out of the way with my foot and opened the door.

The interior stank of fish and salt, a fetid odor that I could not imagine living inside. The odor was not the fresh salt smell of the ocean, but an odor of decay, of fish long dead. The smell reminded me of a chum machine my father had once kept in a backyard shed, a grinding machine that had terrified me to the point where I cried upon seeing it exposed anywhere in the yard. Its odor, without even looking upon the teeth of the gears and grinders, was enough to set me off. That smell of rotting fish flesh was the root of all human fear; I was sure of this. The entire idea of churning flesh into bits, any kind of flesh, was at that time of my life unimaginable: it was my first image of horror, and its smell was the smell of terror.

It was this smell that Spring Robinson and her mother breathed each day, the smell that entered their hair, their skin, their dreams. The smell of years and years of dead sea animals being gutted and deboned had soaked into the wood of their home. I stood in their bungalow breathing the smell they had lived inside, hating the smell, yet breathing the scent of decay as atonement. Then I walked through their house.

It took me a few minutes to realize that their interior lacked walls, or at least the normal number of walls people have in their homes. Only the bathroom had two walls; the bungalow did not have a tub, only a sink, a shower, and a toilet. The rest of the space was as open as the bay. One corner had a small counter and a stove that had turned from black to the color of ash. Assuming this area to be the kitchen, I walked over to see if they had left anything behind. Only a comb sat alongside a faded cereal box on the counter. Such ordinary things. I longed to uncover more exotic items in their house, clues to the danger of their lives: glittery earrings, an octopus statue, pictures of film stars. But a comb and a cereal box, mundane possessions that could be found inside the humdrum of Hannah's apartment.

The whole place was lightless as space. A skylight provided what little light seeped into the dark molar of their cabin; even that was cracked. The windows were obscured with newspaper and cardboard and as I leaned over to examine the windows, I saw the breaks in the glass.

I could imagine the coldness of raw days with wind sweeping the beach and rain gliding down through the places where glass should be. I hurried to leave their house, knowing it was as abandoned now as an unmarked grave. As soon as I stepped into the flashbulb brightness of the day, I heard someone calling my name.

"Magda, over here," the voice said, and I turned, hoping my mother had come back, a mistake in the body identification at the morgue. I had believed this for the first three months after she died, that she had gone for a walk and taken a ferry or a boat somewhere else after suffering a bout of amnesia. All I had to do was wait for her return. My heart beat wildly, a flapping wing, as I turned.

"Here, Magda."

Chito. I had forgotten about him, a grizzled fisherman who lived in a bungalow near the mouth of the bay's gully. He liked to garden and my mother had stopped a few times to speak to him, asking him how he prepared his soil in all this sand. I remembered the way she had stood at the side of his house, her hair pushed forward in an auburn hood of curls, her eyes the same agate-green as seawater, an ocean nymph visiting the land of mortals.

"Come see, Magda," he called. "See now what I've made."

I walked to his garden, the entire side of his house where he grew sunflowers and tomatoes in loamy soil, made that way by a ferment of leaves and fish.

"Not there, Magda, another garden, over here, on the other side of the house."

What I saw astonished me. A series of women, some dressed in beach wear and some dressed in evening wear, had been sculpted into the earth. "Are they made of driftwood?" I asked.

"Driftwood and lots of castoffs I've found washed up on the beach. You'd be surprised what washes up on this beach, what the people from Manhattan and Brooklyn leave behind. I'm like an architect. No, what do I mean, Magda? I'm like an archeologist. I dig around for hidden treasure. In the sand no less, like one of those guys over in the tombs."

I had seen Chito many times walking through low tide, slogging past dead fish that starred the evening's opaque water, spearing up old bottles and clothing so wet that it hung from his pole like hair. Never had I thought he would be able to produce anything from his beachcombing. But here they were, a panoply of faces and expressions rising from the earth like a picture of a pagan burial site I had seen once in the pages of a magazine.

"The newspaper's coming today to take pictures of this," he said. "Someone called my ladies in to the *Advance*."

"Where have you been?" I asked him. Chito's bungalow had been dark all spring, and I did not know if he knew about my mother or not. "I thought maybe you moved."

"I was at my sister's in Cleveland. She wanted to change

me into her brother again." He made an angelic face, rolling his eyes upward. "She thinks she is a wizard, my sister. Always thought she was a wizard, but I'm back here, just like before." Chito laughed, his face crinkling into a cross-hatch of lines and chinks. "She's no wizard. Finally, I told her, Betty Alice, I am what I am, just like Popeye says." He adjusted the hat on one of the wooden ladies.

"See, I have this theory." He laughed, very loudly. "If only I had just one—I have a lot of theories." His face grew serious. "But this theory explains me and Betty Alice. In this world, there are water people and there are land people, and that's it."

"No sky people?" I asked, remembering Mrs. Fish talking to me about the sky.

"No sky people. Sky people are water people; land people are only land people."

"How can you tell the difference?"

"Ah, you know already, Magda. The land people are more locked, but the water people, they are the ones to watch. See, Betty Alice was always an inland girl, even when we were growing up in South Carolina, out on the shoals and in the water, right on the coast. Betty Alice was inside learning how to make a doily look like lace." He shook his head back and forth in disbelief. "We would have this sky right outside our house, this unbelievable salmon-colored sky and the water smooth as glass and I couldn't even sit on the couch looking out at it; you know, water and colors like that, they call to you, they sing like a hymn delivered right to your ears. I would call Betty Alice over to the window, and she would look out and then go right back to her needle, a real, real land person."

"And you weren't," I said quietly, thinking that I could end up like Chito, an oddity, a person living in the drift forever, creating sea sculptures on the lawn for tourists to visit during the lackluster days of their vacations.

"Naw, I was out in the shrimp boats, young with my father. Even down to Louisiana we went, gone for days at a time, then we moved up here and I found a way to fish."

I looked more closely at Chito's women. Their wooden stillness and their grouping reminded me of a triangle of bowling pins. Each of them had a set, vapid expression on her face and a large, frightening ledge of breast.

"You've made a village of women," I said quietly.

"A village, that's right. Someone's gotta keep me company here." He looked at me with such sympathy as he said this, that I heard the unspoken remainder of his sentence: "…especially now that your mother is gone."

I nodded and looked away.

"The water, you know," he said, moving toward his women. "You get gifts from the water and then it takes gifts from the land."

"You might be right, Chito." He held out his hand. I took his hand and shook it, his flesh surprisingly firm and warm.

"All right," Chito said. "I better get back to work. You come back and see me, Lena. I'm thinking of making some men to go with them. Maybe they'll have families, I'll put some kids in, too. Depends on how much driftwood I can find."

"Maybe you should send the newspaper clipping to Betty Alice," I suggested.

This caused Chito to laugh and laugh, and I walked the long way back home, passing by Spring Robinson's bungalow again. The sun had already left its roof and walls, and it stood in the marshes, dim and abandoned, its shadow the same color as the sea.

I woke in the middle of the night to the scent of fire. It came in my room, through the screen, its fragrance touching me in sleep. I sat up. Lights whispered on in other houses. I went to the window. The sky was filled with slate-colored clouds; voices filtered up from the beach. Red lights blinked from fire trucks, the air carried the emergency sound of fire. My father moved behind my door. I went out to join him.

"What's going on?"

"I think it's Chito's place," he said. "I went out to the front lawn and the fire looks like it's coming from there."

"You know Chito?"

"Not really. I know where his house is."

"Is he okay?"

"I'm not sure, Magda. There's no ambulance. And it smells like a wood fire. He has all that driftwood by his house, right?"

"Yeah." His women. I wondered if Chito had set them

ablaze or if someone else had come in the night and struck a match.

"Why isn't there an ambulance?"

"Honey, I think Chito may have set the fire himself. You knew he was never…"

"Yes," I answered quietly, "I knew."

Chito had been saying goodbye to me. Somehow, I had known that, but it was the kind of knowledge you don't realize you have until later, until a thing happens. He did not want to enter the standard. Neither had my mother. And I did not know how to enter the standard. I sat on the small sofa in the sun porch until the lights on the beach dimmed and only the smell of smoke remained in the air, gray and bitter with a woody salt flavor that helped me remember Chito.

"Why don't you join the church camp?" Hannah asked brightly the next afternoon, a slow, yellow Friday.

I had been reading on my bed, thinking how the days of this summer were growing eternal, the weighted days of a hospital stay or a prison term.

"A church camp," I repeated flatly. I imagined myself sitting inside a group of relentlessly upbeat teenagers, each with the face of a hen while we sang "Kumbaya."

"Yes. My new parish has a day camp full of people your

age. Friday after lunch is newcomers afternoon. I bet you'd have a ball there."

"I'm too afraid of everyone and everything," I wanted to say. But instead I said, "Huh, maybe. You never know."

"You're indoors too much for a girl your age," she scolded. "A few friends would do you a world of good. Why don't you give it a try?"

"Sounds interesting, Hannah. Thanks."

I made sure I wasn't home anymore on Friday afternoons.

The following Friday, I went down to the old piers on the shadiest part of the beach where no one went, not too far from Spring Robinson's house. I scaled the rock wall there, an eel-slick jumble of rocks filled with sea moss and serpenty fish that darted and coiled in the warm, shallow pools between the rocks. From my perch, I watched a horseshoe crab skim the sand, then slip back into the sea. When I looked up to see if the creature would make it into high tide, I saw them drop the grappling hook. Immediately, I climbed off the rocks, wanting to be back on the sand.

As I grew up, that boat had replaced the chum machine as my singular image of terror.

I had seen that boat only a few times before, a battered tub, as large and earthbound-seeming as a pyramid. The fact that the boat floated on the water amazed me; it had the appearance of a moving casket. Long scabs of rust shivered down its sides. The boat had other maritime purposes, as it had a spot at the end of one of the marina's docks, but whenever I saw it I only remembered seeing the grappling hook plunging from the side of the boat. The first time I saw it, I had been standing with both my parents on the shore.

"Get her home," my father had whispered as my mother peered at the horizon, one hand shielding her eyes from sun. She did not turn me in time. I saw the hook spill over the side; I watched it sink into the water, a needle passing through flesh.

"Won't be much left of that body after that hook pulls it from the bottom," a man had muttered loudly. I knew then that the grappling hook was how the drowned were pulled from the sea's bottom. The hook moved along until it hit a solid object, then the hook pierced through the flesh to bring the body to the surface.

But my parents were no longer there to turn me away from the sight. I watched the boat prowl slowly through the water, turning in long circles so as not to miss the solid tug of a body on the bay's sludgy bottom.

A crowd had gathered along the shoreline. I never understood how this kind of news traveled so quickly, but already about twenty people clogged our small beach. Cameras snapped photographs of the boat.

"Hello there." A voice spoke from nowhere. For a long second I stared into the water, certain my mother had spoken.

"I don't mean to bother you, young lady, but I was wondering if you could help me."

I felt the woman before I saw her, her shadow falling onto me.

"That boat," she said, gesturing toward the old tub, "is searching for my daughter. She's about your age. I was wondering…" The woman had trouble going on. She looked at the boat, then at the crowd, then back to me. "I was wondering if you saw a girl swimming alone this morning. I know she shouldn't have been alone, but she sneaked away from the house this morning. Daphne told one of her friends, well, actually, it was her boyfriend, that she was going to swim the channel."

A chill went through me. The channel scared even my daring-in-the-water mother. When I first learned that my mother had drowned, I assumed she had attempted the channel. Buoys marked the area and fast, unpredictable currents rippled its surface so that whitecaps there were a constant.

"I'm sorry," I murmured. "There were a few swimmers in the water this morning, but I don't remember seeing a girl alone."

"What am I supposed to do?" the woman asked. "Just exactly what am I supposed to do? Can someone tell me that? Please. What am I supposed to do?"

"Just wait." I said this with sympathy, remembering the morning I sat on our sofa while rescue workers flanked our beach. Luckily, my mother's body had surfaced close to shore and no grapple had to be used. I had seen only the ambulance pulling away from the beach, slowly and without alarm, the same way it had gone up the street with Chito.

"Wait." The woman peered up the shoreline. "That's what I've been doing all day." She began picking her way across the pier slats back to the sand, where I saw a man put his arm around her. I waited, too. I waited until the boat went back into the harbor and the crowd left. I even stayed on shore after the woman turned away and the police left.

I didn't want to tell her that sometimes bodies were never found in this water near the channel. That was the reason I had stopped swimming there; I didn't want to come across any.

My father was home early that night. I had just come back from the beach when his car pulled into the driveway. I could see by his face that he had not heard about Daphne. "There she is, my Magda," he called as he came through the door. "Been down the beach with your friends?"

He really did live underwater.

"I'm going to take you out tonight, down to that new place by the marina, seeing as it's beautiful outside and we can dine alfresco. Hannah's coming and I'd like you to meet my friend, Dorothy Shoane. I think you'll like her."

"What if I don't?" I said, and as soon as the words hit the air, I wanted to take them back.

My father opened his mouth, then shut it before saying, "Well, I like her, Maggie, so I assume you will. It never occurred to me that you wouldn't like her."

"You're right," I said quickly. "I'm sorry, I'm sure I'll like her."

I put on a dress with a lace collar to make up for my surliness to my father. I even embraced Hannah when she came to the car, an act that I could see cheered my father. He drove faster than usual; he walked with a jaunty air. I knew my father planned to marry Dorothy. Catholics never have public meals with anyone of the other gender unless they plan to marry.

Dorothy met us at the restaurant. She had extraordinarily sculpted hair, full of dips and swirls and tiny turrets. We once had a calendar titled "The Earth's Bodies of Water," with pictures of how the seas and oceans looked in each month of the year. The North Sea was December, and its waves and plunges had served as the template for Dorothy's hairstyle. I had trouble keeping track of her head.

"So nice to meet you. Your father always speaks so well of you." We shook hands like diplomats at a summit. "My son will be along any minute now. He's a bit older than you, Maggie; he'll be starting college in the fall."

"How nice," Hannah said, and I could see what she had in mind. If Hannah had been an insect, she would have been rubbing her legs together at that very minute.

The waiter brought us to a table on a patio overlooking the bay. I tried not to think of Daphne, still floating in the water.

"Dorothy's son is going to St. John's in September to study accounting," my father offered in a penny-bright voice. I didn't understand why the adults kept looking at me. Dorothy was a done deal. None of us would be here if she weren't.

"Accounting, there's a subject my Magda would probably not visit too long." My father beamed at me with such a festive expression that he seemed to have transformed from his usual moderate self into a game show host. All he needed was a giant spinning wheel behind him. Dorothy leaned forward with an equally exaggerated expression of interest on her face, as if one of my academic lacks interested her enormously.

My father continued his beaming glance. "What I meant is Magda is more inclined to the abstract, plays and art and that sort of pursuit." Dorothy looked disappointed. I could tell she liked concreteness; she would like the blank solidity of a ledger book, of tax laws, of rules. In fact, though not a large woman, Dorothy's presence was densely large, in the way a mountain or a glacier is densely large, the opposite presence of my mother who shimmered like mist. Dorothy would never shimmer, but she would continue on, and she would continue on in the solid, reliable way of a barn or a church. Perhaps, for now, that was enough for my father.

"Have you selected a major yet?" Dorothy asked.

"Not yet, but I'm very interested in nursing," I replied, though I had no idea why I said this. My father and Hannah blinked over their water glasses. Hannah wore an expression so blank she could have been confused with her plate.

"You have time," Dorothy counseled. "And nursing is such a wonderful career for a girl. A wonderful career. So many opportunities." My father continued to stare at me. He knew the sight of naked flesh, let alone blood, frightened me. "My Andrew, he's been interested in math since grade school. If you can imagine such a thing." Dorothy smiled and gave a short little laugh, a kind of lilting bark that might issue from a lyrically inclined dog. "He saw one of my balance books from the store and when I showed him how it all worked, with the debit and credit columns, he just was fascinated. Not that he would be interested in running a sewing shop," and here Dorothy looked around the table at every individual face to make sure we each understood that Andrew was manly enough. "He was only interested in the accounting part." She smiled and we smiled, tentatively, relieved that she was done speaking, but then she barreled on, "I don't think Andrew even thought about his major, he just fell into it. Lucky, how some people just have a calling. Maybe that's the way it is with your nursing, Maggie. A calling."

"Maybe," I shrugged.

Dorothy rubbed at the corners of her mouth with her napkin. "There he is now, my Andrew." She launched from her chair, excusing herself to go steer her son to the correct table.

"Nursing?" My father raised his eyebrows. "When did you decide this?"

"Just yesterday," I answered nonchalantly. "Yesterday I decided I wanted to be a nurse."

"Does that mean that tomorrow you may want to be, say, an astronaut or a lawyer?" He said this with an edge, an unusual manner of speaking for my father.

"I think it's safe to rule law out," I answered. "We both know how I feel about law. Here comes the accountant."

"That's enough, young lady," my father said in a low, worried voice.

I would have recognized Andrew anywhere. He had the same diamond-shaped face as his mother, a face that spanned very wide just above the lips then narrowed to a chin no larger than a chestnut. The result was an uncanny resemblance to a sheep.

"This is my Andrew," Dorothy gushed. We smiled politely. I fought back the image of Dorothy and her son as sheep, willing my mind to count things: one, the water glass; two, the plate; three, the salt shaker; four, the chair. I did not want the whole place to turn into a barnyard. I knew full well that the architecture of this meeting, of this dinner, would be the architecture of the next meeting and the one after that. I steeled myself to the dinner at hand. I would not let my mind wander or go about in its usual manner, in the manner my mother had admired so much. This dinner, these people were not connected to my mother at all. But it happened anyway.

I looked over at Hannah, at her far-set eyes, at the curls thatched in the middle of her head, at the curving tips of her ears emerging over each eye. As I gazed at Hannah, her features began a slow migration into those of a buffalo.

My father kept his soft eyes on me, and as he did he transmogrified into a dog, a trusting companion dog. I was my usual giraffe, sitting across from the two sheep. I managed to answer questions. I managed to eat some of my shrimp scampi. I managed to listen politely. What I could not manage was willing back my companions' human features. This time was different, and I wondered, only for a moment, if my mother was acting through me, enraged that my father now sat with a new woman and her child. But she would not do such a thing to me. I was sure of that.

I could not explain why this time was different, why the animal faces did not leave. The fish did not leave when

I wanted them to either. I sensed danger in my lack of ability to melt away the bestial images. At the table, seemingly moored between my aunt and my father, I spun the whole time, swirling faster and faster inside eddies I had shared with my mother. I only hoped I would not be swallowed by such fast moving tides.

Two days after the dinner, my father announced we would be taking a vacation. I looked up from a drawing I had been working on, a strange collage of a woman's head with blooming hair, a sort of floral Medusa. I shaded the drawing with my hand, not wanting my father to think I was drawing Dorothy.

"Hannah mentioned that you're too much around the house, Magda," he said as though this were news. "I'm thinking it's time for a family trip. Here we are into August already and I can't name a thing you've accomplished this summer."

"Where are we going?" I asked, snaking a tiny patch of daisies into a curl.

"To the Jersey shore," he announced. "To Ocean City."

"Who else is going?"

"Dorothy and Andrew will be going. But," and my father's entire head reddened as he said this, even the patches of his scalp that were visible turning pink as ham, "of course, they won't be staying in the same room with us. Only the same motel."

"How many days?" I asked, trying to mask the dread in my voice with nonchalance.

"I thought we would only be able to get a night or two, but I was able to book three nights." My father said this proudly, as though he were about to burst into song.

"Sounds like fun," I said in a hollow voice.

"I'm going to work a double shift tomorrow night so I can get the time off. I won't be home until about one or two in the morning. You don't mind staying with Hannah for one night then?"

"No, that's fine." I watched my father swim past me, far into the lightless part of the sea until he was no longer visible.

Looking back down at my drawing, I added more petals to one of the peonies near the woman's ear when Mrs. Fish popped up.

"This is it!" she exclaimed to Baby Fish. "We are finally here." She pushed him along in a stroller with two fins on either side. I could not see Baby Fish's face, hidden by a net. "It's time to see everything."

"Are you on vacation, too?" I asked, but they did not answer.

"Time to run," Mrs. Fish said. "You know what they say, old Magda bones, don't you?"

"No, what do they say?"

"They say..." Mrs. Fish laughed loudly, a snorting, bubbling sound like the spread of slow lava. "They say it's either sink or swim. And we know what you're going to do, don't we?"

"What do you think I'm going to do?"

I waited for her to answer, but she and Baby Fish went around a corner and disappeared.

I waited a bit for the fish to return, and when they didn't I decided to go down to the beach. Already, when I pushed the warm, bleached top layer of sand with my foot, I could feel the coolness beneath. The seasons came and left earlier near the water, I knew. Teachers in Staten Island were always pointing that out, since so many of their students lived along beaches. I knew that water held sun and cold longer than land, yet the fact of it still surprised me. I was sitting on a log, moving the sand around with my foot when I looked down toward the rocky end of the beach. A family strolled toward where I sat, at the marshier end of the beach, and as their faces came into focus, I saw that the family was Julia's. They strolled along the shoreline, their pants rolled up, their shoes in their hands. They spoke to one another, I could see that by their laughter and the way they turned to one another, but they did not seem real: they looked far too ironed and tucked in to be on any breezy beach, as though they walked immune to wind. Their faces held so much light they seemed polished, and as they moved their heads, each of them glinted with angles of flesh and sun.

Never before had I seen Julia walking with all the members of her family, with her younger brother and her father. As they neared, I lay behind the log, tucking my head into my arm and pretending I was examining a shell for fear they would recognize me. Sand surged into my pockets, it poured into my shoes, filling all my spaces in the converse of leaking. I started thinking how the whole idea of leaking reminded me of mourning, of grief, how things just left you, poured out of you in places you didn't know you had holes. I was thinking this just as Julia's family passed in front of me, their long diamond of shadow stretching out in front of me. While their shade fell across me, I could not breathe in or out.

Then they were gone, the four of them, not noticing me as I lay adhered to the log like a barnacle burrowing into sea wood. No wonder the fish had moved into my head. I was growing more like a creature of the bay than a human girl.

"I don't understand," I complained to my father the morning after seeing Julia's family. "Why can't Hannah stay at our house for the night, why do I have to go over to her apartment?" We were driving to her apartment, so I already knew my complaint would not affect the outcome.

"It's just easier for her this way, Magda, you should know that. Hannah's not getting any younger."

"What does that have to do with anything, Hannah's age?"

"The older you get, the more you like things the same. You like your own bed, your own chair, your own bathroom. And Hannah has enough to do without having to sleep in our home. The least she can have is her own bed at night. I don't think that's asking too much. If she stayed at our house, she'd have to give up her bed and transport herself as well."

"But you drive her everywhere," I protested. "It's not like she has to do the cha-cha over to our house."

"Oh, Magda," my father sighed, "can't you make anything easy for me?"

I thought I was making things easy, I wanted to say, by staying out of your way so much. But I said nothing, quietly following my father down the hall to Hannah's apartment. She would not be back from work for a few hours.

The interior of Hannah's place was stark as a desert. It had the same vacant, uninhabited look of a motel room: lamp, table, chair, all done in beige tones. I slumped down on her sofa.

"She's left food for you," my father said, coming out of the kitchen, and I understood that this act was supposed to endear Hannah to me. My father stood there looking so hopeful that I could not disappoint him.

"That was nice," I said. My father beamed. "Hey Dad?"

"Yes?"

"This should be fun, this trip."

"I think so, Magda. They have an amusement park near one of the hotels. That's the one I booked, for that reason."

An amusement park, I thought, waving goodbye to my father from the front window of Hannah's apartment. My father still thought I wanted to go to amusement parks. He was sinking deeper and deeper into the ocean and I could not stop him from going there. I turned back to Hannah's apartment and sat in one of her beige chairs.

Light splintered in front of me, combing in through the slats on her Venetian blinds, so I half-closed my eyes to try and see the colors split and bend. As I was doing this, Mrs. Fish appeared. She wore an apron made of clear bubbles and stood at a sink, her fins elongated enough to function as arms. These arms were immersed in a sink full of soapy water. I heard squishing sounds, though I could not see what Mrs. Fish was washing. "I can't take much more of this. It's like living with an emotional eunuch."

Mr. Fish sat at the round table, a bare table that resembled an industrial spool. It was the first time I got a good look at his face, and I could see that he had crudely etched features, a large nose and flaking scales all over his skin. He, too, had elongated fins, only his were more jagged, as though they'd been caught inside a machine, perhaps a boat engine. He drummed these long fins against the table. "I don't know what to say to you," Mr. Fish protested in a surprisingly thin voice.

"Oh, as if I haven't heard that before, as if that isn't the excuse of the year lately. I don't know what to say. Excuses. Did I ever tell you my theory on excuses?" Mrs. Fish swished her fins inside the sink violently and did not wait for Mr. Fish to answer. "Excuses are nothing more than veiled failures. We fail, and that stinks, then we have this social perfume to flower it all up like it's not a failure. All the words: I can't or I don't know. I forgot, I can't find it, I didn't know that. All failures."

"Why all this now?" Mr. Fish asked. "What has happened that we have all this now?"

"It's not now," Mrs. Fish answered, turning around to face Mr. Fish. Her bubble-apron moved rapidly up and down in front of her though she had stopped moving. "It's been always. Now with Baby Fish it's all coming to a head." She turned back to the sink. "That's the trouble with all men: they never see anything coming, they only see what falls on their heads when it's about ready to shatter. Then they look up at the pieces and say, 'Well, I'll be damned. Didn't see that one coming.'"

"Who are you?" I said loudly.

"Oh, you again," Mrs. Fish said, turning her head to the left. She still wore the bright, heart-shaped lipstick on her mouth. "Not now, just not now. Why don't you go figure it out?"

"Why don't you give me those rules for entering the standard and maybe I will figure it all out."

"The rules. Well, sweet Magdalena of the bay, you think you're such a hotshot at figuring everything else out, don't you? Well, go figure this out and stop bothering us." She turned back to Mr. Fish. "As I was saying, I just feel like I'm living inside a glacier. The coldness is astral, positively astral in its depth."

"I am the way I am," Mr. Fish said. He pulled at his fin, then let go to watch the undulation. "You knew the way I was when we met. I never misled you regarding my nature. You knew precisely what you were swimming into. I was wide open. You can never accuse me of being a clam. Never. Not now, not when we met."

"When we met. When we met all I really wanted was Baby Fish. Any Baby Fish. My mind was filled with babies. Babies, babies, babies. Like a sickness I had, an obsession. Who was I to judge?"

"So then all this is, in a way, your fault," Mr. Fish offered, standing up on his bottom fin. "You wanting the baby so badly you couldn't see who or what I was, is that what you're saying? That you were blinded by your maternal passions?" He whistled, a long, hollow sound. "All I can say at this point, Alice, is it's a done deal now. I never hid from you what I was, how I was. I've been authentic from the start. Now that isn't enough, that's not satisfactory. I work hard, I do everything I do for my family and that's not enough. I'm not sure what is enough anymore." Mr. Fish sighed. "It's not like we both don't have faults, surely you're aware of that."

"I'm not talking about faults. I'm talking about incompatibility. And we haven't even mentioned the dullness, the total dullness of the situation, the way we stay here all the time, the way I'm expected to get along without friends, without family, with nothing but you and the impossible weight of a child and a house."

"I can't fix that, Alice. That would be up to you. You can't expect anyone else to make you happy. You don't have to stay home all the time. And that's not to mention that you have those long periods of low mood..."

"No, I suppose you're right, Preston, I suppose you're right. I can't expect anyone else to make me happy, now can I? And my low moods." Her voice sounded like water rushing as she said the last sentence, like water rushing over rocks. "But how, tell me, am I supposed to get happy when I'm living under the weight of a child and a house? The constant attention I have to pay to both." Mrs. Fish turned to face me, her eyes large and luminous as jewels. "No one can ever answer that, no one."

"Are you sleeping?" Hannah stood over me.

"I wasn't asleep," I answered. I opened my eyes very

wide to show Hannah how awake I was. At the sound of her voice, the fish had scurried off into their recesses and this annoyed me. Hannah seemed to always be interrupting my sleep or my reveries.

"Your eyes are glassy, but they're open and you're sitting up."

"I was watching the fish," I said plainly, wanting to see what Hannah would say to my statement.

"The fish. I don't have any fish here."

"There are fish living inside my head."

"Oh," Hannah said, "I see. The fish that live inside your head. Those fish." She put her grocery bags on the counter. "You know, acting strange doesn't do anyone any good. Your father deserves his happiness. He certainly gives you your share of attention." Hannah sighed. "When you're older you'll understand more."

"You're right," I answered. "I think I'm understanding more now." The fish teach me, I wanted to say to Hannah, the fish are teaching me by running through me like an undercurrent. But I did not say anything like this to Hannah. She had already turned back to putting away her groceries.

"I bought a canned ham for tonight," Hannah said. "I thought we could have that with some potato salad. I asked for no onion this time."

"Have you decided what you'll wear to Dad's wedding?" I asked.

"Or would you rather have the chicken? I could make breast of chicken with the potato salad."

"He definitely has to buy me something new. All I

have are jeans and old shirts. No one's thought about my clothes since Mom died."

"What in God's name are you talking about, Magdalena?"

"The wedding. Dad's wedding."

"Aren't you getting just a bit ahead of yourself?"

"I'm not the one making things happen too fast." I spoke in the same tone as Mrs. Fish.

"I will tell you one thing. I will tell you this." Hannah paused and frowned. "I have always maintained, and I still do, that you should have stayed in parochial school after first grade. You would be a different girl—a more reverent girl today if you had had an education that taught you grace, the grace of manners."

"Do you think I made that decision at six?"

"No, I remember precisely how that decision was made." Hannah waited again. We gazed at each other, two bulls in a pen. "Your mother decided. She told me that if the United States government thought there should be separation of church and state, then there should be separation of church and state in education as well." Hannah pursed her lips until they mashed into a rumple. "Your father took my side, but that didn't sway her one bit. At least he knew St. Sylvester's was a much better place for you than that public school. All public schools do is produce batches of fresh children."

"And so you think that public education ruined your niece, is that it?" We had not moved our eyes from one another's face.

"No, I'm not saying that, and I do apologize if you think that. What I am saying is that you used to be a much more reverent girl and after being exposed to all types of children, and God only knows what type of child is at that public school you go to, your standards are looser. You can't help it. You imitate what you see in your environment. There was never enough of an example set for you at home and then your father agrees to place you right in the heart of public schooling. All I'm saying is, I can only hope your college is chosen with more care."

"I think I like ham more than chicken," I said, turning my gaze away from Hannah. "But it's up to you."

My father was late the next morning. Before Hannah left for work, I politely thanked her for having me. We had gotten through the evening by watching a Fred Astaire movie and acting as though no sharp words had flown between us, embedding in our skin like hooks.

"No one can dance like Fred Astaire," Hannah had sighed the night before. "He moves like prayer come to life, don't you think?"

"He does," I said from under my blanket. The whole movie was eerie: the black and white flickerings inside the blankness of Hannah's apartment made me feel as though we sat in the presence of rhythmical ghosts.

"And that Ginger Rogers. You never see couples like that anymore, never."

I fell asleep on the couch, the spectral couple still dancing on the screen.

The next morning, Hannah embraced me before she left for work. I stood in a sleeve of sunlight that came in through the kitchen window and reached my arms around Hannah's waist in reciprocation, but I did not like the munificent yield of her soft flesh. I pulled my arms back. "Well, then," she said, "I'm off."

I watched her move from the dimness of her kitchen light into the brightness of the day, off to her job.

For years, Hannah had gone to the same clerical job for the archdiocese. She took trips with the people she worked with, to Lourdes or to shrines; sometimes they went on weeklong retreats at monasteries. I could picture Hannah moving inside the scoured air of a monastery, a row of shrubs outside her window pruned with such uniformity that they looked as perfectly strung as a rosary.

Her apartment reminded me of a monastery. Not one corner was softened with a spray of flowers or even an angel statue; I imagined Joan of Arc standing in the middle of the apartment with a clipboard, saying to Hannah, "We need to think sacrifice and doom, add a few more blank angles, bring in some more beige. And those corners should be bald as stone and suggest nothing more than martyrdom and thoughts of doing without."

I walked over to Hannah's living room window to look outside for my father's car. The apartment was small; from any one point, the rest of the place was visible. I waited a few minutes in the sunny, dusted light, then I went into Hannah's bedroom. I realized I had never seen her bedroom in its entirety. The bed had a nubby white spread, and I knew a digital clock stood on her bedside table. Both were visible from the doorway.

The only interesting discovery in Hannah's bedroom was a collection of holy pictures she had placed over her bed. My parents had had two similar pictures, one of Christ in the Garden and the other of the Apostles at the last supper with Christ's feet already hovering above the table in a gesture of ascension. I had stood on my parents' bed as a small child carefully examining the details of those pictures, looking at the gauzy texture of Christ's face, at the edgeless depiction of simple objects, the way the drinking cups and plates seemed to flow into the cloth, at the way one wave of color went into the next. The effect was one of ethereal beauty, of an event taking place underwater. As I grew older, I began to think the pictures were fragments of my parents' dreams, that these dream fragments had risen to be suspended over their bed. Then one day the two pictures disappeared from over their bed. Nothing ever took their place.

Hannah also had two pictures on her wall: one of Christ on a ship with the Apostles, whose faces were turned toward the sea, and another of Mary kneeling before the angel Gabriel. Gabriel's wings were three times the size of Mary. I thought I would try to copy the rendition of Gabriel while I waited for my father; I planned to send the sketch, unsigned, to Julia. She would be sure who had done the drawing and her mother would not have a clue; the idea was pure witchery. I could not wait to get started.

I knew Hannah would not have much in the way of art supplies, so I began rooting around her bedroom desk for some unlined paper. I liked the desk; it was the sole piece of furniture that appealed to me in the apartment. Its two legs were shaped in opposing question marks and the small, flat writing surface had striations carved into the wood that looked like strings, so that the desk reminded me of a lyre.

It was there, in the bottom drawer, while searching for some blank paper, that I found a photo book. The book was small, only slightly bigger than a paperback, but Hannah had wrapped the book in a soft white cloth. I thought the pictures would be of Hannah's friends from her youth, as I could not imagine Hannah taking photographs of anything in her present life.

I opened the book expecting to find group shots of her coworkers standing before sacred walls or handing blankets to orphans. Instead, several pictures of an infant boy met my gaze, a wide-eyed child with short spirals of dark hair. The pictures were chronological; with each turn of the page, the child aged by several months. At about age nine, the photographs ended. No notation was written on the back of any of the photographs and I could not imagine Hannah taking an interest in any child outside of our family. I was still staring at the boy's face when my father knocked on the door. I put the book away carefully, positioning it exactly as I had found it with the cloth folded over its edges in the same manner holy relics were stored.

"Sorry I'm late," my father said. He stood in the doorway holding his cap in his hand.

"It's all right. Hannah only left a few minutes ago. Did you get off work?"

"I did. I think you'll like this vacation, Magda. The place is so close to the beach that the rooms smell of salt."

I wanted to ask my father about the boy whose pictures I had just found, if he were a cousin, but I could see my father was jittery. He kept twirling his cap round and round in his hands. Also, I did not know how to say I had found the photos without revealing my snoopiness. I picked up my overnight bag and walked to the car.

"There is one thing, Magda, about the vacation." My father turned the key in the ignition.

I waited. He cleared his throat: I could see this statement was the source of his jitters. "It's a small matter, but one I feel I should tell you about beforehand." He cleared his throat again. "I was only able to get two rooms at this late date, but they are next to one another. In fact, there's an adjoining wall with a door we can unlock, they are that close."

"And?" I squinted into the sudden brightness. Hannah's apartment was in the middle of the standard, in a particularly treeless area that made the August light splinter into my eyes like shattering glass.

"After talking about this situation with Dorothy for some length of time, we thought it would be most appropriate if you were to share a room with her and I to share a room with Andrew."

"Fine," I said, seeing myself transforming from giraffe to Zulu warrior, screeching and running across the savanna, my face contorted with paint and rage, my spear held high and ready.

five

My father had been truthful about the location of our hotel. On the first day, I sat on the bed in the room I shared with Dorothy and looked out the window. In the distance, out on the Atlantic, two boats bumped into the horizon, so distant that they looked like ghost ships, vessels made completely of fog. I wondered if death were like that place, the seam between water and air, a place that had nothing to do with land, just souls bumping around in gray mist. Or maybe the sensation of flailing inside haze was more a place of grief than death.

"Well, Michael can really pick a room, now can't he?" Dorothy exclaimed as she came over to the bed, ducking her head down so we could share the window. Her head arrived like a solar eclipse, completely absorbing the light. "That's really quite a scenic picture, isn't it? The ocean almost right outside our door like that. He can sure pick a room."

"Yes," I answered without turning my head. I had hoped the room would smell of the sea, but a strong, oily scent of lemons clung to the walls. "It smells a little funny in here, that's the only thing."

"It's the cleanser," Dorothy told me, lowering her voice as though she were revealing a great confidence. "If there's one thing I have to have, and I mean I *have* to have, it's a clean place. I don't care if the place is small or out of the way or even crowded, but it has to be clean. Has to be. Otherwise, I just can't stay. So I don't mind a bit of ammonia smell, if it means clean."

She began to unpack.

This act amazed me. My mother and I had never unpacked until after we had walked around. "You don't want to waste the light," my mother would say, "doing a chore that might as well be done in the dark." Most people spoke of the benefits of sea air; my mother believed the light by the ocean was different from light anywhere else. "Gulp this light, Lena," my mother would urge me whenever we went on a seaside vacation. Even though we lived right next to a beach, my mother pointed out that the light around our house was "bay light," and not the same as light by the ocean. "This light is scrubbed by the openness of the sea," she instructed me. "It's light that has elements mixed all through it, ocean elements. Like vitamins for the lungs, for the heart." My mother had been very earnest in this belief and I had believed her when she explained this theory to me, but I could only imagine what Dorothy would say to such a sentence.

"Might as well get organized early on," Dorothy said. Her voice pleated my brain: tiny, tight pleats like the ones on the skirt of a school uniform ironed into my brain as she spoke. I listened to the muffled whoosh of fabric being folded as Dorothy placed her shirts and shorts in the bureau. "I'm always one to get organized early on," she confided. "That much less to think about while we're enjoying ourselves." She spoke in a breezy, bouncing voice like an orgasmic Barbie. This was vacation-Dorothy. She wore a fuchsia shirt, one pocket pinned in the dead center by a festively jeweled pineapple.

In her white shorts, I could see she possessed a generously rounded belly and thin legs, a combination that caused Dorothy to resemble a gigantic, erectile spider. I looked at our room. I liked the pink and orange tones of the carpet and walls, I liked the lampshades that had little paper fish glued above their plies. Even the ashtrays were molded into cerinth shells. It was the kind of motel where you could find sand in the carpet and tiny land crabs skittering across the lobby where no one shooed them away.

"There," Dorothy said with satisfaction, "that's all done." She slid her suitcase under the bed across from me, then sat on top of the bed, smiling in a dangerous way that warned me she was feeling girlishly confidential. "Maggie, I am awfully glad we have this time together." I looked at her, trying hard not to transform into a giraffe. I hoped the pleats in my brain would keep my thoughts on the conversation and not allow any transformations. Dorothy kept smiling. For a few moments, I stayed in my regular, human form. Maybe being around Dorothy would serve me well: I might be able to enter the standard if I could keep my thoughts from roaming to fish and land animals. Julia's mother had pleats in her brain too, straight, even places to organize her thoughts.

"I know this must be terribly hard for you, losing your mother not even a year ago and now you have to put up not only with the likes of me, but Andrew to boot. I can only imagine what you're thinking, what you think of me." Dorothy lowered her gaze to her knees. "I can only imagine."

Not in a million years could you imagine what I'm thinking, I wanted to say. Mrs. Fish had just moved into my head, pushing the pleats to one side like a stage curtain. In one fin she held a telephone receiver toward Dorothy, but at the end of the receiver a set of lobster claws grasped mightily in the air, opening and closing with a loud clicking sound only to come up empty. But that was not the worst of the images in my brain: Mrs. Fish wore a gigantic fruit bowl on her head. She was dancing around in time to the clicking lobster claws. I wanted to ask her if she still had that tartar cup beneath the fruit bowl. The idea made me smile, and Dorothy barged on, looking up at me once again, "See, now there's a smile. I can't recall seeing you smile, not one time since I've met you, Magda. You are such a pretty girl when you smile. You know, the first time I saw you, I didn't think your dad's description of you did you justice. I thought, my goodness, but isn't she the picture of him with those blue eyes and that hair, a little darker and you would be just like a little Scarlett O'Hara, I thought, the very picture of your father. You know, in my younger days I used to read the movie magazines, and you have the face of a young starlet, did you know that? Really, a young starlet with the cloned features of your dad."

My face was identical to my mother's.

Then Dorothy's face got serious. Mrs. Fish lowered the receiver and held up a Greek tragedy mask. She stopped dancing, bowing her head down low. The lobster claws silenced. "There is one thing I need to make clear to you, Magda." Dorothy frowned. "I have no intention, ever, of replacing your mother. Please don't ever think that of me. Now your father has not told me very much about your mother, but from what I understand, you two were unusually close."

Mrs. Fish put the receiver down and then began dancing a slow hula, putting her fins up to the fruit bowl as though balancing it. I watched Mrs. Fish while listening to Dorothy. I had not realized that Mrs. Fish had on a grass skirt with a belt of hibiscus. My mother had always loved hibiscus and wisteria; we had pictures of them all over our house, close-ups of a single bloom or branch.

Dorothy crossed then uncrossed her legs. "A lot of people have told me that a girl of your age needs a mother, but I was thinking we could be more like friends." She paused and when I did not respond to this suggestion, she furrowed her brow. "My whole life, I always hoped for a daughter, you know, that God would grant me the ability to bear another child, but that never happened. We tried and tried, but nothing.

"And now, well now I'm too old to hope for anything but a granddaughter, but when I met your father and he said he had a daughter, I thought this could be my opportunity with a girl. You know, that finally I would be given a chance with a girl. Not that I would be your mother. Your mother will always be your mother. I would be honored for you to think of me as an older friend, as someone you can confide in. You know, an aunt, an older sister, that kind of thing."

"All right," I answered. I couldn't very well say anything except all right. Dorothy was pushing into my existence in the same way the fish had: uninvited, suddenly, and with evident plans to stay for the duration. Mr. Fish jumped into my head at the exact moment I said "all right." He jumped literally, as though he had just dived from a cliff, and began slowly beating a bongo with hardly any rhythm at all. The cadence sounded like rocks falling into mud.

"Why don't you tell me something about your mother?" Dorothy urged. "Your father did mention that you think about your mother often. Can you tell me something about your mother?"

"She liked harp music," I answered in a voice made of sand. "She said the strings plucked at her soul."

"Oh," Dorothy said, her head moving up and down rapidly. "She sounds like a bit of an unusual person. Very expressive. Very passionate with her descriptions."

"A lot of my friends confused her with Martha Stewart," I answered.

"You mean she looked like Martha Stewart?" Dorothy asked, her voice careful, her eyes open very wide.

"Never mind," I sighed. "Just never mind."

"Well, you don't have to talk about your mother if you don't want to," Dorothy said. "You never have to talk about anything you don't want to, I mean, Andrew never does. Well, to me, anyway." Dorothy paused. "Here's a thought, just a thought."

I waited.

"My Andrew, you know, with his father dying so quickly in the accident and all, well he goes to see a woman once a week, a counselor. Or he did. Right after I noticed he was having some trouble, you know, coping…with his dad dying and all, telling all sorts of stories to, you know, anyone and everyone who would listen, so I found this woman he could talk to and he started going a couple of times a week, then eventually once a week. She's very good, very perceptive about kids and grief. If you think you'd like to talk to Nancy, I can give you her number."

I could tell that she and my father had already discussed this. She was simply the dispatcher, replacing Hannah in her imperatives. I could see my father, leaning over and patting Dorothy's wrist, saying, "Be better if it came from you."

"Thanks. I'll keep that in mind."

"I mean, if you want. No one is saying you have to see Nancy, just if you want. I even went once or twice myself, just to get a few ideas straight in my own mind, mostly ideas about how to help Andrew, how to help him through…things. You feel better after you talk to Nancy;

she has this nice way about her, like anything you say she wouldn't think was strange or bad. She doesn't judge people, I guess that's what I'm getting at. And she really doesn't judge, it's not just that she's being nice or gracious, she is that way, very open-minded. I want to make sure you let me know if you want to see her, I mean really. I won't tell a soul, it can be our first secret together."

I imagined myself stretched out on a small tablet of bed in a New York City hospital, thin, gray lines of trauma being lifted from the area of my solar plexus where I imagined my soul to be housed. A woman who looked exactly like Martha Stewart patted me on the wrist. Mr. Fish kept playing the bongo. Mrs. Fish continued her hula. The lobster claws began clicking again.

"But I'm getting sidetracked here." Dorothy moved her hands around in a quick scrambled way as though that gesture organized her thoughts. "My point was to let you know that in a few years you will be in college, an independent woman, and your father…well," she said crossing her wrists into an X, "he just hasn't had all that much happiness in his life, so far, you know."

I sat up straighter on the bed. "I'm not sure what you mean," I said quickly. "I know he loved my mother."

"Yes, well, of course he loved your mother, but honestly, Magda, your mother was quite a lot for any one man to take care of. I mean, the way she had those long moods where your Aunt Hannah had to come over and pitch in with the housework and the cooking. Surely you knew how, well…difficult, how unhappy your parents were. At times, I mean."

"No," I answered. "I knew my parents were cut from different cloth, but I wouldn't say they were unhappy."

"Well, that just goes to show what a strong man your father is, to have you believe all these years that he and your mother were happy." Dorothy rose from the bed. "I am not saying anything against your mother, I do hope you understand that. All I am saying is that your father has done a terrific job in raising you and making sure your childhood was minimally disrupted."

Minimally disrupted. My father raising me. I sang the phrases in my mind. I looked at Dorothy, at her hair that was calmer than the North Atlantic, that just drooped from her skull in dry shanks, its texture and color similar to wheat. Minimally disrupted. Raised by my father. "They loved each other," I repeated.

"Yes, yes, of course they did." Dorothy went over to the window, her back to me. "But sometimes in a marriage, things wear out." Dorothy turned around to face me.

"Wear out?"

"Yes, they wear out. People wear out, their patience or their ability to tolerate certain things, certain behaviors or situations. This must be awfully hard for you to understand just now, but trust me. One day you'll look back on this time in your life and it will all be very clear to you. You'll look up from your kitchen table one day," Dorothy said this with a faraway look on her face, as though she were no longer in the room, but at my future kitchen table, "you'll look up from your table one day and you'll maybe have your own child or two and you'll think how certain things just wear out. There's really no other way to put it, they just get worn down until they're worn away. People wear each other out when they don't change, or when their problems make family life difficult, they wear out. And maybe," here Dorothy smiled, "you'll recall this conversation we're having on this day and you'll think, Ah, yes, *now* I get what Dorothy meant on that long-ago day when she was talking about marriage." She walked back over to the foot of the bed I sat on.

"Your father and I, surely you know by now, we're not the most expressive people. Neither of us has your mother's gift for expression, but we're doing the best we can. We're all just trying to be happy." She patted my arm. "When I was your age, I wanted the world, too. Then one day you realize all you should try for is simple, ordinary happiness. Your father and I, you and Andrew, the four of us: we're all just trying to be happy."

"Yes," I said robotically, "we're all trying just to be happy."

Dorothy liked this echo of her phrase so much that she leaned over and embraced me, briefly and suddenly as a cold wind. Her embrace was meant as a reward for my future insight.

"You seem like a nice enough kid, a kid who has to understand that her father, after all these years, deserves a chance at happiness." Dorothy's eyes glittered in a way that I could not translate: either she was very happy or close to tears; I could not tell which, and I did not want her erupting in any way in our shared room.

"You're right," I agreed rapidly. "He does deserve his happiness. And I suppose you're right, now that I think about it; my parents went long periods without spending any time together. I never really thought about whether or not my parents were happy." At least, I knew, my mother had been happy when she was with me.

"You're just lucky to have Hannah, to have an aunt like that. Without Hannah, well. I hate to think. After all Hannah had been through herself, then being given a second chance with a child." Dorothy shook her head back and forth while pursing her lips.

A second chance with a child for Hannah? I waited for Dorothy to say more, but she continued without revealing anything further.

"All I can say is it's behind us now. No matter what happened, it's behind us now. You know each one of us has lost a person close to us, each one of us. So the only way I see it is that the worst is behind us now. Your dad has a chance at happiness now and I'm happy to have a man back in my life after raising Andrew by myself for these past two years. So the worst is behind each one of us now; you need to believe that, Magda."

"I should believe that, you're right."

"I mean, it's not like we do anything to get ourselves into these situations. I told Andrew's father over and over not to go out on such a night, that the roads would ice over by the time he came back…" Dorothy looked off into the distance for a moment. "I told him, more than once I told him, not to go out. I mean, for what? To pick up some milk for the morning. Who can't live without milk, like it's the end of the world. Milk. Of all things."

I waited, unsure if Dorothy was done. The fish had

frozen in position, Mrs. Fish in her hula skirt and Mr. Fish holding the bongo. Suddenly, they left my head with a plopping sound. "Enough of that, now, though. No use in going over the past since you can't change it. Or if you can, maybe someone can let me know." She smiled. "Let's you and me go see what the men are doing."

Dorothy knocked on the door adjoining the two rooms. I watched her, the pineapple glinting on her pocket. ("It's the symbol of hospitality," she had said loudly as she first got into our car back on Staten Island; "I thought it would be apropos since I would be sharing a room with Magda.") As she stood sideways, the pineapple jutted out in such a way that Dorothy appeared to have one enormous nipple escaping her blouse.

My father opened the door, and they embraced, chastely, but still they embraced. I could not recall my parents embracing, not once in all my life. I remained on the bed, trying not to let my mind transform their faces into animals, and trying even harder not to let myself fall into a loping giraffe. But the pleats had worked; during the entire conversation, I had not once felt that I would be better off on a grassy savanna than on the bed with my legs crossed.

I had read somewhere that people with trouble getting through life, people missing arms or hands, people whose feet had extra toes or people who had lost their hearing got through life by accepting their diminishment and learning compensatory behaviors. They learned how to maneuver in new ways like brushing their teeth with their feet or sweeping the floor with one arm and their hip. Perhaps I could do that as well. I could learn how to organize my brain in such a way that I would slip unnoticed into the standard and not have such drift, like the fish, in my brain.

At least the thought gave me hope. My mind had begun slipping more lately, wandering further from the people and situations around me that I knew I should be understanding, listening to, and hooking into in some way. The phone rang unanswered as a church bell, mail slid from tables, Hannah and my father asked things of me and my mind barely translated their faces, let alone their words. I swam away from it all. The gauzy place I went to stretched on forever, arcing and bending like a bridge of water. Only on the other side of the bridge, I would have to find an end. Everything ends. My mother and Chito had gone to the other side of this bridge. I sat up, hugging my knees. I had no place to go. I would not drown; that much I knew.

My body would plunge upward. Falling appealed to me, the idea of a weightless plunge excited me, but the mess at the end ruined its grace. I would not die. I knew that now. I would go on. And that was the problem: I had no place to go. I was stranded inside the drift, and my progress toward the standard was stalled.

Dorothy began making clucking sounds over Andrew, pulling me from my thoughts.

She was admonishing him for not folding his clothing in a way to avoid wrinkles. "You roll the fabric," she instructed in an exaggerated singsong. "Then your pleats will stay sharp." Her voice carried like some sort of mating warble, a tone meant to convey her domestic crispness to my rumpled father.

Outside the window, several sailboats tinged the air;

they moved across the water in silence, ghostly crafts born of the drift. I loved the punch of their sails, the way the diaphanous cloth steered the boat. I was, as usual, thinking of my mother, how that is what I had hoped she would do with her own airy ways: just steel herself into a position where she would take charge, where she would show my father and I what to do.

"Come on, Magda, get your shoes on," Dorothy called. "We're taking a walk." My father beamed, clearly thinking that Dorothy had gotten through to me in some way.

I could see, I supposed, why my father would be attracted to a stout and tidy woman like Dorothy. As I watched her close curtains and run a paper towel across the kitchenette counters, I knew that in her presence, no one had to worry about making the most prudent choice. Dorothy gave off an air of such practical knowledge and adherence to the rules that in her presence I felt the same way as I had while taking packages to the post office: this type of tape must be used, this type of paper, the amount depended on the weight, and all this information could be found on a clearly labeled chart, no error could be committed, no margin would ever be crossed. It was not dissimilar to how I felt in school. In such methodical environments, no harm would come. It was the reason none of us took fire drills seriously; the school was just too well-run, too scheduled, to succumb to any force as capricious as fire. Dorothy created that same sense. She was a disciple of the standard, spawned by its conventions and an apostle of its order. Perhaps my father craved entry into the standard as much as I did. We both wanted its safety, its surety, its dependability. We knew what happened to people in the drift. Because we wanted to live, we had to leave.

"We thought we'd take a peek at the area." Dorothy smiled broadly. My father stood next to her, and behind him I could see the top of Andrew's head. A peek. I missed my mother so much at that point, looking at the three of them standing between the two rooms, that I got up from the bed to keep myself from crying out.

"Would you like to buy a few things to bring back?" my father asked as we trotted out to the boardwalk. He knew Hannah had given me some spending money before we left.

"No." I loped alongside him, hopelessly feeling myself all long legs and neck, half human and half giraffe. Pleats, I hissed into my brain, pleats. But it didn't work: I felt my neck rising, my legs growing long and slender. Mrs. Fish rose in my brain, holding out a sheen of leaves for me.

"Go," I hissed telepathically. "You are the last thing I need."

"I bring you delectables from the very top of Kenya's trees and this is how you treat me? Anyway, you were the one who came to the ocean," she said, shaking her hat back and forth. She wore a pineapple hat, exactly like Dorothy's pin, on her head. "Think of all the places there are to visit in late August: the mountains, the lake, there's canoeing, hiking, all sorts of places, and you come here, right where Mr. Fish and I met. And then you ask me to leave." She put on a pair of pink sunglasses in the shape of two hearts.

"Maybe we should get a small gift for Aunt Hannah."

"What?" I said way too loudly. My father put his hands over his ears.

Mrs. Fish sighed, then vanished.

"A gift for Aunt Hannah. Did I scare you?"

"No, you didn't scare me."

"I thought you might like to look around for a little something Aunt Hannah would enjoy."

"I will," I answered. "I will."

Andrew and I stood together while Dorothy and my father examined items in the boardwalk shops, all of them strange, dark holes that smelled of curry and incense. They sold gimcrack like paper fans and bobble heads, large velvet paintings of clowns and Elvis Presley. The shop owners came out from behind the registers and watched us, their faces brittle with suspicion. Dorothy bought all kinds of things: suntan lotion and a jellyfish paperweight, a straw beach bag with large pompoms comprising its fringe that I hoped was not for me, several postcards, and extra soap. "I like to use my own next to my skin," she laughed to my father. "It's how these places economize—on the soap. It dries the skin with all the cheap chemicals." After Dorothy was done, she looked at my father. "I was thinking, Michael, that you and I could take a swim while the kids go off and…well, get to know one another."

A jolt of electricity zigged through my body as though I had just been struck by lightning. It had not occurred to me that I would, at any time, be expected to be alone with Andrew.

"How does that sound?" Dorothy asked. She and my father were already backing away and it struck me that my father was not beginning a new life; he had always had a life apart from me. Only now I could see that he wanted to escape me, to escape my cheerless moods and my face which was so similar to my mother's. He stood on the boardwalk with music blaring all around him and I watched him walk away with the spiderish Dorothy until they disappeared, two ships on the horizon that had nothing to do with me.

"We could go for a swim," Andrew suggested. "Your father told me that you're a pretty good swimmer. Maybe you could teach me."

I looked at him, at his sheep smile and his diamond-shaped head. I looked at him and I said, "You can't swim?" The thought was preposterous. How could anyone live on Staten Island and not know how to swim? We were surrounded by water.

"A little. I mean, I've swum in pools. I had lessons, but I just, I don't know. I just never got it, really. The way the arms and legs have to go together, the head and the breathing and all. I'm just not coordinated that way. And I've never gone swimming in the ocean."

"Maybe we could just walk around the boardwalk then," I suggested, as I did not want to return to the motel and bump into my father and Dorothy. And I certainly did not want to see them in the water together, with all that middle-of-life flesh exposed.

"We could just sit on the beach. On one of those

benches," Andrew gestured toward a scatter of green metal benches facing the water. Several girls in bikini tops and shorts passed directly in front of us and Andrew grinned inanely. The girls ignored him, swinging a tide of hair in front of their eyes. I felt my legs grow even longer, knobs bloomed on my skull, each giraffe leg loped across the boardwalk, then across the sand to the bench.

The bench we found snugged up next to a boardwalk piling. Behind the bench, daylight eclipsed beneath the boardwalk. Fern-colored light pooled in the quiet pocket of calm.

"Do you want to sit there?" I asked Andrew as I pointed under the boardwalk.

"All right."

We sat for a few minutes, our heads turned upward, watching stroller wheels and sandaled feet shuffle over us. "It's sort of like being underwater," I said.

"Is it?"

"Yeah. Like the world goes on around you, but it's far away and all muffled."

"I think our parents went back to the motel," Andrew said. "How much time do you think we should give them?"

"That depends on what they're doing."

Andrew looked at me.

"Oh," I said very quickly. "I guess I have some idea what they're doing. It's just a little weird to think of my father as even having a friend, let alone…"

"Well." Andrew did not smile. "I doubt, I mean I really doubt they're having sex. They might be doing a few other things, but not that. Then it all changes after they're married, it all changes. I can't imagine marrying anyone without having sex first." Andrew said this in a slow, measured way, as though he were speaking of investing in foreign oil. "Imagine you marry and you're completely different in bed, like the sex just doesn't work."

"Hmm," I said, moving rocks around in the sand. I could feel Andrew's sheep-like stare fall over me.

"To me, the sex would have to be right. That's like the first line of communication. What about you, Magda, would the sex have to be right?"

"I guess." I didn't meet his eyes.

"My mother keeps telling me how I should wait, how it has to have meaning. It's just a need we all have, and I say to her, yup, right, Ma, like sitting down to a plate of spaghetti needs a prior commitment, like it's not just satisfying a need." Andrew laughed. "Those two have no idea whether or not they're going to be compatible in that department."

"I'm sure they'll do fine," I offered, insanely eager for Andrew to change the subject.

"Probably. Maybe we can listen in when they're in the new house."

"The new house?"

"Yeah. They're looking at new houses," Andrew said. He leaned back in the sand. A plane went over the water, trailing behind it a cloth advertising restaurant specials. "I heard my mother on the phone the other night, and they're looking at houses."

"I don't want to move. My father hasn't said anything to me about moving."

"It's not like they're going to ask us," Andrew noted, "but your aunt is moving back to Ohio. She wants to be closer to her son."

"My only aunt is Hannah, and she was like a nun or something." I laughed. "She says novenas as a hobby. She couldn't have a son."

"Right. She went to school as a religious history major out in Ohio. But she got married and had a kid. Didn't you know that?"

"I don't know if I knew that," I answered truthfully, thinking of that shadowy time in Hannah's life, the time no one in my family ever mentioned. I had certainly never heard mention of a child. "How did you hear about this?"

Andrew poked at a clot of seaweed that had dried to the thinness of onion skin. "Your father was at our house a couple of nights ago and they were talking about Hannah, how she wants to move back to Ohio."

"Back to Ohio to be with her son?"

Andrew began shredding the seaweed and annoyingly small bits got caught in the wind, flying into my hair, my eyes, onto my arms. "Yup."

"And you're sure this is Hannah we're talking about?"

"Yup." He lifted his hand, allowing the seaweed fragments to blow toward my face. "It was definitely Hannah."

I sat in the sand, perfectly still for a few moments. I remembered Dorothy's statement back in the hotel, how Hannah had been given a second chance with a child during the times my mother could not take care of me. A second chance would have to mean a first chance had been undertaken. And this boy, this hidden son, would explain the pictures of the child I had seen. No wonder I couldn't put the photographs down; the boy resembled Hannah and no part of me could accept that knowledge. Still, it wasn't possible. Hannah somebody's mother; the thought was unearthly, a fragment of dream that belonged inside a different parameter.

"Did Hannah take care of this boy, or is she his actual, his biological mother?"

"She was the real deal."

"You heard my father say that. Those are his words."

Andrew looked up from his seaweed. "Yeah. He said she was married for like a year or two, and she wrote home, pretending she was still a student. She never told her parents she was married with a son. They died never knowing they had a grandson. I heard your dad telling my mom that the other night."

"Did he say anything about how things could have been different for Hannah if she had told them?"

"What?"

"Never mind." No, my father would not say that. Such a thought belonged to my mother. I wondered if she had known the details of Hannah's disgrace, had known my father had a nephew in another state, that Hannah had been someone else's mother all along. I did not think she knew; I would have somehow understood that knowledge in the unspoken, watery dream of our communication.

"What do you want to do?" Andrew asked.

I looked at him, wondering if Hannah had left the pictures there in her desk with the door to her room left invitingly ajar for a reason. Had she wanted me to find the pictures of her son on purpose?

"If she does have a son, who's raising him?"

"Your father says he's with her husband. Ex-husband. He has a big family outside of Cleveland. That's where Hannah's going. She's moving back to see him. Gabriel, I think that's his name. Do you want to go back to the room?"

I shook my head. "Uh-uh." Gabriel. Of course. Hannah's son would never be Fred or Bob.

He would have to be Gabriel or Noah, a name of that sort. I moved further under the boardwalk.

Slats of light angled through the planks in a menacing way, pointed and knifelike.

Andrew leaned against a piling and closed his eyes. His mouth went slack. I examined the wood on the supports. For the first time in a very long time, I began to consider a fire, a long spiral of fire that would swallow everything in sight with heat and noise, the inverse of drowning, but every bit as effective. I could begin it at night, on the beach, I thought, scanning the large expanse of sand filled with flesh and noise. Papers lay in metal baskets; I could use those as kindling, gather bits of driftwood and lead the fire right up to this dry wood of the boardwalk.

"What are you thinking about?" Andrew asked, his eyes opening unexpectedly like a doll suddenly springing to life. I was so accustomed to being alone that for a few moments, I had forgotten about him.

"I guess about Hannah," I lied, taking my eyes from the temptation of the pier wood. Still, the thought of fire did not leave me. I spread my fingers across the dry smoothness of a stick that lay next to me. Making sure Andrew did not see me, I slipped the stick into my pocket.

"Still about Hannah?"

"Yup. How I probably knew she had a kid, somehow, like a suspicion."

"My mother calls those hunches."

"This would be a directed hunch. They wanted me to know, at least she did. That's the whole reason they had me stay alone at Hannah's."

"What, you met the kid?"

"No, no, I found his picture. Forget it."

"We should probably go back up, don't you think?" Andrew stood. "My mother gets worried if she can't find me."

"So where is this house going to be, this new house we're all moving to?"

Andrew yawned. "I don't think it's a done deal yet, but they've looked at one over by the mall a few times. That would be my guess. My mom usually knows just what she wants."

I knew where that was. Far, far from the beach I had always known. No water anywhere except a few old cisterns.

I followed Andrew back to the motel; our parents were not there.

"You okay?" Andrew asked before going into his room. I nodded. "See you later then."

"Okay."

I felt sorry for Andrew in a distant way. I didn't think he cared for my father any more than I cared for his mother, but he was better at accepting situations he was stuck in. And we are both stuck, my mind whispered as I opened the door to my room. I felt strange inside, both thirsty and wobbly, so I drank a glass of water. My head still hurt, so in the middle of the yellow day with all the noise and colors of the beach coming in through the open window, I lay down on the bed. The heels of the curtains blew in and as I watched them, one of the curtains chunked off and came over to me. I sat up.

"Mrs. Fish?"

The curtain undulated. Mrs. Fish appeared slowly, scale by scale, a hologram coming into slow view. She had wrapped a piece of the curtain around her middle section and walked by bouncing on either fin. "If there's one thing I can be sure of," Mrs. Fish said, pursing her lips, "it's that you'll be late every time I want to be on time." She pushed at her tartar cup hat until it sat far back on her head. "Exactly how long are we going to wait before telling her?"

Mr. Fish slid out from under the bed. "In due time. In due time." Mr. Fish stood. "You can't rush into these things. Besides, she has enough to think about now."

"Well, I think she knows already." Mrs. Fish spun around, a slow balletic gesture that allowed the lace panel she wore to flare. "She's more like me than you'll ever understand. She gets what she's not told, what's not visible. I look at her sometimes and I know she speaks the language of the unspoken."

"Huh?" Mr. Fish made circles around his head, indicating that Mrs. Fish had lost it.

"The language of the unspoken, the vocabulary of the soul. You, Mr. Fish, are still looking for the undercurrent in life, and she's already translating it by herself. That's the trouble between you two; it's the same trouble as between us."

"If there's trouble between us, it's not on my part. And I don't see myself as having much trouble with her. She's got some of me in her too, you know."

Mrs. Fish walked over to the window. She turned sharply. "You don't see yourself as having trouble with anyone, now do you, Preston? You just move through your life, simple as a goddamned cod and then you think everyone around you is the same way, simple and unruffled. You have no trouble with her because you don't hook into her. Or into me for that matter."

Then she was gone. I turned to the bed. Mr. Fish was gone, too. I ran my hand under the bed to see if there was wetness, a wet area of sea water, anything left of their visit. There was nothing, not a drop of water, not an imprint on the carpet. The curtains remained straight and still as columns. I lay on the bed, weighted and gritty, full of sand and the effects of too much sun.

Slabs of light coasted in from the outside, skittering silently against the walls. Then I saw Dorothy coming toward me, a saint appearing in a grotto, the pinkish light from the walls dusting her like a benediction.

"We found the nicest place to get a bite," Dorothy said as a way of greeting. "You'll like it; it's right on a pier. It's just the perfect place to get a bite. Your father said you'd really like how you feel you're right on the ocean."

I heard Dorothy splash water in the sink; I heard the toilet flush. I went outside to wait until she was done.

Our motel was only a few yards from the boardwalk

and if I sat on the fence and craned my head just the right way, I could see past the boardwalk and straight to the ocean. I liked the motel's exterior as well as the rooms: the walls were bumpy stucco, painted a pale tangerine mixed with the surprise of aqua, the kind of motel I imagined poets might frequent. Through the parking lot and even in the lobby, puddles of sand meandered up from the beach.

"You look nice," Andrew said coming up alongside me.

"How's that?" I asked. I had not even combed my hair since that morning. I imagined myself closed and expressionless as a clam.

"I dunno. You don't look mad like you usually do. You know, the way your face turns down a lot."

"You mean my mouth. People's faces don't turn down."

Andrew came over and sat next to me, assuming I wanted his company closer. "Some people's faces do turn down. Yours does. Not just your mouth. That first night we all met, at the restaurant, I watched you. Every time you looked at your father with my mother, your whole face turned down. You may not like it, but it does."

"Do you think he sees that?"

Andrew nodded. "He couldn't miss it. A blind guy couldn't. You know…" Andrew turned to look at a bosomy girl oscillate past in a halter top. I waited. "It's okay if you don't like my mother. A lot of people don't."

"It's not that I don't like her, it's just…I think it's all very fast. You know, it's barely a year since my mother…"

"I know. I do know. My mother told me. But it's been a really long time for my mother. And she knows your

Aunt Hannah really well so I know she's met your dad before."

Hannah and her prayer groups. She must have been the one who suggested my father take those trips. Surely, she had Dorothy in mind all along.

"Why don't people like your mother? She seems okay. I mean I know she means well."

Andrew cracked his knuckles before he spoke. "See, she's really organized. She like vacuums before people are done eating and she takes your plate the minute you swallow. Sometimes I can't even put my fork back down on my plate, I'm still chewing and she's already rinsing the dish. It's her compulsion for order that drives everyone nuts. She sees a counselor for it, too. I mean, she's trying to stop doing it. She's trying not to be so organized, trying to not worry about having everything just so." Andrew shook his head slowly back and forth. "My dad was like…he's really hard to explain, but she had no control over anything he did. Not one thing."

"So since she couldn't control him, she controlled the house stuff?"

"Huh?"

A squall of seagulls flapped past us. We both looked up, then back at each other.

"Andrew, do you remember the story about the lilies your mother told that first night?"

"Yeah. She wanted Dad to move the lilies to the shadier side of the house and he did it the minute she asked him. That story?"

"That story. The way I see it, she tells that story so

that we can see she had some kind of control over your dad, that she wasn't powerless."

"You think so?"

"I do. Because no one even knows where the lilies were, only she does. What else would be the point?"

Andrew shrugged his shoulders. "I don't know. I just know she still keeps the house so clean, people ask if we're selling it when they come inside." We both laughed when he said this.

I thought of my mother and how the house had spiraled out of control until I would try to clear some space, to put dishes back in the cupboard or box up newspapers and magazines. We never got anywhere when we started; we would clear a tiny bit of space and my mother would sort of drift off, wanting to go outside to garden or down to the beach.

My father and I had spent hours clearing piles of flotsam my mother had collected. After she died, I helped him throw away bags of buttons and shells she had stored; we donated her clothing and shoes. My mother held on to things. She never let go of anything except me.

"So that's good, that your mother is so neat. I had an English teacher who told us we should always write our essays in a room where there's not a lot of clutter, that our minds would work better in clear space."

"That's the kind of thinking my mother would agree with," Andrew laughed. "She thinks it's sinful to be messy."

"She seems very stable, your mother." As soon as I said this word, "stable," a vision of a barn came to me with several large draft animals standing inside stalls.

"That she is," Andrew agreed.

A clicking sound came from nowhere and I closed my eyes, hoping the fish had not developed exterior sound.

"I'll get copies of that made," Dorothy called to my father, who stood only a few feet behind her.

She had just snapped a picture of me and Andrew on the fence. "That will be a priceless one." I thought of my hair, how it currently resembled desert tumbleweed. "You two ready?"

We walked almost to the end of the boardwalk. Sweet air blew in from the ocean, warm and briny and filled with current that went straight through me.

"I thought you'd like this place, Magda," my father said quietly, "knowing how much you like the water. I picked it for you."

"I do like it. How could I not?" Everyone laughed, though I did not see why my comment was in the least funny. The restaurant was on the pier, directly, and the pier was a straight tongue of wood that went a quarter mile or so into the ocean. Waves broke on a jetty not far from our table and gulls walked arrogantly as emperors between the tables.

"It's great to see you like this," my father said, patting my hand. "I think we all needed a break from the house."

"The house?" I asked.

"The motel, our houses back on Staten Island. A vacation, that's what I meant."

"Oh." I looked away, back at the water.

"Did you want to order?" Dorothy asked.

"Yes, but first I'd like to look at a menu," I answered.

Everyone laughed at this comment, too. I sat in my wooden chair, puzzled.

"Oh, you're right, Magda, of course," Dorothy laughed, "I am rushing you. Here we've barely sat down and I'm coaching you along at breakneck speed. You'll just have to bear with me, I'm afraid. I'm so accustomed to getting so many things done in a day that I have a bit of trouble relaxing. Just bear with me," she repeated. "I'm having the red snapper with dill sauce," she said, turning to my father.

I opened the menu and just as I picked the lemon shrimp with rice, Andrew's hand came down on my knee. I did not know what to do. I felt his hand, the weight of each finger and the palm docked on the roundness of my bone, lodged there as strangely and stubbornly as an octopus on a rock. Very slowly, I nudged my knee to one side. His hand followed. I pulled my knee toward my lap. His hand followed. He did not move his hand during the pre-dinner conversation where I watched Dorothy's words feather into the air, a great eclipse of feathers, followed by the occasional stones of my father's voice holding words close to the table. I smiled and did not move. Nothing made sense. I only felt that hand on my knee.

"Did you, Magda?" Andrew asked me.

"Did I what?"

Andrew's expression revealed nothing, a straight stare with a ripple of a smile. He looked entirely social, not a trace of creepiness about him.

"Did you ever read anything about the theory that deserts were once oceans?"

"Oceans? No. Maybe. I guess so. Why?"

Dorothy snorted a laugh. "Someone, Magda, has been daydreaming." Her voice sounded strange and small, the voice of a gnome or a parrot.

We all smiled. I glared at Andrew. His neutral expression did not change.

In desperation I stood, excusing myself to use the restroom, and as I stood, Andrew's hand did not at first budge from my leg. Using the same flicking motion I had used countless times to rid myself of jellyfish or seaweed while wading through water, I flicked Andrew's hand off my flesh. When I returned, I sat with my legs to one side, far from the table.

"Why don't you move your seat closer to the table, Magda?" my father urged. "You're not going to be able to eat in that position. You look a bit like you've come to fish at the table, sitting back like that."

"I'm fine," I insisted. He smiled at me, a broad, quiet smile that told me he was in a rare mood. I did not want to corrupt his happiness by telling the truth.

"But you're so far from the table," he insisted.

"I'm fine, really." I smiled. He looked at me for a long moment, then shrugged his shoulders.

"Oh, it's their age," Dorothy suggested. "You can't tell teenagers a thing. I don't even try anymore with my Andrew. I don't even try." She shook her head back and forth several times, as though regaining her balance after a sudden seizure. "You'll feel better after you eat, honey."

"Yes," I responded, "I'm sure you're right."

"The one thing about having seafood," Dorothy said

slowly, "is you don't so much mind the fishy odor of the air around here after you eat it."

I looked at her. How could anyone dislike the scent of the ocean?

"I think I'll close the windows tonight and turn on the AC. The last thing I need is to wake up and smell the stink of flounder right outside my door."

"Then I'll be sure to gulp plenty of light before going to bed," I said under my breath. My father sat to my right and he heard me. The look on his face was one of pure pain.

"Magda, that's enough. I'm asking you."

"What's the matter?" Dorothy said quickly. "Is something the matter?" She looked quickly from my father's face to mine then back again. My father and I did not answer her. We sat at the table, motionless and silent as stars. Then my father did something I would not have predicted.

"Dorothy, if you don't mind, I'd like to take a short walk alone with Magda."

"Did I do something?" Dorothy asked.

"No, no, of course not," my father reassured her. "It's just that Magda and I are used to having a certain amount of time alone together to…well, sort of review things, and we haven't done that in a while. We won't be long."

He stood. He waited for me to stand and go with him. He cordially said he would be returning to the table. His calmness terrified me. I wanted him to yell, to grab a piece of scrod from a surrounding table and hurl it at me. But he did nothing of the kind. He continued to be calm and deliberate in his actions. He took me by the elbow, steering me toward the boardwalk. "Wait here." He instructed me to sit on a bench. The people passing by me all wore animal faces; I had already retreated into my giraffe-self.

But my father returned with two ice cream cones. I relaxed a bit. Nothing really awful can ever happen when you are eating ice cream.

"We haven't had dinner yet," I protested weakly.

"No, we haven't," he agreed with no further explanation. He did not smile. "So, Magda, I take it you don't care for Dorothy. But I do, you see. I happen to think she is a good woman. And that seems to be the crux of our problem here. You don't act as though Dorothy is a good woman."

"Did I say she wasn't a good woman? Did I say that?" I took the cone he held out to me.

"No, not exactly. But I have discussed this at some length with my group from the church and they told me to expect this kind of response from you. Magdalena," he said and paused. He rubbed his cheek and looked away from me for a few moments. "Let me make this clear to you— very, very clear: are you listening?" I said I was. "I want you to think, to really think about what I am about to say: it is in no way a betrayal of any kind for me to marry."

I did not taste the ice cream cone. A scatter of gulls rose in front of us, pieces of shadow rising into the air. Ice cream began dripping down my fingers.

"I will always respect and love the memory of your mother, but she is no longer here, nor will she ever be again. That cannot be changed. I need to know that you understand that idea as truth."

"That remarriage is not a betrayal? You want me to accept that as truth?"

"Yes. I do."

"So now that you are marrying Dorothy, you are going to tell me what is truth and what is not? You are going to direct my beliefs like an apostle?"

My father rubbed his forehead for a second. "Maybe we need to back up here just a bit, Magda. Maybe I need to ask you what it is that you already believe."

"Do you? Is that what they instructed you to do in your group? Tell me what else your church group told you to expect from me. I'm curious. What else did they say to watch out for with me?"

"It's obvious that you are misguided," my father continued, as though this answered my question. "You are confusing your reluctance to accept Dorothy with loyalty to your mother. They are not one in the same. Surely, you know that."

The ice cream began lacing my hand, crossing itself over and over in a kind of brocade.

"We were all upset when your mother died, and now…"

"I think you were relieved when Mom died," I said crisply. The words came out of my mouth without my entire consent, water slipping between my lips. I had not even known I believed this until the sentence came. It stayed in front of me for a few seconds, bright red and huge, taking up all the space between me and my father.

"Relieved," my father repeated. "I suppose, in some way I was relieved. Your mother, and I am certain you will agree with me on this, your mother was not the easiest person in the world to get along with. She was very, very difficult. At times. Very difficult. I do believe it is fair for me to say she was impossible at times, prone as she was to her moods."

"Moods." As if that's all she had. Something that came and went like weather. "Most people worth something are difficult," I countered. I was not aware of my brain knitting these sentences together before they left my mouth fully constructed. I wondered if my mother was somehow speaking through me. "Shallow people just drift along on the surface of life. Mom lived way below."

"That she did. And maybe now I want to just drift along and enjoy my life, not wrestle with every thought or have a wife who can't perform the most basic of tasks. Your mother had a generous spirit and there is no doubt that she was an intelligent woman, but she refused to learn how to drive or to spend any time cleaning the house, and dinner seemed to drift in with the tides; I never knew from one night to the next whether there would be dinner on the table or not, whether or not she had decided to walk to the deli and get some milk and bread, whether or not she had been able to locate the phone bill. These are basic activities most men take for granted. If it hadn't been for Hannah, I'm not sure what would have become of us. Your mother certainly had no interest in anything domestic."

"She had interest in me."

"She did have interest in you. But you see, Magda, most mothers are interested in their children, but they still manage to run the house and get meals out and shop in the store. Your mother would spend two days putting in a single patch of dahlias."

"I know. I remember. The dahlias in our yard caused people to stop their cars and ask about them. I remember that, too. You're forgetting that part. It wasn't like she was moving slowly or she was simple-minded: she created paintings in the yard."

My father sighed. "You're right and I don't mean to make you have to defend your mother. You are like her in many of your ways, but you still manage to do well in school, to do what is asked of you. Your mother had those long moods where she would just lie on the couch. A woman with a house and a husband and a child needs to tend to things and..." He closed his eyes for a long moment. "It's as if my ability to live with such...an artistic person has been used up. I don't know how else to put it."

"Used up," I repeated. I recalled Dorothy's conversation back in the motel. "You mean, like worn out?"

"Yes, that's right." My father looked out toward the ocean for a long minute. "I have no more interest in suffering, in working so hard just to get the basics of my life accomplished. I just want to get along now, have a stable home, an easy life at home instead of a battleground. You must remember all that."

"All what?"

"All the battles, the battles between me and your mother."

I shook my head. "I don't."

"You must," he insisted. "Although we argued mostly at night, after you were asleep. Do you remember hearing voices at night, yelling?"

"I don't remember any voices at night. Nothing." Mr.

and Mrs. Fish glinted in my brain for a moment, each wearing a pair of boxing gloves. "I know Dorothy believes all this stuff about things wearing out, getting used up." I crossed my legs. The fish began jumping up and down in stunted leaps, stabbing the air with their boxing gloves. "And she told me how you were not happy with Mom. Only this is all headline news to me. New facts from a new land. I don't happen to remember this war."

"Well, you're probably better off." My father's neck began flushing. "But Magda, don't take out your grief on Dorothy. She's not responsible for what has happened to us; she's not responsible for your mother's getting sick or for her death."

"Then who is?"

"I beg your pardon?" My father stood up, the pink flush of his neck rising into his face.

"I asked, Who is responsible for her death? You think she fell from the pier? Mom? The one who swam to the barge and back for fun? You think there wasn't something you could have done?" I stood to meet my father's gaze, to meet the flash of his eyes.

"Yes, I do think your mother fell, of course she did. No one is at fault here, Magda. Isn't that what everyone said, that she fell?" His voice rose as he spoke the last three words, slowly.

"Oh, she fell, that's what everyone says. Mom comes home from the hospital, she sleeps almost all the time, she takes pills the size of jelly beans, then she falls into water, Mom, the best swimmer I ever knew, falls into the bay and forgets to surface. Right. It just slips her mind to come up and breathe again. Just plain slips her mind, the breathing part. Oh no, looks like I forgot to breathe again, guess I have to just die now. Who wouldn't believe that?"

"Magda, you are forgetting that your mother was on some very powerful drugs for her mind. All kinds of tranquilizers, pills to quiet her."

"They worked then, didn't they? To quiet her. They sure as hell worked." I was yelling. People stopped on the boardwalk to look. "You don't hear much from her these days, now do you? You give her medication to make sure she's quiet or all mixed up, then you don't watch her?"

"I won't hear this," my father said loudly. "I won't hear this. Do you think I could look after an unstable wife twenty-four hours a day, keep you away from real harm, and still do my job? Is that what you want?" My father was shouting, his face pink as a ham.

"How is my mother dying keeping me from real harm? Do you think I don't know what she did, do you think I am not harmed?"

"Is that what this is about? That you wanted your mother safeguarded to the point that if she wanted to hurt herself, I was there to prevent it? Is that what you think? Tell me, Magda, is that what you think?"

I looked at the small knot of people paused in front of us. They wore masks of jackals and elephants, the long jaws of alligators and mules. "No," I said more softly, "of course that's not what I think. No one wanted Mom gone to make their life easier. That's not what I'm saying at all. That would be awful, to want someone gone who was difficult. It's so much easier to have a woman around who gets the wash done and puts out a meal every night, one of those nice standard women you can buy from Sears and Roebuck. I hear those kind don't break like Mom did."

I tossed the ice cream cone into the trash and ran into the herd of animals, past the herd, past benches and tarot card shops, past the motel, past bars and arcades, past a patch of carousels and roller coasters. I ran all the way to the other end of the boardwalk, to the rough surf where I dove in and went under the water, still dressed in my clothes, swimming beneath the water with my eyes wide open, swimming until I could no longer stand the ache of the salt filling my eyes.

I came back to the motel that night wet and sandy, puddling past Dorothy and my father. They were sitting outside on the wide planked fence wearing a collective expression of worry. I did not answer them as they cooed and clucked over me; I shoved past them to the opened door and went into the shower. I had no idea what they had done with Andrew.

"Hey," I said, coming out of the shower in my bathrobe.

"We got a pizza," Dorothy said. "Your father said you'd be hungry after swimming."

"How did you know I went swimming?" I asked my father this question in a tone much more combative than I felt.

"I've known you all your life, Magda. Where else would you go when you're upset?"

I took the pizza and the glass of soda from Dorothy. I waited. Dorothy smiled. My father smiled. "I'm glad you're back is all," he said. "I'm glad you're back."

I did not answer them. I simply sat, eating the greasy pizza with my hair dripping onto the plate, an errant octopus returning to the cave.

My father sat across from me and gazed into my face. "In a way, Magda, it's good that we have things out in the open now." He patted my shoulder. "Though I have to tell you I'm a little too old for this kind of fighting. Takes a lot out of me." He leaned closer. I knew he had told Dorothy about our fight and she had counseled him to do this. "Things happen in life. They are unfortunate, tragic, but they happen. There's no stopping them. You might feel better blaming someone, but you have to see what's true and what's not true. That's the important part."

I nodded, not looking at him. At that moment, with Dorothy clucking about the room wiping surfaces and keeping up a steady static of motion and my father sitting right across from me, I did not want to tell him that right then, I wanted the fish to come more than I wanted to talk to him.

That night I woke inside water. I sat up, liking the sensation. Dorothy moaned softly in her sleep, a nestling sound that reminded me of something blue and feathered. In the darkness, the humid air felt like tongues of water licking my skin. The curtains split in the middle, providing just enough of a chink for me to peer outside. People were everywhere on the boardwalk; it was lit up like prom night. I waited by the window, watching as I had during the spring, but this time I did not wait long. Finding the room key hanging from a hook by the door, I dressed rapidly and slipped into the night.

Strolling past the shops and vendors on the boardwalk, I thought how much my mother would like this moment: an illuminated night inside time that would ordinarily be only a long pocket of sleep, a treasure found. All those hours we had spent beneath the water with masks and goggles, investigating plants and creatures we found, collecting strangely swirled shells. And here was darkness, a place I had always thought of as a pause, alive as the undersea. I found a vacant bench on the boardwalk and sat down, content to watch people walk by. Mostly couples walked past me, young couples without children.

"Do you want a reading?"

For a moment I thought Mrs. Fish spoke to me, but I did not see her.

"I can give you a reading for half price." A girl, just a few years older than me, sat at the other end of the bench. She wore softly glimmered earrings, two pieces of moon in crescent shapes. "I can read your palm for five dollars. Do you want me to?"

"I don't want to go anywhere," I said, thinking of the tiny, dangerous-looking card and tea leaf shops scalloped around the edges of the boardwalk, the kind of places where people could disappear. "Can you do a reading here?" I remembered Hannah's spending money; it remained untouched in my pocket.

"I need more light," she said. "Just move underneath the lamp so I can see your palm." I did as the girl instructed. "Do you have the money?"

The girl's expression remained blank as I handed her a five dollar bill. "Okay, now let me look at your palm. First, tell me your name."

"Maggie."

"Maggie." She pressed her fingers into my palm. "What is that short for?"

"Magdalena."

"Right. You are not a Margaret, that much I could tell." She pressed more firmly into the heel of my palm. Nothing seemed real. Looking at her shimmering earrings, at the long water of her braid, at her dark eyes, I felt I had fallen into a dream, that this girl, this setting were more dream than event. But I could smell food from the many stands, motes of sand blew into my hair, the bench I sat on pressed knots of metal beneath my knees; I knew the girl was real, that this was happening, that she sat in the middle of the night, a few hundred yards from our motel, lightly kneading the valleys of my palm.

"So, Maggie, why are you out all by yourself so late?"

"We're staying at the Sandlight Motel," I answered, pointing to their sign that rose over the boardwalk, "and I woke up and decided to come outside. I've never really been outside in the middle of the night before, have you?"

"Yes," the girl said, "I've been outside in the middle of the night before. Lots of times."

She leaned forward, squinting her eyes as she moved her fingers across the base of each of my fingers. "So you couldn't sleep?"

"No. I mean yes. I fell asleep around ten o'clock. Then I woke up."

"Do you think there was a reason you woke up, tonight, for the first time?"

I liked the question, it was the kind of question my mother would have posed. "I guess there was." Years of spending time with my mother had trained me to never shut the door on these types of queries.

"Can you open your hand up, nice and flat?" The girl looked right into my face. I waited to turn into a giraffe, but I did not. I stayed myself. And I had not thought of the pleats. But I was still far from the standard. No standard dweller would be outside in the night's belly, sitting on an oceanside bench with a fortune teller. Still, my mind remained intact; no images came, no one transformed into an animal.

"You know, when I touch your hand, you sort of curl it up, away from me, like you're afraid of having anyone touch you." The girl spoke very softly. "You pull inward like a caterpillar. Did you ever see a caterpillar curl up at the touch of a leaf?" I nodded. "Well, that is what it is like to touch your hand."

I looked back at the girl, still myself and not a giraffe. She could rob me now, I thought; she could slit my throat and leave me on the beach and disappear into the lights and the crowds on the boardwalk as easily as she came. She had rolled up to me like a wave, silent and without shadow, and she could leave that way as well, a silvery flash of fish diving back into the untraceable sea. But I did not believe she would; I began to think there had been a reason I woke up in the middle of the night and met this stranger. "Sorry. I'm just not used to anyone touching me I guess."

"It's all right. A lot of people are like you." She looked into my eyes for a long moment, and I looked back as though her eyes were hooks pulling me toward her. "Look down," she instructed me, "and I'll show you how this works. There are three lines in the palm, the heart, the head, and the life lines. See here," she said, brushing her fingertip lightly over one of the crosshatched lines on my palm, "your heart line branches early on. So what woke you, Maggie?" Waves broke behind us. It struck me that the boardwalk was a margin, an animated margin between the standard and the drift, much in the same way the boulevard was a margin between the two. Only the boulevard had no life, no quirky sense of honky-tonk to it like this boardwalk.

"What woke me? I'm not sure." The girl held my gaze. "Fish live inside my head," I told her. The sentence came from my mouth without intonation, a fact, a statistic; I was stating the exports of Guatemala in a geography class. I expected the girl to get up and leave, but her eyes did not shift their gaze. "They speak to me, they seem to have a life of their own, a will of their own. They even have a child."

"What do they tell you? Do they tell you to do anything?"

"No, they just…well, they just sort of bounce around

and speak to me, this pair of fish and their child. The child, he doesn't speak."

"The child is a fish, too?"

"Yes, the child is a fish."

"And the fish speak English? You understand them?"

"Yes, they speak English. They wear costumes sometimes and…" I smiled. "You don't think I'm crazy?"

"No, you're not crazy. Listen," she said, "don't worry about the fish. You'll figure out why they're here, why they came into your head. There's a reason for them to have come to you and somewhere, maybe not now, but somewhere deep down, you know that reason."

"Sometimes I miss them, when they don't come for a bit."

"See. The fish are part of you now. Actually, they've always been part of you." The girl dropped her gaze, looking back down at my palm. "I do this in the summer, I give readings and do tarots and I learn a lot about people. You'd be surprised. Your fish are unusual, but not all that crazy, not compared to what I hear." She turned her head back to my palm. "You know the fish are only inside your brain, right? They don't exist anyplace else."

"Right. They're sort of like dreams, only…"

"Was it the fish who woke you?"

I shook my head no.

"So what is it that you need to do that worries you so much?"

"I can't die," I answered.

"No, you can't. But there's something else here."

"If I'm not going to die, I have to go to a place where

I don't understand the people, where I feel like I can't even speak the language. See this place...I can't translate anything that goes on there." The girl moved her head slightly so her earrings glimmered against her skin. I waited, but no more words came.

"There are places between life and death," she said softly. "Did you know that?"

"I did. My mother knew that, too. And that's sort of where I am. Only I can't stay here, and I can't go to the other place because it's too foreign to me."

The girl picked up my hand again. "See though, right here." She pointed to a short line. "Here, this line here shows direction and you've already begun your journey. You've already made the choice to go to a new place. You just haven't gotten there yet."

I looked at the line. "You can tell that?"

"Yes, look." She traced her finger across a line in my palm. "What woke you has to do with this line then, right here," she shook her head, "this branching off of the heart line. But do you see," she said, moving her finger across my palm, "this? How long this continues, your heart line, without breaks? This is where you are now," and her face was earnest, "at this point where the break is. Once you move beyond this...see, your heart line intersects with your journey line, and that's unusual...there was a break in the heart line that stopped your journey. I've only seen that a few times before. You're in a pause, I think. With the fish and all that you described. When the heart line has small featherings around the journey line, it's a sort of stopping."

She straightened up and took her hand from my palm.

"That's really just a quick reading. If you want more, I work at the spiritualist shop on Atlantic and Ninth. We don't open until about two in the afternoon, but if you want to know more, you can come in and see me. I can explain more about the branch lines, how I can read them."

"I probably can't come. I'm here with my dad and two of his friends."

"Magdalena, you are going to be all right, you know that? I can tell these things. And since you can't come to my shop, you know I'm not saying this to you to get you to do anything." She patted my hand, then she slipped off. I stayed on the bench for a few more minutes, looking at the houses on the streets surrounding the boardwalk. They were row houses, each identical to the next, stoop to roof, like the houses above the boulevard.

The standard. This summer, I had done little to enter that world, and I knew talking to a girl whose name I did not know about the fish in my head and my future according to creases on my hand was not going to help buy my ticket into that world of sleepover parties and dinner schedules. And no matter what she said, I would forever be a visitor to the standard, a person looking in through the window at the party guests.

I glanced away from the xeroxed rows of doors and stoops and opened my palm, putting my fingers on my skin in the places where the girl had touched me. I had never paid any attention to my palm before, to anyone's palm, but the lines seemed so deliberate that I could see how people believed these lines to foretell, to be a map of some type. My thoughts were dreamy, tired; they came slowly, stones dropping through muddied water.

The girl had come from nowhere and spoken in the kind of strange spirit-speak that my mother had so often used, she had come from nowhere then vanished, like the sighting of a phantom. She left nothing behind her but her words. That was all. I had nothing to prove I had even seen her.

Yet I felt different after she left, as though I had gone swimming in uncharted waters and stumbled upon an ocean current pulling me toward shore with subtle gravity. In the standard, I would find a compass, an instrument devoted to direction, to mapping: its purpose would be clear and singular. But here, on the water's edge, I would be offered only current, a graceful pull that would only suggest destination then vanish, a glint of sun on a dark wave. I would have to become better at detecting compromise. I could be one of those people between Chito and Dorothy, between my mother and Hannah, a girl like the one I had just met, a margin-person who straddled both places.

As I thought this, I felt something lift from me, not weight or worry, but more the sense that I had been swimming alone in a dark, unmapped sea and I had at last spotted land: I believed I had found a destination, a place I could not yet name, but as I sat on the bench with the traces of the dark-haired girl's touch still upon my skin, I knew I would not remain in the netherworld of the drift forever. And on that night, I could not have asked for more.

Lack of sleep the next day made me feel light, as though my bones had been replaced by feathers. Only an expanse of sky filled my brain. Dorothy brought bagels and fruit into the room; she poured orange juice into foam cups.

"It doesn't pay to go out to breakfast," she said, her voice falling on me like a rain of glass splinters. They scraped my skin and fell off. "For what? A little juice and some coffee?" My father smiled patiently at her, then went back to his car magazine.

"At least the way I do it, we have fresh fruit," she said to no one. "And if there's one thing you need when you're traveling, it's fresh fruit. If you get what I mean." She laughed to herself.

She was right to do this, I thought expansively, generously. On trips to the ocean, my mother got up early to go on shell hunts. "You get the best ones before the crowd comes," she would whisper conspiratorially, as though the shells were jewels. We hardly ever ate anything until noon or later.

"There you are, Andrew."

"Hey." Andrew stood in a welt of sunlight, his hair wet, his face puzzled. He looked at me, then at my father, as though he had forgotten we were on this trip too.

"We thought we would go to the lighthouse today," Dorothy announced, "if that's all right with everyone." She kept wiping at the ring my father's orange juice cup made on the glass table every time he picked it up. "Lighthouses are one of my passions. I love the whole concept of beacons."

I said nothing. The day was bright and promising;

I stretched and felt the lightness of my bones; I looked down at the sinewy shimmer of my calves, admiring the muscles of my calves, the sheen of my skin.

"I want to go swimming," I announced. "Why don't we save the lighthouse for this afternoon during low tide."

Dorothy's face crumpled.

"I don't see why we couldn't do that," my father offered. "Would that be all right with you, Dot?"

"Of course," Dorothy said, changing her expression rapidly, a stoplight changing colors.

I could see how she ran a store, how she dealt with customers all day. "But maybe we should get going since we're all going to need showers before we go to the lighthouse. I know I for one can't go anywhere with that sticky salt from the ocean on me."

"I'll stay here," Andrew said.

"Are you sure?" Dorothy asked. "Don't you want to go for a bit of a swim with Magda?"

"Next time," he said sleepily.

"Well, I'm going to hold you to it," Dorothy said. "You can't come to the ocean and then not go in the water. I can, but not at your age."

I waited outside while Dorothy packed a large mesh bag with drinks and crackers. From where I stood, I could see the bench where the girl and I had sat last night, vacant now, with a couple of seagulls pecking listlessly around its bottom. The bench was unremarkable. Shadows pooled beneath its rounded rectangle; the filigree ironwork on one side was missing. Yet when I looked at it the sense of lightness came over me again, similar to the sense of weightlessness I had whenever I floated on my back in the bay. I did not think it possible to experience this cessation of gravity on land.

"You should see my Magda swim," my father told Dorothy as they came outside.

"Dad, I'm not a promotional item," I said quickly.

"I know that, but you have to admit, you do know your way around the bay."

"Oh, that's nice. Swimming is the best exercise anyone can get. It strengthens every muscle in the body. " The whole time we walked to the beach, Dorothy kept yanking at the flappy little skirt covering her bottom. I looked away from the poverty of her flesh, from the weave of veins that crossed her skin. For the first time, a stirring of pity for her rose in me.

"I'm going to stay here and relax a little," Dorothy said, spreading a blanket. "My idea of enjoying the ocean is to sit and watch the birds." She gave one of her short, barking laughs and unfolded a plastic chair. "I'm just never sure what little creature is going to come up and say hello when I'm in water, or if it stings or pinches. And I am not one for surprises, no siree, not one for surprises."

Sun sparked the water; waves hilled and broke in the rhythm of my own breathing. I dove into the water, swimming out in a long orbit of strokes until I heard the shrill call of the guard's whistle warning that I had gone too far. Without acknowledging the lifeguard, I turned, my final stroke breaking into the foamy head of a wave that rode me back to shore. My father grinned from the chair. He sat next to Dorothy and as I looked at him with salted ocean water stinging my eyes, the two of them blurred into one person for a moment, an edgeless mingling of color and shape exactly like the sighting of a school of jellyfish, who vanish the minute you recognize them and stop in the water to take a closer look.

The lighthouse was airless as an urn. We had to stand on line inside long slabs of sun for tickets, then we were herded through a door into a sudden eclipse of light and noise and air. The sensation panicked me; the abrupt loss of day and the plunge into night reminded me too sharply of the way I felt after being told my mother had died, how light changed into permanent shadow.

I had trouble following the winding stairs. My breath came in short gasps; my lungs felt close to rupture. At last, the guide stopped his rain of words so the tourists could pause to look out small rectangular windows. The sea churned beyond the lighthouse, restless with the fevered drumming of waves.

"The lighthouse keeper lived like this, in this solitude for months at a time," the guide said. "Imagine this kind of solitude during the winter months, your only hope of human contact being the supply ship. Originally, they had no radios, no television."

"I'd lose my mind," a gray-haired woman behind me

said to her husband. "I'd just lose my mind in a place like this."

"No one said they didn't," the guide said and the crowd laughed.

I pulled away from the window, thinking how this shape, this hulking tower full of interior with virtually no light, this closed and dark place of solitude, this circular place that just spun round and round with no boundaries, with no beginning or end, was so like grief. This was the shape of grief. I went next to my father. I stood there, looking at the guide but not hearing a word he was saying; I stood there feeling the lightness of my bones, knowing now this was not only lack of sleep that had transformed my bones into feathers, but my body's recognition that soon I would be leaving this place I had inhabited for one year, this place made entirely of grief.

"Does night come from the top or the bottom? What do you think, Lena, from the top or the bottom?" I heard my mother's voice while I stood inside the lighthouse, one of her last questions to me, a question I did not understand at the time. She had been inside the house for days when she asked me this, my father off at work for long hours. I remember thinking that she had not changed her robe or bothered to comb her hair in two days. Then she asked me that question: "Does night come from the top or the bottom?"

I knew the answer mattered to her, but I did not know what she had wanted or needed to hear. I looked at her on the couch and I said, "I don't know, Mom. But I'll bet it comes from the top sometimes and from the bottom other times."

"So both then? You think night comes from both places?"

"Yes. From both places."

She had nodded, and in a crooked kind of way, I knew my mother had been satisfied.

And I knew that my night, after she left, had come from both places as well. What I needed to find out now was where day came from.

Andrew walked out of the shower with a towel wrapped around his middle. I had fallen asleep after the lighthouse, and I woke as he dropped onto the edge of the bed.

"Hi," I said, as though this visit were not intrusive. "How come you skipped the lighthouse?"

"My mother has dragged me to just about every lighthouse on the eastern seaboard at this point. Someday I'll understand what she sees in them."

They are small and closed and a bit pointless now, I thought, just like Dorothy, but I willed my mind to be more generous. "So where did they go?" I asked Andrew.

"To get something to eat, and they're bringing it back to the room."

"Oh," I answered nonchalantly, hoping Andrew would see my question as an end to our conversation. "I just hope it's not pizza again."

"Mom said something about Chinese. She's like mad

for these little dumpling things they make." My legs were inches from his.

"Chinese. My parents hardly ever ate anything from restaurants. My aunt came over every weekend and made food for the week, stews and stuff. We just took them out of the freezer and heated them since my mom hardly ever cooked. I mean, she cooked sometimes, but most nights she didn't feel like it. She wasn't so much into food, really, which is why she was so thin I guess." I wanted to keep on babbling, to keep Andrew securely in his spot, but I could think of nothing else to say.

"You're pretty thin yourself," he said to me in a way that made my stomach churn. He looked at me, his eyes round and dull as buttons. He shifted his legs. As he did, the towel shifted and I saw a weave of auburn hair, darker and richer in color than the reddish brown on his head. His penis lay curled in the nest of auburn, a tender, boneless thrush of pink whose soft shapelessness reminded me of a clam's interior.

"You know," Andrew said quietly, "when you lose a parent you get lonesome. One thing I've figured out is that sex is the opposite of loneliness."

"How's that?" Light banged into the room, combing through the blind slats and under the doors.

"Well, loneliness is an empty space where someone should be. Sex is filling up all those places. It's connecting instead of disconnecting. Death is a way of disconnecting."

"You know, Andrew, I just haven't thought about guys or anything in that way since my mother died. I just haven't. It's a little like I'm dead, too."

"But you're not."

"I am aware of that; I just don't feel…you know, interested." I moved my legs up under me and away from Andrew and sat up. "I think, too, that if we're going to be in the same house together, and it does look that way, I should tell you right now that I want a room far away from you with a locking door. There's nothing wrong with you, Andrew, it's just that I am not interested in anything like this with anyone."

"It doesn't have to be that way, Magda, you know that."

"Yeah," I said, loudly, "it does have to be this way. I don't know what on earth makes people assume that just because they get married, their kids are going to want to cozy up, but no one has asked me, and as far as all this goes, a family is not an equation. You can't put different factors into an equation and still get the same sum."

I went to the bench where I had met the moon-girl, the one who had offered to tell me my future. It was late afternoon. Gulls circled overhead; amber light had begun gathering beneath awnings, softening edges until the colors had a richness that seemed to be vibrating. The beach began to empty; kids slept in strollers while their sandy parents rolled them along the boardwalk. I would stay on the bench until my father and Dorothy returned; I would not stay with Andrew. There were certain choices I had to make and adhere to if I wanted my life to leave the shade I lived in and enter the light of the standard, of any standard.

Then you should return the sticks, the ones you've been collecting since you came here, the stone-smooth, sleek sticks you keep in a raft-shape beneath your socks in the motel bureau, the ones you've picked up on the beach, as you walk, all those sticks you are keeping. You should take them and return them along with the matches that came centered in the motel ashtray. Gather them all and then go to the beach and scatter them on the sand. Set nothing, plan to set nothing, no last fire, no last ring of stone. Break the sticks so you cannot go out and find them again, break them and toss them into the wind.

"There she is, our little mermaid," Dorothy said, her voice gliding into my thoughts like an injection, "sitting all by herself. Why didn't you ask Andrew to sit out here with you?"

I shrugged. My father stood next to Dorothy, holding several containers of greasy-looking cardboard.

"Let's go eat," Dorothy said. "We were so lucky to find a Szechuan place down here. Andrew told me he just can't eat any more Mandarin, so we were really lucky to find this place."

I followed them back to our motel room where we sat, all four of us, at the Formica table with the golden starbursts. Dorothy set out little dishes of sauce and rolled paper napkins to resemble birds. I could see how she took care of people, how nothing around her would ever grow sad or frayed or neglected.

"I thought tonight maybe we could take in that amusement park down the boardwalk. There's going to be a bonfire and fireworks." My father smiled at Andrew and me. "And a couple of those rides look pretty good."

"I like the magic acts," Dorothy said. "Not just the magic acts, but all those little sideshows they have running along the midway, the puppets and the sword swallower, those kind of shows. Do you like those, Magda?"

I wanted to tell her no, of course I don't like those, I have a sideshow running inside my head far too often. Andrew sat with his head down, hunched over his food as though nothing had happened between us. "I like some of them," I answered, spearing a snow pea with my plastic fork. "I'm just not all that familiar with them."

"We are," Mrs. Fish said, rumbling into my brain with the sound of motorcycles. She and Mr. Fish got off two Harley motorcycles and I watched as Mrs. Fish removed her helmet, her paper cup hat still intact. The bikes melted behind them, into colored bubbles of water that rose around them like a psychedelic aquatic show. Dorothy's voice drifted far away from me, long spirals of sentences moving across the air. I chewed and watched the fish swim through the light beads. When they came back to my line of vision, they wore black wigs and began moving to music I didn't hear, the colored bubbles bursting into flower blooms.

"We should probably stop," Mr. Fish said, stopping and going over to Mrs. Fish. She stood perfectly still while he embraced her. "Does it mean anything anymore when I say I'm sorry?"

"You underestimate her, you really do," Mrs. Fish replied. "You say the rest of the world is sealed off to her, you say that as though I had some kind of choice, as though I could enter into that kind of life. I never misled you about the kind of person I was."

"No, you didn't," Mr. Fish said quietly, gently swaying. Mrs. Fish's body remained still. "It's just this, Alice: what will become of her being raised like this? The only occupation she'll be suited for is...I don't even know, a beachcomber maybe. She spends her days walking the beaches. I mean, if that's all she does, she doesn't have a chance, now does she?"

"A chance to do what? You act as though she is being stunted, as though children somewhere else will flourish and she won't. I just don't buy it, Preston, I just don't."

"There are parks, there are dance classes and things like that. It's all so...quiet around here."

"You've been hanging out with the eels far too long," Mrs. Fish threw her head back and laughed, "if you think the beach is quiet. That's the last place..."

"Magda, are you ready?"

I looked up. My father and Dorothy stood at the doorway. I could see Andrew already waiting outside. No dishes remained on the table; the napkins had been tossed away, the table wiped clean as sunlight. I did not know who had spoken, so I stood and walked over to them.

"You are a dreamer, Magda," Dorothy said, squeezing my forearm as though we were on our way to the junior prom, two giddy girls in baby pink pumps. "Your dad always told me you're the dreamy sort, but now I really know what he means. You really sink into your thoughts."

"Yes," I said. "I sort of go underwater."

Everyone laughed, and again, I had no idea why they

laughed. The sentence did not seem funny to me; it was true.

"Well, never mind," Dorothy said as though I had asked for approval or forgiveness. "I think it's a good quality in a person, to be able to sink into your thoughts like that. Lots of people think it's a good quality."

We walked to the end of the boardwalk, the sky now dark and sprinkled with stars. I kept looking for the dark-haired girl, but of course I did not see her. I would probably never see her again, and I had known that I would never see her again that night, but still, I hoped for one last glimpse.

"No takers for the Ferris wheel?" Andrew called, looking at me and my father. "You sure?"

"We're sure," my father said. "You two go on ahead. We'll wait down here."

My father and I sat in two ridiculous plastic octopus chairs. I wondered if the fish would show up now and make a comment, but only my father spoke.

"I'm glad we were able to get away like this, Magda." Andrew and Dorothy disappeared into the crowd.

"Me too."

"You miss the house much?"

"Just the beach. I miss the beach."

"I'm glad you don't miss the house." He reached over and patted my leg. "Magda, we're putting the house up for sale. I thought you should know that."

"Andrew already told me that. You guys are buying a new house near the mall. I know."

"So you're not going to run off and dive into any rough

surf now, are you?" He meant this sentence lightly, as a means of winning me over, but I just looked at him, blank as wood.

"No. My days of running off into rough surf are over." He nodded. My father and I looked up at the same moment to see Dorothy wave to us from her Ferris wheel car. Andrew looked out over the water. "I'll miss the house, probably, Dad, but I'm kind of used to missing stuff now."

My father waved back to Dorothy. "That's too bad. I was hoping you would like the new house, like the bigger room you'll have."

"I might. I definitely want a lock on my door."

"Right. At your age, I can understand that."

"You know, Dad, I see why you like her now. Dorothy."

"I'm glad."

"Don't you want to know what I mean?"

"Nope. I don't want to argue with you."

I laughed. "Well, you should know." I wanted to say, after all I've put you through, but I didn't.

"All right then. What is your reason? Or reasons, as the case may be?"

"She's sort of the opposite of Mom. The way she makes you feel like you're all sewn up when you're with her, like everything is planned, nothing is left to chance. The way she always has a tissue or a drink right with her, that kind of thing. Mom made me feel more like I could draw or understand music without really trying and I liked that. To be honest, I liked that more, the way Mom was."

"Yes," my father said, a slight smile on his face, "we all know you liked that more. You are far more like your mother than Dorothy, and that's understandable, since you are not related to Dorothy."

"But still, I do see how you would want to feel taken care of now. Mom didn't do that. She made me feel taken care of, but I guess not you."

"Something like that," my father agreed. "It is something like that." He waved to Dorothy again. "She likes you, Dorothy does. She thinks you're very deep. She said you seem spiritual for your age."

"Sure. That's what they all say." My father smiled. The moment seemed to open, like one of the holes I had been falling through ever since my mother died, only this time I was not afraid. The walls of the hole seemed soft, warm, as though I were falling through my own body. "Dad, I was thinking about all those fires in the spring, the ones around our house."

"That was some headache." My father craned his neck to see Dorothy and Andrew rocking at the top of the Ferris wheel. "Then the drought. I was so worried that one of those fires would get to our house. So close to us in the woods like that."

"The last one, when the cars were exploding, do you remember that one?"

"I do. I could never forget that one. The fire was spreading close to houses."

"Do you know who set those fires?"

"No, I don't know who set those fires. The girl they suspected just disappeared. They had no real evidence on her either. Then she just vanished."

"Dad, I meant I know who set them, I'm not asking you. I know because I set them."

My father turned his gaze back to me. He looked at me for a long moment, his gaze steady as a beam. He put his hand on my hair, near my throat. For a moment I thought the gesture was a menacing one, that he was going to put his hand around the bloom of my throat and strangle me. But he only caressed my skin, moving my hair back behind my shoulder. "Not for a minute would I believe that, Magda. Not for a minute would I believe that you would do such a thing. I know what happened to your mother really sent you reeling, but not for a minute do I believe you capable of such an act." He shook his head back and forth. "You're just not the type, Magda, you're just not the type. You're the type of girl who would put a fire out with her own hands, that's the type of girl you are, the type of girl I raised. A girl who gets As in school and has a gift for drawing, that's who you are." He picked up my hands and held them.

"You are far too young to understand this, but I have seen children who are arsonists: they are nothing like you. Nothing. They are disturbed children who mean to do harm. That girl, what was her name?"

"Spring Robinson."

"Yes, Spring Robinson. Now she was the type of girl to do harm, to be an arsonist. But not you. That's a ridiculous thought." He squeezed my hands. "It's over now. We don't always know who set every fire, but we do know that's over. We can move on, and that's the last thing we are going to say about that time."

Dorothy and Andrew came over to us, pointing to a snow cone stand they wanted to visit.

We stood and my father leaned over me. "Now let's forget you ever said that. You've been through a lot, Magda, an awful lot and it's beginning to show. You've even got your Aunt Hannah worried with some of your behavior, but let's forget the fires for now."

We ate snow cones and went on rides that nearly sickened me with their spin and smell of exhaust. My father and Dorothy walked ahead of Andrew and me back to the motel. Andrew did not speak, so I just listened to the schlop-lop of waves rupturing against sand.

"We only have one more night here," Dorothy announced as all four of us filed into our shared room. "And there's something I'd like to give you." She held out a rectangular package wrapped in shiny pink paper. "Michael, would you put on some coffee?"

Dorothy had given me a blank hardbound book. "Thank you," I murmured.

"I just saw it in one of the shops and I know how you are always daydreaming. I thought isn't that just the thing for Magda to draw or write in. I'm glad you like it." She turned to the small coffeemaker and began stirring powdered creamer into two cups. "Do you want to tell them?" she asked my father.

"Magda, knowing Magda, already knows, but I'll tell them." My father grinned. "You two kids probably figured this out weeks ago, but Dorothy and I are going to be married come this Columbus Day weekend, the first Saturday in October."

"Congratulations," I said.

"That's great news," Andrew said and I searched his face to see if he meant this sarcastically, but his features were too sheep-like to read.

"To celebrate, we're treating this whole family to a barbecue on the beach tomorrow night. There's going to be a bonfire."

I thought of the sticks in my bureau. I would take them with me; I would toss them into this fire and I would be done. As soon as I resolved to do this, the lightness returned to my body, the floating sensation I had woken up with feathered through my bones down to the soles of my feet. It was the weightlessness of grace. I had heard my mother say those words once and now I knew what she meant. The weightlessness of grace, I repeated silently to myself, will be my compass, an idea born in the drift of those willowy days spent with my mother, now a kind of compass that will help me know what to do.

We got to the beach early enough to see the first fireworks spark against the night air. I could not recall ever getting to a fireworks display this early before. Dorothy had already packed our room up, encouraging me to fold my belongings back into my suitcase. "Everything but what you're going to wear tonight and tomorrow morning when we go back to Staten Island. It will just make checking out that much easier."

I wore jeans with large, deep pockets. Inside each pocket, the sticks rested and I could feel their hollowness, as though I carried shells. They were noiseless and tiny and when my father and Dorothy began setting up chairs in the sand, I strode over to the bonfire. It was an average fire with simple architecture. I stood in front of it, appraising its engineering. This fire, about six yards in height, would never grow any higher. It was circular and contained, with a man standing at either side to ensure it never became wild. I cast each of my sticks into the fire. I could not explain why I had gotten the sticks, an old habit, a way of bringing light into my world, I could not be sure. But as the crowd watched the jarring fireworks, I watched the bonfire, standing before it as though it were an altar. I liked the leap of each flame, the happiness of the hissing sound, the way sparks rose into the air like illuminated bells and flew out of sight. I stood in the warmth of the fire, noticing the ripeness it gave to everyone's skin, the pleasantness of its heat radiating in circles from its center like a benevolent goddess of the hearth.

"Yoo-hoo, Magda," I heard Dorothy call. I turned. She and my father motioned for me to come back to their circle of chairs. I sat with them, watching the sky flash, thinking how much these lights were like the fish. They came from nowhere, filling up the dark recesses of my brain with light and sound, filling up a piece of the void like a cactus flower in miles of arid sand. Then, as if I had summoned them, the fish began cartwheeling through my brain, taking on the light and bang of the fireworks, first Mrs. Fish, then Mr. Fish wearing costumes of every kind: clown suits and scuba gear, Renaissance hats with velvet smoking jackets. Mr. Fish donned a pirate's outfit while Mrs. Fish paraded past, wearing Little Bo Peep's frock and carrying a small shepherding staff. I closed my eyes, willing them to stop. It was a meteor storm of fish. People all around me sat on sand or folding chairs, probably only mildly worried about traffic congestion after the show, and I sat there with the fish misbehaving inside my head, utterly powerless to stop them.

"You can go now," I willed them. "I have an idea where I'm going."

"So do we," Mr. Fish laughed, dressed as a Medieval minstrel. He strummed a mandolin. "We know just where we're going." Then the scene slowed. A slow bend of turtle-brown water came into view, some kind of river or creek. Mrs. Fish had on a gingham dress; Mr. Fish wore a straw hat and overalls with no shirt beneath them. Baby Fish played happily on a wooden swing. He wore a diaper with dancing cows.

"This is just terrific," I said to them. "Just what I need right now."

The fish moved further away, as though I watched them in a film. I saw a cascade of branches skittering down, their tips grazing the brown water.

"The way I see it," Mr. Fish began, putting a piece of hay in his mouth, "is that folks take themselves much too seriously lately. Much too seriously."

"Isn't that the truth?" Mrs. Fish said, shaking her head

back and forth as she rested on the riverbank. "You said it, Preston."

Mr. Fish grinned, his needle teeth entirely exposed. "Me? I've come to a decision, one I made while watching the sky yesterday. I'm taking my new direction from the clouds. Whatever I do, the wind will just push me along and I'll end up where I end up is all. Some people around here, and I'm not naming names, worry entirely too much about where they'll end up, which way they are going to go, and how they're going to get there. Oh my, oh my." He held a fin up to his cheek in mock distress.

"What did you think of the show?" Andrew asked me.

I jumped.

"Sorry," he said, "I didn't mean to scare you."

"Oh, it wasn't you." I had forgotten he was next to me. "I was just a little lost in the show. It was great," I said, a gust of exhaustion welling through me. Mrs. Fish smiled with her needle teeth, a baleful smile, full of exuberant malice. Now she wore a dental-white martial arts costume, complete with a black belt. Her little tartar cup hat was still on, though she wore a wig with a black topknot. Mr. Fish came up beside her in a fifth-century Japanese emperor's gown and a silk hat shaped into twin cranes. I remembered the outfit from a picture Mrs. Keith had near her desk.

"Who's up for pizza?" Dorothy asked me. We had just finished a basket of chicken and hamburgers before the fireworks.

"I'm really tired."

Again, her face crumpled. "Oh, maybe we should just go back."

I glanced at my father, whose face looked as though I had struck him. "Maybe I'm tired because I'm a little hungry," I suggested. I walked with her, and when she linked her arm in mine, I did not protest.

Dorothy chose a gleaming Italian place on the boardwalk, full of steel and white tile, where she ordered two slices of pizza. "The men have decided to go back to the room, so I told them we would catch up, if that's all right with you."

"I thought they were coming." I wished I had turned around during our walk.

"No. I wanted to just talk to you alone for a little bit, just for a few minutes. Is that all right?"

"Sure." I watched the fish bow and leave. The pizza came. I waited for Dorothy to speak.

"You remember how I spoke to you about Nancy, the therapist who helps kids who've lost a parent?" I said I did. "Well, there are just so many ways we can grieve or feel guilty that sometimes we don't even understand what we are doing to ourselves. But I wanted to share this one idea of Nancy's with you, one that has helped me with Andrew." She took a bite of pizza, then scraped the corners of her mouth with a napkin. "No one is responsible for the death of a parent unless they shot that parent. Or they mixed poison into the parent's apple juice. It's just something Nancy had to keep reminding Andrew of, over and over. For a time, Andrew blamed me for his father's death, and according to Nancy, that's a natural feeling. After he saw that I had nothing to do with his father's death, he, well…we sometimes blame ourselves for things, for evil things that there are no answers to. Sometimes there just are no answers." She took another bite. I watched her chew, each lip moving in time with the other like a gear on a clock. I pushed my piece away.

"It sounds like Nancy thinks emotions are pretty orderly."

"Maybe they become orderly when we understand them better."

"My emotions have always been messy," I countered, "very difficult to understand. They just seem to occur, like weather fronts."

"Nancy interprets them. That's what I would say. A meteorologist of your emotional landscape. I kind of like that." She swallowed and smiled, obviously waiting for me to speak.

"Dad told you I started those fires, didn't he?"

"He did not say that. He did not say that you started those fires." Dorothy shut her eyes as though I were a particularly nettlesome task. "He told me that you are confessing to a crime you did not commit. He's worried that you are either seeking attention or taking on responsibility for an accident that no one had control over. That you have some kind of guilt problem."

Accident. The code word for failure between my father and me. How my mother, supposedly, ended: in an accident.

"But I did set them," I said, very slowly, very deliberately, as though Dorothy were a retarded child I was helping learn the names of birds. "And my mother did not have an accident."

She wiped her mouth. "Well, who's to tell what happened when you get right down to it? It's the same story with Andrew's dad, who's to tell? No one was there when either one of them died."

"I'll never believe she had an accident. Never. And the fires were no accident either. I set them as intentionally as I would set the dinner table. Every one of them. I planned them out in the same way my English teacher showed us how to plan an essay. I gathered my thoughts, pondered the beginning, how I would stack the wood. That would be my thesis. Then I developed the fire, flushed it out nicely, and made sure it came to an end where people would notice."

"Magda, you are such a sweet and silly girl, with your father's highly developed sense of duty."

Duty. I raised my eyebrows. Was she referring to my father's sense of duty toward me or my mother?

"I have been around long enough to know that the daughter of a fire dispatcher would certainly never be foolish enough to set fires. That much I know. Remember, Magda, healing takes time," Dorothy said and stood up. "Everything takes time, sweetie. That's how we heal."

chapter

·

six

September came, golden and warm with an amberous light that I could not stop staring into. I found myself bathing my arms in the polished light, watching ropes of muscle that I could not remember seeing before twine beneath my skin. In school, bees thronged into our classroom and I watched them as they flew inside honey, inside the pollenish dusk of that light. It was while looking at that light pouring through our living room windows and jeweling the air to topaz that Linn Pear crashed through the door of our house with her clipboard.

I sat up on the couch, surprised, thinking her quick knock and entry to be Hannah puddling through the door with her uninspired groceries, a turnip and some cans of tuna fish. Or worse, that Mrs. Fish had taken on human form and would be entering my daydreams fully incarnated.

"Ahoy!" she called, a word I could never, ever envision from Hannah's lips. The woman stood over me as I sat on the couch, her hair cut in an angled way so that it moved like perfectly hewn grass struck by wind, each piece clinging to the next in one unified arc. The strands themselves shone an improbable blonde, and she wore a clingy green shirt that clearly displayed her nipples. I kept looking at her erect flesh beneath the thin silk, unsure why I could not look away from her tiny breasts with their pointed salutations. Willing myself to stand, I shook her hand.

"Hello, Magda. Your father told me you would be here. I'm Linn Pear, the agent from Raritan Realty."

"You're here to sell the house." I said this plainly, and when I spoke the words aloud, the fact that the house would vanish struck me, both dreamlike and astonishing at once.

"Hopefully I'm here to sell the house. And quickly." She tapped her clipboard with a pen. "I like to get down to business pretty fast. First, I'll take some measurements of the rooms, get an idea how many square feet you have, the features of the house, you know, anything unusual or remarkable about the structure."

The structure. I looked around at the rooms that I did not see as rooms but more as a landscape for my emotions, a biography of memory.

"This house is haunted," I said.

"Well, if you mean that someone has died here, that's

all right. We all have to die somewhere. Probably whoever died here wasn't the first to die in this house. Ever think of that?" She went on without waiting for me to answer. "It's not what you'd call new, dying." Linn pulled a tape measure from her pocket and began working with rapid, clipped motions, a squirrel stowing nuts into a winter nest while gale winds blew. She did not look up from her work. I continued standing in the living room, my neck growing long, knobs on my head budding. "Other than this place being haunted, anything I should know? Prone to floods or leaks? Termites? Any kind of infestations?"

Infestations? "Didn't you speak to my father?"

"I did, but only briefly. He had to get back to work, but he did say you wouldn't mind if I got started today. He called just at the point when I had a free afternoon. I was thinking of going over some files, cleaning out the office a bit, but then he called and it fit the whole curve of the afternoon. I couldn't have been happier." She looked up from her clipboard, directly into my face.

"If you know what I mean by that. The curve of the afternoon being that it was so nice out, I didn't have to waste such a sunny day doing chores that could be better done in darkness or in rain. I even managed to get this listing in Sunday's paper. I had to be quick, my specialty."

"So people will be coming through to look at the house?"

She nodded. "What I usually do is call ahead a few hours before showing the house. That way the owners have a chance to clear out. You know, it's so much easier to show a house when the owners aren't home." She narrowed her eyes and glanced at the ceiling. "Attic a walk-up?"

"Crawl space."

"Basement?"

"Nope, just sand and air under the house. And the ghosts."

"Well," she said evenly, "they have to live somewhere." She made notations on her clipboard. "When I'm done here, I'll have to take some pictures of the house. The gardens are such a great curbside feature. What are those purple flowers all trellised out there?"

"Wisteria."

"Now there's a mournful word if I ever heard one. Wisteria. Kind of the name of some Southern woman who never married, don't you think?" Without waiting for an answer, she moved to the left of the sun porch, into the small room my mother and I ignored. I followed Linn and waited on the room's precipice. "Now what is this? I see, what do I see here—the possibility of another bedroom or a sewing room. Look at that, a bassinet. I like this, a sunny little nook, very precious. Small, but so sunny, almost like it's not part of this house. What's in here, a daybed and infant furniture. Interesting." She wrote on her clipboard again, then took out a measuring tape. When she came back out to measure the sun porch, I walked into the room I had rarely entered. Linn had been right: a wicker bassinet stood in one corner filled with baby clothes and tiny, dusty hats, items my mother had probably meant to donate but never got around to.

Linn came into the small room again. "Magda, honey,

give me some clues as to how your family used this room. There are little blue socks peeking out from that bureau, there's the daybed with some hand-painted pillows." I followed behind her with the precise wobble of my giraffe legs. She walked over and picked up the pillows my mother had silk-screened. After examining them closely, she put them back down, but a little straighter. "Very nice use of colors on those pillows. I studied art for a short time, and these are well done. What did you say this room was used for?"

"A guest room," I answered.

Only guests never slept there; no, except Hannah. It was where your father slept, had always slept, away from you and your mother, as though he lived inside another house, revolved inside another orbit. You never went into that room; your mother never went into that room. You only sat together, in the part of the porch where your mother kept her plants, listening to sun whisper across the floor in the languid sweep of aloneness. You smelled the dusted scent of unhappiness leaking out from behind the door and now the room had lain abandoned, left alone since she died, a place that collected nothing but sun and silence, a room gone useless as a broken basket. Right after she died, your father took over the room they had once shared, before you were born. He slipped back into that room, leaving the small room off the porch, the room that had never been named or spoken of, leaving that room, with the daybed and the stark luster of its bare walls, alone as an echo.

"Ah, a guest room." Linn Pear glanced at me and I wondered if she could see the truth of how we had lived in this house, if as I approached the standard, people would look at me and see all of me, all I contained as though I were shallow, a sunlit segment of the shoals with my rocks and shells glittering in the bottom for all to see. But she simply bobbed her head up and down quickly, in the manner of a cork bouncing back up from beneath a capsize, and said, "Seems like what I personally call a 'whatever room,' you know, used for whatever but another great find nonetheless. Every room is a feature, a selling point." She wrote on her pad in spare, clean strokes. "There's a lot more to this house than meets the eye. To tell you the truth, when your father first called to say you'd be moving out in a few weeks, I thought, Oh boy, here we go again, another bungalow that will stay on the market until spring. But there's a lot more quirky character to this house than in the usual bungalow."

Quirky character. A few weeks. We would be moving out in a few weeks.

"Let me just get a sense of the kitchen and bedrooms and I'll be out of your way. The rest I can do with your dad."

"That would be great," I said politely. Hannah had come in and stood behind Linn Pear. When Linn Pear turned to see who I looked at, her small breasts bounced. I watched Hannah's eyes assess the motion.

"I'm going down to the beach," I said to them both without looking behind. Walking slowly, I held my arms in the light, admiring their thin strength, their sculpted hollows.

I had not been to the beach since returning from

Ocean City in August. The wind was still hot, but it was stronger. Chito's garden of women had frayed, their clothing burnt off their charred bodies, their faces filled with scorch marks. His house looked deserted, a husk left for the wind and the water to swallow. I stood outside Chito's old house for a few minutes, remembering how happy he had seemed that day when he talked about the women, how he was going to find mates for them. He had spoken of the future. Perhaps that is the way people leave who want to leave: they pick a good time, then they sort of dive into the black at that moment. Maybe they swim around for weeks, months, knowing only that they want to leave but not sure of the precise moment to go. Then that moment rises up, larger than anything they have ever known. I wondered where they went, those souls. My mother always said she wanted to come back as wind, that she would come back as wind and find me as an old woman. I had laughed when she said this, the idea of my child-self growing into an old woman as absurd as the idea of my mother's leaving.

Now I would be leaving, but not for an unknown place, not to become wind or light or anything of that nature. If anything, I was to become more solid. I would enter the new house with my father and Dorothy and Andrew and be removed from the drift once and for all. But I would find my borderworld, that place between the two worlds. I would be able to salvage parts of the drift I wanted to keep, even if they had to remain hidden, no matter how seamlessly I entered the standard.

I stood near the beach I would soon be leaving, as close to the water as I could manage without getting wet, looking out over the bay at a few sailboats coasting the wind, at small lathers of whitecaps churning in the still-calm water, at the buoy that clanged in a desolate way, beginning to sound further away than it had in high summer. Sounds on the beach traveled across the water differently in each season. In the summer, bits of conversation and radios journeyed across the bay and the beach clearly and with ease, as though the air were empty and waiting to be filled with sound. In the fall, even in late summer, sounds became more muted, traveling inside air that seemed thicker and more resistant to the weight of sound, and they were harder to identify.

Just a few weeks ago, the buoy had rung as though it were behind me or next to me. Now it seemed distant, a sound I recalled in memory or dream, not a sound that had the strength to enter day. Turning from the bay, I decided to walk to the shaded part of the beach, to the eel-dark place where Spring Robinson's house had been. I knew this would be one of the last times I would walk on the beach before we moved, and I wanted to pay special attention to the things I had always taken for granted: the shuffling sound of horseshoe crabs as they scuttled the sand with their claws and spiny tails, moving slowly and with a kind of primordial grace, simple, spiderish creatures that were the stuff of nightmares to most people who came to our beach, but to me, they were animals I had grown up near and had always known. I looked at logs holding scars of summer fires, their once smooth flesh blackened in scales and scorch marks, evidence of their final use. I put a few of the bladder-shaped reddish rocks that lined our shore into my pocket; I selected a few disinhabited mollusks for my new room.

I was reaching for a small glisten of a jingle shell when I saw her, the woman I had not thought of in weeks: Daphne's mother. She sat on a log close to the rocks, staring out into the water, all the light gone from her eyes, her pupils dark and large, her corneas turned to ash. I did not recognize her expression, though her mood entered me like a jolt of electricity, swift and unmistakable. Never before could I remember looking at an adult and perceiving their mood so instantly. Of all the times I had looked at my father after my mother's death, not once was his mood so readable. On the rare occasions when he spoke of my mother, my father's face reminded me of clouds moving across a sky, changing by the moment, their shape and direction unpredictable as ether. This woman sat before me, a river of pain, her face eclipsed by grief.

"Hello," I said levelly, wondering if she remembered speaking to me on the day her daughter drowned.

"Hi." She kept staring. I assumed she did not remember me; I did not expect her to recall our meeting or much about that day, yet I wanted to speak to her, to touch her in some way.

"We're moving in a few days and I thought I'd take a little of the beach with me." I did not know if she would respond to me, I only knew I wanted to speak to her, I needed to speak to her before leaving the beach for good.

"Where are you going?" she asked, her voice flat and exhausted.

"My dad is getting married, well, remarried, and we're moving over by the Staten Island mall."

"The mall. I know where that is." The woman did not

take her eyes from the water. "I'd rather be here," the woman said, "by the beach." She continued staring out into the water. "My daughter comes here all the time," she said. "This is where she is so I like it here the best. I stay with her now."

A plume of wind came up behind me, stirring the top layer of sand. "Then you're better off here," I said quietly, believing I understood the woman, knowing that she was not mad or lost. Her grief for Daphne had forced her into a lonesome, windy place where she could see nothing except more lonesome days filled with wind, just a tunnel with no end. She could not yet see around her or above her. But she would; I wanted to tell her that, though I knew she would not believe her view would ever change. She would find her way out of the continual grayness. I knew that to be true, as I had begun finding my own way back into the bright surface of day. It would never look the same, but it would not be the same gray space.

"Maybe I'll see you here again sometime," I called, knowing she would not answer me, but wanting to acknowledge her before I left her sitting there inside her own weather. I walked all the way to the end of the beach, to the most lonesome spot where Spring Robinson's cottage stood, and when I turned, the woman was still in the same spot, her eyes out on the water, watching. I had moved beyond the point where she was, but it seemed I could never tell where I was until that point passed. I did have a sense of my own navigation. Unfortunately, it worked only in the past tense.

The fish decided to move. I was sitting in math class watching the earnest young teacher explain a question regarding the hypotenuse, and Mrs. Fish suddenly stood up wearing white carpenter pants and a painter's cap.

"It's about time," Mrs. Fish complained to no one I could see. "This place has been too small for years now and to think we have eels right down the way, I mean really, eels. Walk outside my door and there they are, oily and writhing, an entire sea of eels. Never in my day did I think I would be neck and neck with eels." She shuddered, and as she did, her scales glinted.

"It's not so bad," Mr. Fish said. A light went on overhead and he stepped out from behind a jumbled tower of chairs. "It wasn't a bad run as far as runs go. I could think of half a dozen worse places to live, easy, right off the top of my head. Half a dozen."

"Is that a fact? I could think of half a dozen better places to live," Mrs. Fish snapped, tugging a box out from behind a rock. They did not look as though they were in water, just in weighted air. Bubbles rose around them, brilliantly colored bubbles that had an element of noise, not quite a hum, but a slow purring sound, the kind you might hear when riding an elevator. "To think we'd be staying here, now with Baby Fish starting school. He's all yours," she said to Mr. Fish. "It's your turn with Baby Fish." Mrs. Fish pushed at her tartar cup hat with one fin. "You might think it's a crazy sentiment, for a mother to want to take a break, but since the day Baby Fish was born I've been here, every step of the way, every bite of food, every tooth, every morsel of food and now I just want a little breathing room, a chance to see how I do on my own."

Mr. Fish began taking the chairs down. "I can do more. What you're asking for is excessive, very exaggerated, but I'm done arguing. We can just split up the furniture." He made two piles with the chairs. "I'll need more furniture for the baby." He turned, his eyes hugely silver, and stared at Mrs. Fish. "Does it ever occur to you what your actions might do to Baby Fish? Does that ever occur to you?"

"Don't forget to account for his growth," Mrs. Fish said dryly, in a voice that could be quoting insurance statistics. "He'll grow out of that furniture in no time. They have spurts where they grow, it's not a linear thing. It's not like they grow an inch a week or anything along those lines. They blossom, all at once, much more like an explosion than a change that can be predicted."

"Sort of like his mother's behavior then," Mr. Fish said.

Mrs. Fish wheeled around on one fin, a movement that she executed with balletic precision.

"So, Maggie, does that explain the equation a bit more clearly to you?"

Equation. Mr. Frank stood only a foot from my desk, his shadow creating a moving umbra over my body.

"Yes, I think it does," I said quickly, falling back into the class, listening to bees just outside the window, a weal of sun pouring onto my hand. "It clears it up." I put my head back down, unsure of what "it" might be. Hands around me shot up, students sure enough of the lesson to ask questions.

That afternoon, I remembered only the word hypotenuse when I opened my geometry book. As I glanced down the page my head clattered with angles, then the angles turned to bones, then the bones turned to dust. Nothing stuck. A creaking sound sprawled lackadaisically though the air, and for a panicky moment I thought the fish might be coming through the door, that they had vacated my head only to move into my living room.

"Ahoy!" The door shut. Linn Pear stood before me, clearly not an apparition, holding several cardboard boxes, one nested into the other like one of those magical Easter eggs you keep opening until you get to the candy inside the smallest egg.

"I brought you these so you can begin cleaning out some stuff. This morning I talked to your dad and he thought you might want to go through some of your mother's things by yourself, sort them out. You know, when you're selling a house, less is more, you have to remember that." She started arranging the boxes in size order, putting the largest ones behind her. "I've pretty much adopted that as my life philosophy; I gave away all the extra dishes in my cupboard, all the extra clothing and books I could never find room for. Did you ever read about those monks over in India, the ones who live with only one bowl and a mat?" She arranged the boxes in a line straight as railroad cars.

"I think so."

"They're my ideal. The simplicity of that lifestyle, the ability to get so much done in a day."

"But what do they get done in a day?" I asked. "I thought they only prayed."

"Of course, I know not everyone can live that philosophy, but I do like helping people pare down. Simplifies everything. You'd be surprised how paring down, weeding out simplifies just everything in your life."

"There's not too much stuff left of my mother's to bring to the new place."

Linn looked at me quickly, then looked away without blinking. I understood: Dorothy did not want any of my mother's belongings ghosting her new home. This life, the life my mother had so clearly centered, was to be cut off cleanly, and with the same regard as a jagged swatch of cloth from one of Dorothy's projects in her shop. I was to keep only a small amount of my mother's belongings. My father had left me to choose.

"I'll take care of my mother's possessions," I told Linn, standing and closing my geometry book.

"Oh, that must be them," Linn exclaimed as we both heard a knock on the door.

"Them?"

"I talked to a family from Queens yesterday and they wanted to see the house this afternoon, but they said they would drive past first. I always tell my clients that, to drive past the house first to see if they like the overall look of the place, the location. Then call me, let me know if they want to continue the exploration. Buying a house is a lot like going out on a date, that's one of my jokes. Take a look first before you even consider leaping. Saves time." She put the last box in order. "Want me to get the door?"

"Sure."

But it was not the family from Queens. Two girls from

school, Katria and Peg, girls who had been in my class since the second grade, stood on the front stoop. Linn came and got me. "Must be friends of yours," she murmured. "I'm going back to the office, see if there were any calls." She straightened a box that was already straight. I heard Peg singing my name. "So," Linn said, "I'll call if that family wants to come. Your dad gave me a key, but I'll call first anyway so you know people will be coming to see the house. That can be our policy, okay?"

"Fine."

"Hey, Maggie, you coming?" Katria hollered through the door. I turned from the room, from the boxes and the quiet, and went out to the front yard to join them.

"We're going over to the mall," Peg informed me, smiling, "and we were up at the bus stop when I remembered you lived right down this street and I said to Katria, 'how come Maggie never goes out anywhere?' and Brilliant over here says, 'cause she doesn't.'" Peg had the face of a cat, triangular and tiny with slanting green eyes. I had never paid any attention to either girl, and I could not imagine why they had come down my street except out of curiosity.

"So now you have to go with us," Katria added. "We are so sick of hanging around with just each other that we wanted to liven things up with someone new."

"Liven things up with me?" I laughed.

"You know, we called you a lot this summer. At least I did," Katria said, playfully shoving Peg. "I actually called you a lot."

"Why?"

"Why?" Peg laughed. "I don't know, we've known you

like forever, Maggie. I even have pictures of you at my eighth and ninth birthday parties. It's just you got so quiet in ninth grade, I mean after…you know, we had to wait to call you up again. Give you some time."

"And your time," Katria said, "is up. And I want to know why you never pick up the phone in your house."

"It seems like an intrusion," I answered, honestly. "Like people can call and whatever you are doing, you are expected to stop. I don't like the idea of telephones."

"Well," Katria said, "you are going to end up in a convent if we don't get you out of the house."

"I could think of worse places," I said quietly and they both laughed, far more robustly than I thought the comment deserved.

Katria put her hand on my shoulder and it stayed there, a cold octopus tentacle resting on my flesh. It had been so long since I had felt the touch of another person, since the girl that one night in Ocean City, that I felt nearly paralyzed by the pressure of her palm. She turned sideways and as she did, she looked exactly like Neptune, with a bank of swirled mythical hair rising from her forehead and her chin jutting into air.

I tried to recall information about her as I stood there with her hand planted on my shoulder, but I could recall only that Katria had written an essay on the possibility of William Shakespeare's bisexuality. Mrs. Keith had rolled her eyes upon seeing the title, but she had quietly given Katria an A. I knew that since Katria had handed me the essay and I had read it, marveling at the quickness of her associations and the ease of her assumptions. My own assumptions were heavily supported by quotes from the book, but Katria had been able to skim along, using only a minimum of examples and ending up with words that were light and playful, not filled with Gothic weight as mine were.

"You're nearly my height," Katria commented. Her gaze lingered on my abdomen, on my hips. I shifted uncomfortably. "But you're a lot curvier."

Peg laughed at this, loudly and with a croaking sound. "Like that's hard."

"Oh." I stood next to Katria, unable to think of any kind of response to her comment.

Turning away, I looked at my mother's garden, at the clumps of purple flowers ripening the air; the sky held starkly white clouds against its cerulean cloth. How could I tell them that people went past me like so many fish in the water? But I had to say something. Part of leaving the drift would be to speak to people, to go places with people. Everyone in the standard spoke and acknowledged one another pleasantly, this much I knew from sleeping over at Julia's house one weekend. They said good night to one another, they greeted one another regularly, they smiled all the time. No one was allowed to sit in silence in the way both my mother and I had, sometimes for hours at a time. I would speak, I would join them, I would put one foot into the first corner of the standard.

"I do think it's weird that you don't answer the phone," Peg commented. "I like can't wait to get to the phone. In fact, I, personally, cannot stand it when someone else gets to the phone before me."

"I just…usually don't feel like talking once I get home

from school." I smiled at their quizzical glances. We had to move away from any examination of my life; I needed to enter the standard without a past. "So what do you do at the mall?"

"Guys." Katria removed her hand from my shoulder and I exhaled. "Shoes. Both."

"Both?"

"Yeah," Katria answered. "We check out guys sometimes, sometimes we go buy a shirt, look at shoes, nothing really. Just come, okay?"

We walked to the bus stop. Ignoring the notions shop, I listened to Peg detail a babysitting episode, two children who took turns urinating on the floor to get back at her enforcement of their bedtime. Small children terrified me; never could I imagine an undertaking as normal as babysitting.

We took the bus to the mall and I walked through aisles with these two girls who contained no weight, no fear, and I thought of them as sails, cutting through the wind while I was ballast closer to the ground. Still, never before had I participated in such a standard activity and never once did I think the standard would come up to my door and knock on it, never once. But it had and now I moved alongside them, a girl with friends, a fish on land, learning to breathe.

"So what do you think, Maggie?" Peg asked me as we stood in the middle of the mall with a fleet of baby carriages wheeling past. She looked at me as though I were a captured native from a primitive land hearing opera for the first time.

"It's great. I mean, every time we go in and out of a store,

I feel more and more like a fish-tank fish, swimming through one of those neon castles with the holes all in them."

"What?" She looked at Katria who stood next to her. Katria shrugged.

A bubble of panic welled in me. My mother would know exactly what I meant by that. Would everyone I met from here on require translation?

"What I mean is how we go in and out of the stores and still come back out to this main strip here, like fish swimming all around their tank, but still ending up in the same rectangle of water."

They both laughed. Katria put her hand on my shoulder, squeezing it slightly. "One day," Katria said, "we'll figure out why you're so quiet in school. I remember when you were a little kid, how funny you were. Before you got so quiet." She ran her hand over my shoulder a few times before dropping her arm to her side. "I mean, we all know what happened, but you got really quiet even before anything happened in your family."

"Things happen in every family, you idiot," Mrs. Fish said, barging into my brain. She wore a maid's uniform, baby pink with blue stitching around the collar. On the pocket, scrolled letters read: *Alice Fish*. In one fin she switched a feather duster back and forth. "It's not like the loss of a parent makes you festive. What does she expect? A goddamned party?"

"Not now," I told her, "you need to go back. I have to do this. I have to learn how to be around people my own age. Go. I have to do this, really."

"Do what? I can't think of a bigger waste of time than

walking around this place. And to think you compared this to fish!" She pushed at her paper cup hat. Dangling from her ears were tiny feather duster earrings, matching the blue feathered one she swished in the air. "Fish are more complex than that, surely you know that, Magda-pie."

"Please go."

"You're just lucky that Mr. Fish and I are meeting with the lawyer right now, that's all I can say."

Katria leaned closer to me. "Do you remember how you signed everyone's sixth grade yearbook with the principal's stamp you found in the hallway? That was hysterical."

"I remember that," Peg nodded. "Even my parents asked me about that. But I remember the dog you made out of toilet paper in art class. That's what I remember."

"God, that was funny," Katria agreed. She looked at me.

I was watching Mr. and Mrs. Fish walk into mist inside my brain.

Katria peered into my face. "Yes or no?"

"What's that?"

"I said, are you coming here again with us?"

I said I would. I liked the mall. The long tunnel in the middle with skylights and plants had a hushed quality that reminded me of the moment right after a dive underwater, the way the day disappears behind you with all its sounds of radios and traffic and you are in a different place, where nothing is regular and everything is possible. I preferred places where anything could happen.

Geometry went on like bad weather. I sat in the class while the teacher spoke first in Farsi then in Hindi. At times, he ventured into Latin. The fish kept returning, particularly during geometry, small snippets of their conversation playing in my head like song lyrics. They took ages to move, pulling bits of their lives out from behind rocks, exposing coral reefs and caves, heaping helter-skelter piles all around them. They spoke more in aphorisms now than in sentences.

"Can't take what you don't have," Mrs. Fish murmured one day while unscrewing the lids of gigantic jars and letting shells and flat white rocks go by in a current of water.

"A man's got a job to do and a job needs a man to do it," Mr. Fish said while pushing boulders together to make a wall. I had no idea why he was building a wall, but I no longer questioned what happened to me. I just watched him build the wall. He left one chink open that he swam through, sometimes enlarging as he came through the wall until my entire brain was filled only with the image of Mr. Fish's face, grinning with his needle teeth in the way of the Cheshire cat. I did not will his image away, I just watched him then I sank underwater, slowly drifting along, brainlessly amorphic as a jellyfish.

"I could help you with this," Katria said, interrupting Mr. Fish's brick cementing. It was the day after we had gone to the mall and she had asked Mr. Frank if she could change her seat to sit next to me. I was gazing at the D I had received on our first unit test when she made the offer. Never had I failed a test or even come close. "You could come over this weekend and I could help you with this.

Would you want to do that? I don't mean like a date or anything," she said, laughing.

"You mean sort of tutor me? Understand, I get like not a word of what is going on in this room. It's utterly foreign." I glanced back at the test. "I take it a cosine is not a Russian pastry?"

"No. But we can go over all the stuff on the test. I'll call you with directions to my house, okay?"

I nodded. Whenever Katria was near me, her presence fell across me in a way that immobilized me, like one of those viperish fish that sting its prey to keep it alive long enough to eat later. And I could not figure out why I felt reduced and stricken in her presence: never had she said or done a thing to cause this. It was probably a result of my hours of aloneness after my mother died, all those days of silence affecting normal interactions. I wanted to believe that, but there was also the issue of the way Katria touched me. She sort of rubbed against me too often, or too long, or both, but there was something in her mock-massages and the lingering of her hands that made me squeamish. Only I could not say this; to say anything would be to acknowledge that she was doing this, and I did not want to bring it up. I had to move forward in meeting people my own age no matter how uneasy the process made me.

That afternoon Katria called and I sat holding the phone like a rock next to my ear, eerie ripples of paralysis ringing through my body. I listened as she spoke about her mother's hysterectomy, the way the halls smelled in the hospital, how her mother's nail beds had stripes of blue lining them and the doctors could not figure out why.

"I kept wondering what they did with the organs they took out of the women," she said. "You know, like where does all that stuff end up?"

I said I didn't know, that I had never thought about it before. Then I told her I had to go.

Linn Pear had left a note on one of the boxes asking me to fill and label them so my father could transport them over to our new house. My father was picking me up at four thirty so I could see the house and my new room; it was already three thirty when I hung up the phone, and I had not begun on my mother's closet or bureau.

I had just opened my mother's nightstand when the door opened and Hannah walked in.

After months of feeling separate from people, after floating away from them and in silence, suddenly I found myself thrust into an eccentric kind of dance hall. Hannah stood before me with a clear, sparkling look in her eyes.

"I just wanted you to know that I'll be taking you out to lunch on Saturday," she announced nonchalantly, as though we were in the habit of going to lunch, two old college buddies ready for a chat. Hannah and I had never so much as eaten at Burger King together. "Let's go to Peggy Noonan's," she suggested, "just you and me. We can take the bus. You'll be in the new house by tomorrow, of course, so I'll pick you up there on Saturday, about one."

"That will be nice," I agreed, wondering if the point of this lunch would be to tell me she was leaving.

"You can't wear that." Hannah pointed to my faded jeans and peasant blouse. "A skirt would be nice. Maybe a dress, but not those kind of clothes."

"I have a red dress," I told her. "The one I wore at Christmas."

"Yes, the red dress. That would be a nice choice." Her expression changed with such obviousness it was like witnessing a squall interrupt a placid sky over the sea. "Why are you in your parents' bedroom? Is everything all right?"

"I have to clear out Mom's stuff. I get the impression that Dorothy thinks the belongings of the dead are unclean." The sentence was out of my mouth before I could retract the words and they stained the clear air between us, first blue, then red, like blood appearing on a patch of perfect skin.

"I'm not sure it's that," Hannah said in her thoughtful voice. "Maybe she just wants to make a clean start, not have reminders around all the time."

"So what am I then?"

"Oh, Magdalena, I'm certain no one looks at you as a reminder. You're his daughter, for heaven's sake. People are not trinkets." Hannah coughed, a dry, delicate sound like lace tearing. "Now don't be difficult. I have a million errands to run before tomorrow. I'll see you, young lady, around one. Don't forget."

"I won't."

Mrs. Fish swam into my head before the door shut.

She wore a bus driver's suit, the gray hat snugged beneath her little tartar cup hat. "To the moon, Alice," she said in a booming voice.

Then she swam off and I watched Baby Fish enter onto a wooden stage. I sensed an audience, though they were silent and unseen. Two clamshells held the curtains parted, one on each side, and a single, clear light beaconed down from the stage top, lighting Baby Fish in a circle. All around him it was dark, opaquely dark, so that the absence of light had an unspoken substance like water. He stood in the circle of light, his head bowed, his fins close to his fish body, his long eyelashes, which I had never before noticed, casting an arced shadow onto his face. He had grown.

"Do you have a voice?" I asked him in the silent language I always used with the fish. "I've never heard you speak."

He did not respond.

"Or is it that you can sing? Maybe you cannot speak, but you can sing. That must be it."

He looked up. A single note on a cello was plucked, then Baby Fish raised his head and opened his mouth. At first, his mouth was open in a choir boy pose, an O-gape with no visible lips or teeth, a posture of clear, potential energy. Then he moved his head back a fraction and from his mouth issued a baritone, a voice deep in its richness and scale. I could not identify the language he spoke; it was more a collection of sounds than anything recognizable as a spoken language, though it made sense to me. I followed the story he told: he was lost inside a cave, only the cave was made of water. Without sides or any apparent doors, he could never find his way out.

"But you found your way in," I said in an unspoken whisper. "All you have to do is find the shape of water. You know the shape of water, you do. Once you remember that shape, you can leave."

The shape of water.

Baby Fish looked up at me and bowed, then swam up and out of my view. Then I looked down to see what I held in my hand: my brother's birth certificate, the month and the year twenty months after my own birth, a single piece of paper my mother had kept in her nightstand all these years, beneath a pile of old gardening magazines, a paper she kept with these old publications that I had boxed up while watching Baby Fish perform. The air rustled with dust; chips of paper flaked onto my hands. I turned the paper over and saw there were two sheets. The other paper was his death certificate, two days after his birth. His name had been Brian Michael.

I thought of the small room off the porch where my father had slept on the daybed, the room so filled with the presence of absence. It made more sense to me now. That would have been Brian Michael's room; perhaps the sun porch would have served as his playroom, or combined to make one large room for him. Somehow I knew there had been another child in my parents' lives, but again, it was knowledge I understood only after having the facts presented to me. My thoughts still lived mostly underwater.

But yes, I did know. That was the reason Hannah had come. My mother lost the baby after nine months of waiting and then his delivery. Hannah would come to a place where such loss existed. And she would arrive with gray luggage and a pronounced sense of duty.

I put the magazines in a pile and placed the only proof of my brother's existence into an empty folder in my desk. I would keep that with my own belongings, separate and away. Then I went on, putting items into the boxes Linn Pear had labeled: *New House, Donate, Toss,* as though everything in life and after life had a place, as though it could all be sorted and stacked or at least coerced into forms that made sense.

When my father arrived, I asked him why Dorothy did not want my mother's effects. He looked at me, the blue of his eyes milky in the sun. He reminded me of an Old Testament prophet when he looked at me with those blue-milk eyes, as though he had been given the gift of inner sight as restitution for not being able to see the world. We were taking boxes over to the new house and the car smelled of cardboard and dust. I had not yet seen the new house.

"She never said a word," he replied. "Not a word about your mother's things. Never came up between us." Then he smiled. "Well, you know Dorothy. She would never wait this long to…organize a person's belongings." He said this with admiration, as though my mother's lack of practicality was evident even after her death.

"So you don't want her things there."

"Right. I don't."

"I'm not used to you being quite so bald." All this honesty, I thought, in a family where even births were hidden in pockets of silence.

"Am I bald?" He laughed and looked in the mirror. "You've got no sense of play anymore," he said and patted my knee. "Listen. It's not so complicated. Your mother and I lived in that house for almost twenty years and we had a good life, at least in the beginning. The thing you don't quite get these days, Magda, is that the rest of us have to go on living even after our loved ones die. Your mother would not have wanted you to moon about so much, for so long, and I think you know that. When it comes time to make a clean break of it, you have to do exactly that: make a clean break."

"I think I read that in a fortune cookie once."

"See, now you're getting your sense of humor back. As soon as we turn onto your new block, your sense of humor is restored."

I stayed in the car while he unloaded cartons, staring at the house. It was plain, gray, and shaped like a toaster, the kind of house a child might fashion out of discarded boxes.

"What do you think?" My father poked his head through the passenger window.

"It reminds me of Dorothy," I answered truthfully.

"She said it was the most house for the money." My father opened the door. "I thought you might want to spend some time getting your room in order. Your bureau and desk will be here later on when the movers come, but you can decide where you want them placed. Tomorrow will be our first official day here, Magda."

We went inside. Small patches of light filtered in through the blinds Dorothy had already installed. The light seemed to swim and the result was a ferny feel: the house reminded me of being on the edge of a swamp. My room was at the end of the hall, the top of a T-shape, and thankfully, had a lock on the door.

"It's bigger than the one you had back at the old house," my father announced in his tour guide voice.

"Yup. The room is definitely bigger." A bed served as the only furnishing in the room. I watched him go down the hall, the square of his back growing smaller and smaller until he disappeared inside the room he would share with Dorothy. I sat down on the pink carpet in my new room, looking at the walls, at the tiny dings and cracks near the baseboard, feeling the ghosted presence of all the girls who had lived in this room before me and had gone on to other places. The room had the impersonal, disconnected feel of a waiting room on Jupiter.

After school the next afternoon, I took the school bus to the new house for the first time and opened the door to my room. The desk and bureau had been placed neatly in the corners. The effect of their symmetrical placement gave the room a staged look. New, gauzy drapes had also been added, pinned back in twin scallops with a frothy valance resembling the headdress of Little Bo Peep. A mirror edged in shells shone from a vanity I had never before seen.

"She's here," I heard Dorothy sing from my doorway. Andrew stood next to her.

"Where's Dad?"

"Oh, sweetie, he won't be staying here until after the wedding." Dorothy's face took on a florid sheen. "Just don't even mention such a thing in front of your Aunt Hannah."

"So where is he?"

"He's staying at Hannah's. For the time being." She moved into the room.

"What I want to know is if you like your new vanity. And the curtain. I always wanted to do curtains up like this in a little girl's room…I mean not that you are a little girl or that I think of you as a little girl, it's just that having had only a boy, I always wanted to do some pink tulle as a window treatment. And I had just the thing in the shop."

"You sewed the curtains."

Dorothy nodded.

"Thank you. I do like them."

"I'm glad. Then your Dad and I were at the Englishtown flea market and we saw that vanity together, and we just said, there it is, just the thing for Magda in her new home." She walked over to the vanity and flipped up the top, revealing a mirror and a wizard's apron of tiny circular holders and built-in containers.

"That's very nice."

"I'm glad you like it. I knew you would. So did your father."

Dorothy slid out some hidden drawers and spun a lazy Susan with locking triangular-shaped separators. Andrew and I watched the demonstration in silence. "I just love the way this is done. Such planning. All your cosmetic needs in one spot, and out of the way. Some girls' rooms are such a mess the way they keep them with hairbrushes and nail polish all over the bureau tops, even their deodorant out as though they want to display their personal hygiene items."

"Right," I said, understanding the warning.

"Well," she said, closing the vanity's top, "Andrew and I have made a batch of buttermilk pancakes if you'd like some. I know it's the middle of the afternoon, but we always make a big batch of pancakes when we celebrate anything, and a new home certainly qualifies for that."

I smiled. "Yes, it does."

"And your father dropped off a few boxes for you to sort through. If you get a chance today to organize the boxes, that would be great. I mean, only if you have the time." She smiled at me, and her mouth had changed, the teeth not larger, but more noticeable, as though she had sharpened each cuspid in preparation for inhabiting her own swamp.

Hannah came as promised on Saturday and we took a bus together to Peggy Noonan's, a restaurant that seemed to serve only items made from ground beef. Plant life had no place in this restaurant anyway. Inside, smoke replaced air and the tables were dark oak and enormous, tables fit for raucous Viking banquets. Even the salt and pepper shakers were the size of fists. Had a lightning bolt been hurled across my head inside Peggy Noonan's I would not have been shocked.

"You've always liked this place," I said to Hannah. I knew she had met my father here for lunch several times while I was at school. "And it's strange, I never would think to bring you here."

"No?" Hannah took off her straw hat. "What kind of place would you bring me to, Magdalena?"

"A less beery one, maybe," I said, nodding toward the barge of men who sat in the bar area, their faces shiny red as berries, each one of them holding steins.

"I don't think of Peggy Noonan's as beery." She placed her hat on top of her purse. "I think of Peggy Noonan's as a practical place, one where you get a good meal for a reasonable price."

"You're right." We studied the menu for a few minutes before ordering what Hannah told me she always ordered at Peggy Noonan's: the hamburger plate with a root beer float.

"You know, Magdalena, that there are a number of things I need to tell you today, and I only pray that I do everything justice. In the absence of your mother, I am trying to do the best I can." She stopped for a few seconds, her eyes locked into mine, then she went on. "If there was one sentence I could leave you with, that would be the one."

"Which one?"

"That people are doing the best they can."

I nodded.

"That we are all doing the best we can, especially your father." She took my hand, only one, and holding it aloft, she began rubbing her thumb in circles around my palm. "You understand he needs to marry Dorothy."

"I don't know that I understand that," I said quickly, then regretted my words. "What I mean is, no one really *needs* to be married."

"Your father does. He needs looking after."

"Couldn't he hire people to clean the house? He and I could surely figure out how to make a few meals."

"There's more than that to a marriage," Hannah said softly. "There's so much more, but you're too young to understand what I mean by that. You have to try and see that Dorothy…"

"She's just so different from his first wife. I can't think of anyone less like Mom than Dorothy."

"Yes, I do know. She is just so different from your mother. One day you will realize that your father needs a woman who is simple and easy, after living with a woman who was so much more complicated and difficult. Maybe difficult isn't the right word. Your mother had a restlessness about her, an almost ticking quality of impatience. Do you remember that?"

"I don't." I thought of the long hours my mother and I had spent in the garden, three seasons of the year, separating bulbs, transplanting seedlings, weeding patches until the earth shone bare and dark as outer space; I thought of the hours we spent drawing while we listened to music. These were not impatient pursuits.

"Don't you remember the way she used to pace the yard, peer out the window during rainstorms, as though she were always waiting for someone, something to occur?"

"I really don't. She liked to watch clouds during rainstorms, she worked in the yard, and she would check on her gardens a lot, but I don't remember any restlessness."

"You may not have noticed. Kids don't always notice. I remember right after I met her, your mother and father had gone on a date to Kendallsburg Village, that colonial simulation place in Massachusetts. They drove all the way up from Staten Island for one date because your mother had heard there was a Christmas tree up there lit entirely by candles. She thought nothing of doing things like that when she was young." Hannah shook her head back and forth. "I was home from college for the Christmas break and your mother walked in wearing a holly print dress and a red bow in her hair, and I thought she was a knockout. I told my mother, your grandmother, that she would cause Michael heartbreak. No woman who looked like that would be happy with a regular life. And Michael, you know, he wanted a regular life." Hannah picked up her fork and rubbed it against the napkin as she spoke.

"But she had a regular life. I mean, I think she was happy. She seemed happy with me."

I waited. A cheer rose from the bar area.

"They watch a lot of sports here," Hannah explained.

"I figured that. You know, Aunt Hannah, when you talk about a regular life, going back to my parents, I do think my mother was happy when she was with me."

Hannah's eyes grew wide with concern. "I didn't mean

to say she wasn't happy with you. You made your mother very happy; you were so much like her. We all knew that. You were all the things she wanted to be." Hannah put the fork neatly on the napkin as if to signify that her focus was completely on this conversation.

"Me?" At that moment, Mrs. Fish popped into my head carrying a tray of small French fries, each one with the miniature face of one of the men at the bar on its top.

"Go, please!" I said silently to her image. "I thought you had moved away."

"Oh, and your thoughts, Magda-pie, are always so true." She did not leave. Instead, she lowered the tray so I could see each man's features more closely.

"Oh, Magdalena, yes. How could you think any differently? Your mother had that shy way about her, all her gentleness. She could barely deal with the outside world. And you went to school and you had friends, and everyone said you were funny and gregarious. You were like your mother in looks, and in your artistic streak, but you were what she wanted to be: at ease with the world."

"At ease with the world," I repeated just as Mr. Fish began eating the French fries with the men's faces. "Mom thought that?"

Hannah took my hand. "Yes, everyone thought that. My point about the regular life is that your mother would have been better suited as a museum curator or a fine artist commissioning portraits, a life of that nature. After a point, we all believed she found the life of a housewife, of domestic chores...well, unsuitable."

"Not the life of a mother."

"No, not at all. I think if she could have left to be an artist, she would have taken you with her."

She did leave, I wanted to say. And she did not take me with her or even tell me she was going.

"I'm not sure I'm following you on the unhappiness thread."

"You, she loved. The housework, the isolation of the house's location, the day-to-day dishes and laundry and dust, she could have done without."

"Apparently. Except Dorothy explained it differently: she told me my parents were unhappy. Period." I shifted in my seat as a cloud of smoke tendriled my face.

"Dorothy only means to show you that things will get better now." Hannah nodded as she said this, as if approving Dorothy's intentions. "That's all she meant."

"I know. I just wish I could remember them unhappy. I know when Mom was in the hospital, they couldn't have been happy, but…"

"They were not always unhappy, and that's the part you remember and you should always keep that. They were very happy in the beginning when you were first born."

"So I made them unhappy? My growth?"

"No, not that, of course not, Magdalena. Just…you are very young, and it is difficult to explain situations to someone with so little experience, but suffice it to say that many people drift apart after years of marriage. They grow in different ways and not always together." She tried to make her face appear soft. "You always made your mother very happy, that much I know. Never doubt that. You were the apple of her eye and I see so much of her in you. Then you have to ask yourself, where does that leave Michael?"

I waited. A few shouts came from the bar area and then, strangely, a long pull on a whistle.

"Remember, you are going off to college in a couple of years, and after that, he would be alone."

"I guess." I wanted to stop looking at Hannah now, to stop studying the crookedness of her teeth and the darkness of the pores around her nose.

"And you forget how in the next two years, you're going to be off, out with your friends, driving, going to parties and movies. That's what I did when I was your age."

I knew what was coming. "Want one?" Mr. Fish held a French fry face out to me.

"I'm ignoring you," I hissed telepathically.

"No, you're not," Mrs. Fish said, "that's why we're here. Wouldn't it be nice if you could be more like your family and just say what you want to be true and—whoosh—it's true. But you're not like that, old Magda-bones, you're just not."

"Magdalena, I made a good many decisions when I was younger that I regret now." For a moment, I was not sure whether it was Hannah or Mrs. Fish speaking, but Hannah met my eyes in such a way that I knew it had been her. "All I can do, all anyone can do, is their best at the time. It's so easy, so very easy to look upon others and judge them for what they've done wrong, or for decisions they've made that have not been the best ones."

"I know you have a son, Hannah," I said quietly, "if that's what you're referring to. Andrew told me when we were in Ocean City."

"Actually, I was hoping you knew. I stopped putting the pictures up in the closet and I just left them out, as any mother might."

Mrs. Fish took out an easel. Imagining a boulder in my mind, I tried pushing her from my mind's eye, rolling the boulder down over her, but the boulder only bounced down then back up. I understood that Mrs. Fish was protected by an invisible layer of strong water. I decided to ignore her, and just as I thought this, she turned her face to me, her needle teeth visible over the rim of her lips, her eyes ignited with rage. Her face grew enormous. Then she held up her painting. In bright red letters, she had painted one word: *MOTHER.*

"Magdalena," Hannah said loudly, "are you listening?"

"Yes, yes I am. Sorry."

"So I have this boy out in Ohio, just a few years younger than you, really, a boy I don't even know. He thinks I'm ill. Too ill to take care of him. Jake's family told him his real mother is ill, but she might get better one day.

"At the time, twelve years ago, I thought his family was making a mistake by telling Gabriel I was still alive, that they should just raise him as their own, but they wouldn't. They always sent pictures and had him make me drawings. Some days, especially the darker days in winter, you know those days when the trees redden at four o'clock?" Hannah's face softened.

"Yes, I do."

"And you know it's going to be dark very early and for a very long time, that's what you know. The mail would come sometimes on those days and I couldn't even go to the mailbox for fear I would find something from Gabriel, a class picture or a drawing or a letter from his grand-mother describing his last cold or a slip he'd had on the playground. Sometimes even when the envelope came, I would put it away to read at another time. At least that's what I did in the beginning and I would think, his grand-mother is right, I am too ill to take care of him. Only I had no name for the sickness that plagued me."

"Except now you're better."

Hannah looked up at me, her face resuming its regular expression. "Yes, now I am. But the main point here, Mag-dalena, the most important aspect of all this that I want to explain to you is how it was, back then. Before you judge me, before I leave and the one feature of my life you recall is my abandonment of my son, I need to tell you how it was. I don't want the most shameful event of my life to be the defining act of our relationship." Smoke curled into a wreath around Hannah's head as though she were a spirit from the fairy world. Music began playing, a bluesy song whose bass came up through the floorboards and entered my feet. Han-nah did not raise her voice so I leaned forward.

"I was only twenty-four at the time he was born and while I realize that may sound ancient to you at this point, actually I was closer to twenty-five, and we're going back a few years now."

Mrs. Fish put the sign to one side of her easel and held up a portrait of Hannah, much younger, wearing strands of beads and a half pound of eyeliner on each eyelid.

"Gabriel is already…it's hard for me to even grasp, but he's in the eighth grade this year. Imagine. I've managed to send him gifts every year for his birthday, a few pictures of me, but I haven't seen him or touched him since he was eight months old." Hannah sighed and began folding her napkin into accordion pleats.

"My parents told me you went out to Ohio and you were a nun. They never actually said that, maybe I just sort of assumed you had been in a convent."

Still folding her napkin, Hannah said, "I went out to Ohio to get a degree in religious history at a women's college. No one thinks of you meeting anyone at a women's college, of meeting a husband at least, but then no one realizes the number of dances and social events there are at a women's college, when they bring men over from the university on the other side of the river. But that's not why I went."

"I didn't think so." Mrs. Fish shook her head and her entire rear area as she held one fin up. "No, no, no," she chanted.

"I wanted to teach religion at the high school level. I always saw myself teaching the parables to teenage girls, and about a month before graduation, I met Jake at a dance and we married. I called home and told everyone I was going to begin Master's work at the university. I'm not sure why I said that, I guess I thought they would say I was too young or oppose me in some way, so ten months after that, I had Gabriel and we were living in this apartment...you can't begin to...you see, there was this laundromat in the back of us and I used to hang out his little shirts and sleepers on a line and I could look down into the parking lot of this laundromat. In the kitchen, where I sat most of the time with Gabriel, there was this fan, this black fan with dust all over the blades and I would put the laundry out and sit by the window giving Gabriel his rice cereal and I would watch the fan. Every day. That was the shock of having a baby: how the work was there, the same work, every day, each day, without any kind of change. The same sleepers, the same shirts, the same cereal. Over and over."

Hannah's eyes took on a distant look I had never seen before, as though she were watching a film play over my shoulder. The bluesy music stopped, suddenly as it had started.

"Every day, that's the way it is with babies, with children. Every day I would give him his bottle in the morning and the laundry would flap on the line outside the window and yesterday's bottles would be drying on the sink rack, the fan would move, all that dust on its blades, thick with dust, and clouds would roll in over the valley, and I would think how I had all this day to fill up now that I was home with this baby. So much day. And I had so little energy. I should have found the time, the energy, to at least clean the dust off the fan blades, but I was in this kind of surrender mode. If there was dust, there would continue to be dust; if the floor needed mopping, I would only do it when I saw Jake look down at the dirt on his socks. I spent a lot of time gazing."

"Gazing?" I thought of my afternoons in the spring, how I gazed out at the world without moving.

"Yes, gazing. And there was always this silence. Jake worked on campus, at the library, and he left early so he could be done in time to take afternoon classes. He was going to be a librarian, and he eventually became one. I would think how there he is, in silence, but with other people around him and with his day defined so sharply, what time to eat, what time to take a break, to read, to come home, and I just had to figure out how to organize my day…"

Mrs. Fish drifted past, her feather duster running across a wall of clocks.

"Are you following all this, Magdalena?"

"Yes, but I can't imagine you having a problem with the house. You always organized our house, our meals, took care of so much of the domestic stuff. I thought it was my mother who had trouble with the house, with meals and organizing closets and that sort of task."

"That was different; I had no other life utterly dependent on me. And I've been seeing a therapist. I thought it would be a good idea for me to consult a psychiatrist before going out to see Gabriel, so I don't do him any further harm."

"Oh." I thought of Dorothy and Andrew seeing Nancy.

"Your father went too, for a time."

"Dad went to a therapist?"

"Yes, mostly…"

"To figure me out, right?"

Hannah looked startled, then she smiled. "I think to some degree. You can't really ask people what they talk about in therapy. It reminds me a lot of prayer, of the way confessionals work. Only instead of saying any number of prayers, you go into more detail, talk about maybe why you made certain decisions or what you can do to avoid certain situations in the future."

Hannah paused for a few seconds and I tried to see if she was praying, but her eyes were turned from me, her gaze gone vacant. "I talked a lot in therapy about my time with Gabriel, about those months I stayed out there in that small apartment, how this strange sense just didn't go away, this sense I had of..."

"Drifting," I offered. Mr. and Mrs. Fish floated past, stretched out on clouds. "Go," I told them sternly. "Leave now."

"Yes, something along those lines. Nothing seemed definite. After a time, I began to hear this low hum. At first I thought the hum was the fan, maybe one of the dryers from the laundry, a noise from somewhere I could trace. Sometimes Jake came home for lunch if his afternoon class started late, and I would ask him about it and he kept telling me he didn't hear any hum. But I heard it the whole time he was there, I heard it after he left and when he came home again at night. I heard that hum.

"I was okay for a time after that. I just stopped asking Jake if he heard the hum. But it got louder and louder until it developed a visceral presence."

"Visceral?"

The waitress silently placed our food in front of us, then left. Mrs. Fish imitated the waitress by swimming back and forth inside my head, then silently delivering the tray of French fry men to the floor.

"Yes, visceral. The hum began to touch my arms, my face, it began to move over me like wind, in pulses of wind, like a heartbeat. Every day I did the wash, I rocked the baby, I put soup on, I washed the bottles, and then I sat staring at the fan. It went round and round and it just didn't go anywhere, ever, exactly like me."

"But," I began quietly, "didn't you have to go out to buy food? Didn't you ever put Gabriel in the stroller and take him out for a walk? Didn't you ever go to the doctor or to the park?"

"I did, only all the stores were right on the street below the apartment and the doctor was on the next block since we lived right in the town. I never saw a park; I never spoke to anyone, I never exchanged a word with any of the other women with babies. They all seemed to know one another, to have grown up in the town with aunts and cousins and generations of memory in that one place and they would just nod at me and move on through their busy day."

"But your day wasn't busy." I thought of my own mother, sitting on a distant bench in the playground during one of our few excursions to the park. She would read or gaze off into the sky, clearly not part of the great throng of mothers who laughed together and called to one another's children with relaxed affection. My mother sat on the bench, a penguin stranded in the Caribbean.

"I should say," Hannah continued, "in the interest of honesty, that once in a great while one of the shopkeepers would talk to me about a storm coming or about a news item, or Jake's mother would come by and bring us some chicken or a pie, but mostly, I stayed in that apartment with the baby."

"And you watched the fan."

"And I watched the fan." Hannah squeezed concentric circles of ketchup onto her burger. "Then finally, it occurred to me that I had begun to inhabit the hum."

"Inhabit the hum?"

"Yes. That was my word for the place I was in at the time. A kind of moving, pulsing vacancy that had no path, no end." She bit into her pickle as though this last sentence was not in the least surprising.

"But you had a husband; you had a baby," I pointed out.

"I saw none of that. I saw only the fan and the hum. And it got worse: the baby had begun to panic me. He stopped sleeping all the time and he would put things into his mouth, anything he found, and the more I was with him the more worried I got that I would look away and he would die, that he would choke and die.

"Then there was one morning when the hum became deafening and a hissing sound began beneath the hum. I looked at Gabriel, all propped up on a pillow, and I picked him up. I gave him a bath, I nursed him for the last time, I put him in new clothes and I took his picture. Then I drove the two hours to Jake's mother's house and I asked her to watch him while Jake and I worked a few matters out. And I came back here. You were already walking, a toddler, and your dad was having a tough time with your mom, managing it all. And I knew Gabriel's grandmother wanted him, that she was young enough to raise him."

"So you left your own baby to come and take care of your brother's baby?"

"I wasn't alone here and I wasn't cut off from everything

I'd ever known. I understand that it's difficult for you to absorb all of this, that you have a cousin, that your aunt who you thought was single all these years turns out not only to be married but to have a son close to your age. I know all of that must be tough to take in at once. Try to think how it will be for my son, that I am returning after all these years."

I picked up my hamburger as the waitress cruised past. Mrs. Fish swam out of my head, allowing her lettered sign to clatter to the ground, the picture of the heavily made-up Hannah dissolving as she swam off.

"Hannah, I don't judge you," I said. "And I'm not sure anyone is in a position to judge you. You did what you had to do."

It was the same line she had told me when I asked her if my mother's death had been a suicide or an accident. She had looked up from her dusting and said, "Either way, what's done is done. People do what they have to do."

"So what happened to Jake, your husband?"

"Oh, he remarried, years ago, more than seven years ago. He has two little girls, and he keeps in touch with Gabriel. Gabriel thinks of them as his sisters and they have Christmas together, holidays, all at his grandmother's house. Jake's off in the summer, so he takes him for two months."

"So you're divorced?"

"I am." Hannah bit hard into her hamburger. I watched her chew for a while, trying to picture Hannah as a young mother. Only the image of my own mother appeared in my mind.

"Now," Hannah began, "my only hope is that Gabriel

will accept me into his life. I couldn't bear it if he resented me after all these years."

"He'll be happy to see you," I said in a flat voice made of dust. All around us, people laughed and spoke happily to one another. Hannah had taken me here so she could leave, unfettered.

That seemed to be the story of the women in my family: they jumped ship early, at the first sighting of white-caps and wind, never sticking around to weather the rough seas.

Hannah walked me to the top of my new street, where we embraced. I watched her walk to the bus stop. The minute I turned down the unfamiliar street, the day dissolved. I liked this feeling, as if I had dived underwater. The heavy leafiness of the trees blocked out the light in the same way the water blocked out the light. On this hot September afternoon I shivered, but I walked slowly, inspecting each house. Nothing was awry. Anywhere. Shutters matched doors, cushion mums bloomed obediently at doorways. (I knew these houses had to be inhabited; cars were parked in driveways, laundry fluttered on backyard lines, morning newspapers were taken in by the time I got home from school, but I never saw our neighbors.) The silence of the standard reminded me of Julia's street.

"You have to watch silent places like that," my mother had laughed one day when I told her how nothing surprised me at Julia's house. We had just jumped back as a throng of mean-eyed seagulls descended on a fish. "There's probably someone up there slowly turning into an assassin."

"Not at Julia's. People up there turn into brides and secretaries, things like that."

"Like in that movie." We laughed together. We had stayed up late the night before watching a black and white movie where the mother wore an apron in every scene. Most of the time she had oven mitts on as well, but the apron did not come off.

"It's actually grown onto her," my mother whispered. "A hand or an extra thumb. She can't breathe without it maybe, a necessary appendage, like something a fish might need to breathe on land. Yes, yes, I think that's what it is, Lena, a gill disguised as an apron. That woman is really a fish."

I smiled, remembering my mother. The next house looked like all the others surrounding it. A series of curtains hung with the look of envelopes in a box. It took a few seconds for me to realize this was our new house, so similar were the homes in this development.

The wedding grew closer. I could tell because Dorothy spoke less at dinner, and her meals grew simpler each night until she served us tuna fish sandwiches.

On Friday afternoon, the day before the wedding, I came home to see both Dorothy's car and my father's car parked in the driveway.

"I have a surprise for you," Dorothy sang as I walked through the door. Andrew slouched in a chair, reading a magazine with a giant marijuana leaf on its back cover.

My father winked at me from behind Dorothy, a knowing wizard.

Andrew continued reading his magazine, his eyes glassy and swollen. How could my father and Dorothy not see what he was doing?

"Now I hope you don't mind surprises," Dorothy said in a feathery voice. "I have taken it upon myself to whip up a little something for our wedding." She walked over to a circular box, a gray and white box that reminded me of an enormous clamshell. I waited for Mrs. Fish to appear on the box, dressed as she would be in a little shimmer of a mermaid outfit, but she did not show up. I stared at the box.

Dorothy just about twinkled. "We all know that your favorite color is purple." She pulled out a diaphanous material that was sheerly iridescent in the exact manner of fish scales. I gasped; the fabric looked alive. Any minute it would wriggle out of Dorothy's hand. "And since my passion is sewing, this is my small gift to you."

The style of the dress was one that Heidi might have worn while skipping through the Alps: the bodice had a back-and-forth stringing pattern that tied in a loopy bow, the sides had a bow at each hip and the skirt flared into a gauzy dirndl.

"See this?" she said, pointing to the buttons in the back. "I thought these looked a bit like those wisterias you liked so much at your house."

"Yes," I said, grateful for a focus, "they do."

"And I heard that little gasp when you first saw it, so I know you liked it. Now, if you don't mind, could you try this on?" She grinned and I realized there was no escaping this room, these circumstances. I would be expected to wear the Heidi dress. "Let's go to my room." Dorothy followed behind me and the dress traveled with sound, a kind of bristling fullness that allowed me to know what feminized static sounded like. "Here we go," she said, placing the dress across the bed. "If you just slip off those jeans, down to your panties and bra, I should be able to pin this for a final stitching." I did as she said, quickly, my skin damp with anxiety.

"My, the first item on my list is to buy you a new bra." Following Dorothy's gaze, I saw the swell of my breasts spilling from the top and the sides of my bra. "That might have fit you last year, but breasts do have a way of changing." She pulled a tape measure out of her pocket. "Don't be embarrassed. I do this all the time in the shop, especially around prom time. Girls just don't always realize they need new underpinnings. But you know how important those undergarments are to a dress. I always tell them, that's why they are called *foundations.*" She laughed while I stood in her room, the shadowy light from outside dropping down from the high bedroom windows without warmth or motion, the kind of light I had only seen before emanating from the moon.

But Dorothy's bedroom had nothing to do with the spare beauty of the moon. Every inch of space that could be covered had been padded with layers of fabric, so the room had a pronounced sense of quilting. It was not only the dress that threatened to swallow me, it was the general fabric envelopment of Dorothy's bedroom. Even framed photographs of Dorothy and the baby Andrew had fabric-swaddled frames. (Photographs of her husband were conspicuously missing.)

"Magda, if you turn, there's a mirror. You can watch your transformation."

When I turned, I saw my reflection in the long windshield of mirror Dorothy had over her bureau. "Step in," she instructed, and I did, watching the puffed sleeves billow at my shoulders, making my face appear dour and swollen as an adder fish's. "There, you see. Perfect."

Dorothy dove all around me, pinning here and there, marking the fabric in chalk, criss-crossing ties of fabric then letting them drop. "If you are thinking of wearing this dress to the prom, that would be fine with me, just so long as you wear it first to our wedding. That's the only condition of wearing this dress. If you don't mind."

"All right."

"Any ideas who might ask you to the prom this year? Maybe someone from the in-crowd?"

The in-crowd?

"No, no one has asked me so far," I replied. Though, I thought, smiling to myself, I could hold a private prom night with the fish.

"If you knew how many perfectly good dresses I've worked on only to have girls put them in the back of their closets...oh, it just makes me cringe. All that work." She unbuttoned the back and I slipped my arms out, the watery flesh of my breasts bellying around the lacy fabric of my bra. "And don't worry about the bra. I'll pick one up the next time I'm in Sears. I'm very good with size."

I nodded, a fish on land, a motherless girl. "Thanks," I said, hoping this covered the dress and the future bra.

"Oh, you're quite welcome. Your dad was kind enough to clue me in that you had not a thing to wear to the wedding. That's one of the things I love so much about Michael: he is so perceptive."

"Perceptive." I repeated the word and blinked.

"Yes, the way he remembers every little detail, the way he notices the absolute tiniest of details."

"I don't find that," I said with exaggerated slowness. "I find he misses an awful lot."

"Well, that's because you're his child. Andrew says the same thing about me. And it just isn't so. You know that. No one could be more devoted to their child than me. Heaven knows."

I smiled. I had to; Dorothy stood before me as expectantly as a game show contestant. That was one of the tricks of the standard; I understood it now. You just had to find someone who believed what you wanted them to believe. You could walk past your stoned son, ignore the stunned horror of your groom's daughter as she stands in an ocean of organza, then congratulate yourself on a day's work well done.

"Now why don't we go see what there is to eat?" Dorothy folded the fish-scale/Heidi dress back into its clamshell and took my arm. "I made a lobster salad," she said in a low, conspiratorial voice, "fattening as all get-out, but the way I figure it, how many times do you have a pre-wedding brunch?"

"Is anyone else coming?"

"No, just our family."

We sat in the glassed-in porch. The previous owners had placed a bubble over the patio so they could use it in all kinds of weather. It was like eating inside a glass bubble that had been darkened by trees.

We looked out over shrubs with edges as sharp as bricks. The trees held precise aprons of white azaleas. I remembered Julia's house, the way her mother had placed the tulips and the flowers in a ring at each tree's base, the way the house was large and organized down to the arrangement of the towel colors in the linen closet. I remembered walking into her pink and white room with the homemade curtains and the butterfly lampshade her mother had stenciled and thinking, this world is too different from where I come from; it will never be mine.

Only now I sat in this world, eating lobster salad, drinking soda, listening to Dorothy describe a beach in Bermuda where they were going for their honeymoon. I had thought I would trust this place more, but if the table suddenly dissolved or the shrubs shot flames from their neat tops, I would not have been particularly surprised. The oddness of these surroundings, the strangeness of the inland feel, with no gulls or salted scent in the water, reminded me of the mall I had gone to with Katria and Peg, a place closed and inured from air, from wind, from wildness. I had never thought the drift, with all its irregularity, or my mother, who planted a garden she believed might attract fairies (wood sprites, she had called them when my father laughed at the bank of delicate flowers on the edge of our lawn), or the erratic ebb of our days there, with my parents leading lives away from each other, never had I thought all of that would provide comfort of any sort. But I longed for it as I sat in the bubble. I did not feel that I was anywhere inside the new house; I wanted the small, dark house I had always known. Even though I sat inside this new house with its matching carpets and drapes, I had the definite sense that I was in mid-air, diving from the house of water where I had been born, from the place where anything could drift in, where no boundaries or edges could be found, where no day was like the next or the one before it. I was diving from that place to this new place of ringed flowers and mossy quietness.

I missed motion, the motion of waves and clouds, the savage gyre of the gulls when they spotted a piece of bread in the water, the motion of boats and currents and the openness of the drift. The standard was safe, but it was closed. But this was my new world now. I would inhabit days bordered and predictable as calendar squares, meals would come on time, beds would be made and parents would remain. I was slipping into the standard, silently and without fanfare, with no one around me pointing out that I did not belong, that I could never belong, that there were many things here that I did not understand; I did not possess the necessary tools to inhabit this place. My mother had left me perfectly useless. I had to translate this environment into a habitable place despite the crushing sense that everything around me had stopped.

"Oh, there's the phone," Dorothy said.

My father nudged me with two fingers. "Where did you just go?"

"What do you mean?"

"You left the table."

"No, Dad, I was sitting right here." Andrew smirked at me from across the table.

"I know you were sitting right there, I have eyes in my head, but you left; you were off somewhere. Magda, do you have a boyfriend?"

"Whoooa," Andrew hooted, "a boyfriend."

"Dad, stop."

"The phone," Dorothy announced, coming back to the table, "is for Magda."

"What's his name, Ma?"

"It's a girl. Kat-something."

Katria wanted to meet me at her house. I said I would go. I knew she lived near the ferry.

At least going there, near water, I might be able to breathe again, to feel my lungs open again.

chapter

seven

"So you don't like your new stepmother-to-be?" Katria asked me. "As if I know anyone who likes their step-parent."

"It's not really so much that I don't like her or that I do like her. It's just that when I'm with her, it's like standing next to an explosion, when all the oxygen is momentarily sucked into the fire." We were sitting on the highest step of a narrow spine of stone stairway leading up to her house. New York Harbor spread in front of us and the motion of the ferries going back and forth, back and forth, with the gulls and the waves soothed me.

"So what are you saying? That you like her or you don't?"

Katria waited, looking at me with an impatient expression. I could see why Katria was successful at math: she saw solutions to problems, answers. And they were immediate. I saw problems more like collages, entities that shifted and showed new dimensions every time I looked closely at them.

"She means well, Dorothy. At least I think she does. She just doesn't get people. Like her son is smoking pot all the time, drinking stuff from this little bar she has in the living room, and she doesn't notice."

"Does your father notice stuff?"

"Not really. He wants to, but I was a lot closer to my mother."

"My mom always said if the Salem witch trials came back, your mom would be the first one tried." Katria stretched as she said this, arching her back like a cat. "She used to see your mom sometimes at the school plays or at the market, and I remember she would always say that about the witch trials."

"Excuse me?"

"She didn't mean anything, you know…*bad* about your mom. Just that she was different, sort of…"

"Artistic."

"Yeah, that would be the word. The way she had all those nice plants in front of the house and she wore all those nice clothes, but she never really socialized with anyone, did she?"

I shook my head. I did not want a summation of my mother from Katria. When I said nothing more, Katria went inside to get some sandwiches.

"You know, Maggie, I'm glad you came over today. I

really am." Katria sat down next to me, a tray of chips and sandwiches to her right. "It's not like we ever get that much chance to talk in school. And I like the way you talk, the way you say things. There are," she said, moving closer to me, "so many things I like about you."

"Thanks." As she moved closer to me, I saw that her Neptune hair had been slicked back some and I noticed tiny diamond studs in her ears. Light chipped through her hair. "So how come you never do anything? Like go to the stuff at school, or go out to the movies? Is it 'cause you're like your mom?"

"I don't know. It's not how I was raised, I guess. My mom didn't go out so much." As I said this, I thought of Julia and her mother, how they would go shopping and to the movies, always talking about restaurants they went to for lunch. A pang came over me with such force that I had to sit up and change position.

"What is going on?" Katria asked.

"Nothing, just a little grief for the living." I had not realized how much I still missed Julia and her mother.

She laughed. "Why don't you have a sandwich?" She handed me dark bread rilled in lettuce. I looked at her, at her gray eyes and straight nose, at the way her mouth turned up at the corners as if the world amused her, at the way she sat with her legs akimbo as a child's.

I looked back out at the ferries running between the Manhattan and Staten Island terminals, and I understood that I had little feeling for Katria; she was a person who existed in the border land where I abided for now. No gravity held me to Katria, as it had with Julia. I did not know why. Katria was a perfectly nice person. She had never done a disservice to me. I wondered if it was because Julia had known my mother. Would the rest of my life be measured by association with my mother?

"I was thinking," Katria began, "that today I could help you with math."

I remembered her offer of math help a month before, and how I had never responded to it. Something about her bringing this up again made me distrust her.

"What made you think of that?"

"Just the way you were looking at the boats crossing the water. It reminded me of how that strange mind of yours works." She smiled at me and as she did, her face glowed, oddly lambent in the middle of the amber afternoon. I was in the onerous position of knowing someone who liked me far more than I liked her.

"Not strange, just not inclined to geometry. Something about the whole system makes my brain ache."

"Achy brain." She gathered up the paper plates we had been eating on, gesturing for me to take the soda cans inside. "Let's go into my room and we can look at the homework he gave over the weekend. It's kind of a lot."

"I think I pretty much get it."

"Well, let's just go over it together."

I could think of no more ways to protest; Katria had netted me with her polite insistence. I could not possibly tell her I had only come to her house to avoid Dorothy.

I followed her to her room and I liked it immediately. Her entire house was small and narrow; the hallways and rooms reminded me of a ship. Even the windows were done in octagons, small and high, looking out into the harbor. Her room had a circular area to one side where her mother had placed a cushioned seat; books lined the shelves and her bed was white and plain as a tablet. Her house did not remind me of Julia's house, yet it was clean and orderly, with light and air moving inside it. Had our house on Raritan Bay been cared for properly, it could have looked a bit like Katria's house.

"My mother always complains how irregular the windows and rooms are in this house," Katria said apologetically. "A ship captain built it and she tells my father all the time that it wasn't meant for family life, that the rooms need to be wider."

"But I like your house," I said sincerely. "It's like one of those old ships with the galley kitchens."

She shrugged. "My mother sells real estate and she sees all these new houses in the developments all the time and she thinks they're better."

"The standard houses," I laughed. "All the houses look the same there."

"I know. But that's what she likes. Houses with basements and laundry rooms. She says the rooms here are too vague, that she could never tell what was meant to be a bedroom and what was meant to be a living room 'cause they're all around the same size."

"Vague rooms. I've never heard that expression before."

"I grew up with that expression." She took some paper from her desk. "Anyway, do you want to start this math? I have graph paper."

I watched as Katria explained terms I could not follow:

tangents and planes, cotangents and proofs, right angles and sines. I nodded and made small, guttural sounds Katria took for comprehension. Then she put her hand on my breast.

The move was not fluid or graceful by any means. We were sitting on her bed, our legs crossed like opium smokers when she closed the book softly, put the paper and pencils to one side, and grinned. I smiled back, worried. I had no idea what she had planned, but her expression was cryptic as cuneiform. Then she lunged, her upper body pinning me between the wall and the bed, her hand reaching to my pear-shaped breast where she squeezed the flesh between her palm and fingers.

"Katria."

She did not move. Her breath was hot and moist on my ear. "Katria," I repeated, "you have to get off me. I don't want this to happen."

"Why not?" she asked in my ear. "Why don't you want this to happen?"

"I just don't." The room suddenly seemed small and closed; the air pressed on me. "I have to go. Dorothy wants everyone there tonight for some kind of dinner she has planned, and I have to catch the bus back."

Katria sat up. She handed me the two papers with the incomprehensible numbers written on them. Her eyes glittered in a dangerously moist way.

"Listen, I'm sorry. I really am. I just…"

"Don't," she said, holding one hand up, palm side out, as though my words were pelting her.

"I'll see you in math on Monday," I called, hurrying down the stairs and into the last few warm minutes of the afternoon. By the time I boarded the bus, chill veined the air and I shivered while walking in the shade of our new street. I wanted only to close the door to my room and figure out what had just happened at Katria's house. I did not want conversation or dinner or anything: just monkish solitude, long and dark and undisturbed, the kind of solitude I had had only back at our house on the bay. I walked quickly down the street, not bothering to notice anything about the other houses or the neighbors.

"It's Andrew," my father said, coming down the driveway. "He's in the hospital."

It took me a few seconds to translate my father, there in front of me, his face white and smooth as the inside of a shell. "The hospital?"

"Yes, Saint Vincent's." He rubbed the palms of his hands together. "They think he'll be all right. Physically, at least."

"Physically? What happened?"

"He had an accident."

Accident. The word sprung out in front of me in bright red electricity. Once again, that code word.

"An accident?"

"Yes, Magda. He's not really talking much. Dorothy and I are going over to see him now."

"She didn't go with him in the ambulance?"

"It didn't happen here. It happened at Jason's house."

Jason. I dimly recollected seeing Jason at the new house one day, a shaggy boy who resembled Kurt Cobain.

"Listen, she's in the car. I'm taking her over now. Magda…"

"Yes?"

"Did you have any idea this was going to happen?"

"The accident?"

My father nodded.

"No, I never would have thought he would try to do anything to hurt himself."

"Good. Dorothy can't seem to stop blaming herself, that she didn't see it coming."

"Most people don't," I assured him. "You better go to her." My father turned away. Cold wind clattered down the street. "Hey Dad, tell Andrew I said hello. I'll go and visit him when he's feeling better."

"I'll do that, Magda. And thanks. We'll call you later."

I waved. They drove past, Dorothy's face small and red in the passenger side. She held up one hand to me in a short, queenly wave, still polite in the face of disaster. I waved back and went inside the house, where a long hiss of silence filled the rooms.

Monday came and went. Katria glanced at me with a weak smile, then did not look at me for the remainder of class. My paper came back, clearly marked with another D. The entire classroom took on a watery feel, slow moving with light filtering through a substance that could not be seen but that made us all seem as if we were bouncing toward one another. I sat watching the teacher mark up a rhombus.

The strange light fell every which way in feathers of warmth and coldness, and I imagined how an astronaut might feel, swimming through space, connected to the ship by only an umbilicus of tubed line.

This was my mother's way of thinking. I also knew that I sat in a tenth grade geometry class that made no sense to me while Katria, a girl I had thought launched from the standard, sat across from me, as far from the standard as I was. In an odd way, it comforted me. There were more of us walking the earth than I might have thought: people who floated more toward the edges of gravity than near its center. Now Katria and I would walk past one another in the hallways, as had happened this morning, to begin the process of unknowing one another. I had heard my mother speak of this once or twice, when we went to the supermarket and she saw a particular woman.

"We're in the process of unknowing one another," my mother had whispered, "so don't even look at Mrs. Alexian."

"But she came to our house that time," I had protested. "And she brought us a cake."

"Unknow the cake," my mother had instructed, "unknow Mrs. Alexian."

I remembered the strange tightening that came over me as my mother and I passed by Mrs. Alexian. I could not imagine what might have occurred between Mrs. Alexian and my mother to create such a chasm, but we never did speak to or look at Mrs. Alexian again. It would be the same with Katria.

Just as the teacher passed out a work page, the fish decided to throw a birthday party for Baby Fish. They drove up to my brain, Mr. Fish with Baby Fish, in a red Jaguar. Mr. Fish had on one of those British caps, at an angle, and he wore World War II Flying Ace sunglasses and an aerial scarf. Baby Fish had on a birthday hat and an enormous lobster bib. Willing them to stop only made Mr. Fish drive faster, all the while grinning at me with his needle teeth. They turned a corner, and there stood Mrs. Fish at a table with a dozen more fish, all the size of Baby Fish, all wearing lobster bibs. Large dinosaur bones cluttered the table. As soon as the twelve small fish saw Baby Fish, they each picked up one bone and began banging one end on the table in a gleeful racket. I had to force my attention to the worksheet.

"Go," I said in a silent shout to the fish.

"Oh, since when are you the social director?" Mrs. Fish said, swimming up to some kind of window in that way she had of bouncing from the left fin to the right. "If I were you, and I guess I am to some degree…anyway, if I were you, I would certainly work on my manners. You're always butting into our business."

"No, actually, you are interrupting me right now. I have to focus on this math and you are in the midst of a birthday party."

"Fish don't have birthdays," she said firmly. "What a ridiculous idea." Then she pulled down a shade on the window.

My father and Dorothy had been away most of the weekend visiting Andrew, who had tried to undo himself with a combination of Jason's mother's sedatives and a wrist-slashing that resulted in little more than scratches a few inches below his thumbs. The phone rang all weekend in the new house, and I let it ring, not wanting to talk to any of Dorothy's relatives or to Jason's family.

Dorothy and my father kept leaving takeout food in the kitchen for me: lo mein and pizzas, small bags of Mexican salads and cut-up fruit in containers. On Tuesday afternoon, Hannah showed up. She stood in the doorway with her winter coat on, despite the day's warmth. I stared at the haired nubbiness of the coat's fabric: it looked as if it had been sewn from goat shag.

"I couldn't get through on the phone," she complained in her goat-coat, "and I was worried about you and your father."

"You forgot to say you're worried about Andrew and Dorothy," I pointed out.

"Well, of course I'm worried about them, we all are, but I am more concerned that you are getting proper food and rest."

"They leave me food on the table," I said with far more malice than I felt, "the way a cat or a dog is left food when its owners go to Reno." I gestured toward the litter of bags and paper containers. "Dorothy wouldn't want dishes."

"This anger won't do you any good," Hannah warned. "It won't change anything."

"What's going to happen with the wedding?" I asked.

"She's moved the date back, Dorothy has. The wedding will be just after Halloween. Andrew needs time in the hospital, and he has to work his way up to day passes." Hannah stepped gingerly into the kitchen, as though she were stepping onto the surface of Venus.

"What happens to me?"

"I'm going to come by after school and stay here with you. I've left my job, so I just have a few odds and ends to take care of before I leave for Ohio." Hannah came into the kitchen and began throwing bags away, wiping the counters, all the while wearing the brown coat with the gray whiskery nubs.

"Do you want me to hang your coat up in the hallway?"

"No, didn't your father tell you? We're taking the bus over to see Andrew. He's ready for visitors. You better bring a sweater; they're predicting frost tonight. Early in the season, but that's just our luck right now."

Hannah and I boarded the bus to St. Vincent's Hospital. Many of the houses we passed had pumpkins on their stoops; leaves clung to the bus windows when the wind blew. An early spatter of stars jeweled the sky. We sat without speaking for a few minutes.

"Gabriel can come to the wedding."

"Who?"

"Gabriel. My son."

"Oh, right. Sorry."

"That's all right. He's coming in through LaGuardia the day before the wedding and he's going to stay with me."

"Oh. Good. For a minute, I didn't..."

"I know. You forgot I had a son. It will take some getting used to."

"Does he want to come to their wedding? I mean, he doesn't know us."

"The wedding is going to be small, you know that. Second weddings are usually pretty small. But he wants to meet you and your father; he wants to see where his mother has lived for most of his life, he wants to meet the people I've spent most of my time with. And a wedding is a nice way to start off. Start over, I guess." Hannah laughed, a nervous, twitchy laugh that I had never before heard.

"Are you nervous?"

"A little. I mean, exactly how does one go about...I mean, you have to realize I'm not exactly the standard-issue mother here."

Standard. I turned my gaze to Hannah. "Who is the standard-issue mother? My mother certainly didn't fit in with most mothers either."

"No, she didn't, but she stayed with you and no one ever doubted how she felt about you."

"They might now."

"What do you mean?"

"Whether or not she felt...she abandoned me," I said softly. "I was not enough to keep her here."

"Oh, no, Magdalena, that just isn't so. You don't understand at all. Your mother...listen, people lose their balance." Then, in a lurch of her arms and upper torso, Hannah hugged me as I sat in my plastic, cupped bus seat. "You must never, never, think that your mother abandoned you. She would never do such a thing."

I blinked. A voice in my head chanted, "This place is temporary, temporary, temporary, temporary as weather." It was not the voice of Mrs. Fish. It was a voice I had never heard before; I wondered if it were my own voice. Of course my mother had abandoned me. How could Hannah say such a thing?

"She would never abandon you, Magdalena, if she had any choice. She lost her balance in many ways, but 'til my dying day I will know that she loved you more than anything, more than anyone in her life. She would have given her life for you. She lost…your mother lost her balance is all."

Her balance.

I waited for Hannah to stop embracing me. When she did, she placed her hand over mine. I turned to look at her. "You can't blame yourself, you can't blame your mother or your father for the way anything turns out. Do you think it's easy for me to forgive myself for leaving Gabriel?" Hannah, who usually spoke in a composed manner, spoke rapidly now, as though she had only seconds to transmit vital information. "The only way I can face myself is to remember, to always remember, that we are fallible beings, that we are prone to error, all of us, whether we are parents or children or friends. It's taken me years to truly believe that, to work up the courage to contact my son, to tell him how at that time I could not raise a child, I could not stay in that place where I saw only wind and blankness, but when I finally and truly accepted that we are all flawed, all of us, that we will always make mistakes, I was able to forgive myself. I would never want Gabriel to stay in a place to care for me if he had the feelings I had when he was an infant. You have to forgive, Magdalena, you have to. You can't hold things inside you forever, right up against your soul in the way you do. You'll only live in torment. I know. I recognize some of your moods. And you can't imagine how much I want you not to be in such a state. You really can't imagine."

I patted Hannah's hand and turned my gaze out the window, stunned by her sudden outpouring. A black sky pressed down on the last lines of blue horizon, and as the rubber lips of the bus door opened, bitter gusts of air gasped through. People boarded the bus with red cheeks, their eyes glittering with cold.

"I hope I've helped you some," Hannah said, speaking again in her regular tone. "That's all I hope."

"You have," I answered. I did not want to end up like her, my life stranded and filled with regret. Only I could not say this to her, to anyone.

"That's all I ever wanted to do," she said, and I could see her pull herself back in, her face regaining its normal vacuity, her eyes growing dull as a doll's. "Is help."

"You have," I said, feeling very, very far away from her.

But not as far away as that day, the day you had to walk in and see your mother as she lay stilled as a mirror, her face looking exactly the same as when she slept. Then you were in the stratosphere of the drift, rocketed into the furthest point. You stood in the hallway watching Hannah come down the hallway toward you, her feet slipping over the cabbage roses on the carpet, her arms held out to you like a receiving angel, like a being who longed to be made of light, but it was Hannah, only Hannah and you stood there, looking at the hooks on the wall, at the jackets hung there, at the suede collars and thick puffs of lining. You stood there looking at the coats and not at Hannah, wondering why there would be coats there in the middle of August with heat rising from the boulevard in woozy vapors.

You wondered all this while Hannah waited for you to come to her, but you could not go to her. Had you gone, she would have interpreted the act as acceptance of her as a mother, and you did not want that. So you stayed far from everyone, from the people speaking to you, from the people touching you, and Hannah kept coming toward you as if she held bowls of light in each hand, coming toward you those three days and never once did she see the skin sliding from your bones, the exposure of your veins, your nerves to the elements, the way your thoughts, your words kited away from you and skidded into the air, allowing fish and fire to enter your dreams, your silence.

Then you went into the room, at the very end, with the priest and the people, sitting in front, you raised your eyes to say an unimaginable goodbye and the coffin was closed. You had never seen your mother there, stilled as a mirror. Yes, your father said, the coffin has been closed the entire time. You had never seen her, yet you remembered the vision of her, floating in a netting of white veil exactly like her summer nightgown, her face allayed as if in sleep.

You feared a connection with her now only slightly more than you wanted one and when you walked out, you looked at the coats on the hooks again and you wondered if these were the garments of the dead, unclaimed and unremembered as you felt.

"We're here," Hannah announced.

We walked out into the night, wind stinging tiny veins in our noses, our hands reddening in the cold. Before we found Andrew's wing, we had to walk through a catacomb of corridors. My father met us at the nurses' station, then escorted us to Andrew's room. Unfamiliar with medical procedures, I had only a vague idea of what to expect: a couple of tubes with clear fluid pulsing through them, charts of vital information attached to the bed, worried faces, images all culled from television. Instead, Andrew sat on a sofa in a room decorated with framed pictures of geese in flight and an oval rug. Dorothy sat next to him. Plants in macramé holders hung from the windows; the bed and dresser were as normal and bland as furniture in a motel.

"Hey," he said to me and Hannah.

"How are you?" I asked.

"I don't know," he answered and we both laughed, a nervous, scattered sound that broke in the air. "They come in every coupla hours and tell me." All the light had left Andrew's face and I thought of the woman I had met on the beach who was looking for Daphne. Her face had reflected no light either.

"I brought you these," Hannah said, removing some oranges and pears from her bag. "They never give you enough fresh fruit in a hospital. And that's the last thing you need, not to have enough fruit."

"Thanks," Andrew said, his face puzzled.

"You know, you're right about that, Hannah," Dorothy said, standing. "The food here isn't so bad, but there's nothing fresh, I can tell you that." We all watched Hannah arranging fruit on paper towels as if it were a magic act we could not tear our gazes from. Finally, Dorothy cleared her throat and said, "Michael, let's you and me and Hannah take a stroll around the halls. I can show you the solarium, the rec room; we can get a cup of coffee in the snack room."

The adults did not look at me as they left, and I understood that this was planned before my arrival.

"I take it they want us to talk alone." I still stood near the room's entrance, unsure of where I should sit.

"Magda, why don't you come in?" Andrew motioned toward a chair. "Your dad didn't mention that to you, about us talking alone?"

"Talking to me is not...you know, a strength of his. Communication."

"Doesn't he work in the fire communications dispatch office?"

"He does, but that's only information for emergencies. I'm never an emergency."

"I was the other day." He moved his knee up and down in a rapid volley of motion.

"So I heard. But again, I heard that since it was an emergency."

Andrew moved his head around as if clearing water from his ears. "I get these weird sensations, like there's pressure in my neck, my ears," he explained. "They said it could be the medicine, different people have different reactions." He opened and closed his mouth quickly. "So your dad isn't the world's best communicator?"

"It's just that I used to talk to my mother a lot more than my father. We kind of got stuck with each other." I looked up to the plants, at the paper cups on the radiator. People shushed by outside in the hallway. "You have no door, do you?"

"They don't want me to hang myself. No shower curtain, no drapes, no cords." Andrew looked down at his hands. "Sorry. I shouldn't be so graphic."

"It's okay. I kind of figured they set the place up for reasons like that." He kept looking at his hands. I cleared my throat. "So, Andrew, what are we supposed to talk about? Did they tell you that?"

"It would be easier for me if you came in and actually sat down. You look like you're getting ready to flee the scene."

"Oh. Sorry." I took a chair across from Andrew. "So what are we supposed to talk about, again?"

"They told me to apologize, so I'm sorry, Magda."

"Okay, but what are you apologizing for?"

He moved his hands so the palms faced upward, and I saw his wrists were bound with gauze and white tape.

"For coming on to you like such a creep. Half the time I was drinking and just…not wildly drunk, but buzzy all the time, not in control."

"I don't recall you being out of control. A little weird, but I wouldn't say out of control."

"My dad was an alcoholic, too," he went on as though he had memorized a script and had to recite it. "Only my mom would never say that. She doesn't drink. Never did. But my father was drunk all the time. *All the time.*"

He paused. "My mother acts all normal, like we're this happy little family, but the truth is my father was drunk so much of the day and night, and she would tell me he was tired or had a headache. One Christmas morning, he crashed right into the tree. All the bulbs, the tinsel, the whole tree came crashing down on him, and he was sitting there with all these needles and tinsel on his head and there were all these broken ornaments around him, and he started laughing. He just kept laughing and my mother looked at me and said, 'Andrew, can you be a dear and find the dustpan?' Then Dad went to bed and my mother and I sat there with this huge turkey between us."

"But you can't blame her for what he did," I offered.

Andrew nodded slowly. "You're right and I don't. I don't blame her for anything, really. It's just that…she's all upset that I told the doctors here about Dad, that he was such a drunk."

"It's all confidential, though," I reminded him.

"I know. I just don't want to end up like him is all."

"No, you don't."

Andrew plucked at the tape on his wrists. "The worst part is, my father was drunk that night he went out in the car, only my mother doesn't want to say that. She goes on and on saying how you never can tell when a mishap is about to befall you, when your number's up, it's just up, like he wasn't drunk and he died in a regular car wreck."

"Yes, I know how that is."

"You do?"

"My mother didn't fall off a pier."

"I figured she didn't as soon as I heard it. So in a way, they both had…"

"Similarities," I said, finishing the sentence for him. "Which probably means each of our surviving parents are fairly similar. Or maybe it doesn't. Who knows? Sometimes I think other people, other parents, would get better in different families, but…forget it," I said. We smiled at one another.

Andrew said nothing, so I went on. "You know, on the way over here, Hannah was telling me how the one thing she's learned in her life is to forgive people, but mostly I think what she meant was she had to forgive herself. I wanted her…I guess, when she was telling me all this, I wanted her to stop talking, but now I sort of see what she means."

"The shrink here thinks I have to talk to you more, that you are part of my problem."

"Me?"

Andrew nodded. "How you came through losing your mother and never did anything out of the ordinary?"

"You don't know that I didn't do anything out of the ordinary."

"The way you are so perfect, with the good grades and listening to your father, never drinking or going out with guys."

"All that may be true, but after my mother died, I didn't go anywhere. I didn't want to be around anyone.

Maybe I would have gone out more, but my best friend just kind of dropped me."

"At least that's normal. At least you didn't go around drinking and trying to feel up anyone you saw. I can't even remember all the stuff I've done."

No, I thought silently, I only set the woods on fire and let fish take up residence in my head. Andrew began crying, quietly, more a leaking than anything else. "You know, Andrew, if it helps, we can start over again. Forget everything that happened in Ocean City, forget the stuff about drinking, forget all that stuff and maybe we can help each other get through the wedding."

"Mom thinks I did this now to prevent the wedding."

"No, you can't prevent this wedding; you only delayed it. Your mother is like a force of nature; her course can be changed, but never stopped."

Just then a nurse came in and handed Andrew a fluted cup to drink from. She smiled at me and I smiled back, uncomfortably aware that the cup containing Andrew's medicine reminded me of Mrs. Fish's hat. I waited until she left, then got up to peer out the door. I saw no sign of my father or his retinue.

"Andrew, there's something you should know. I mean, if you look at me, and you believe too that my mother wanted to die, and I'm okay, you should know that for the first few months after my mother died, I didn't go anywhere. I stayed in bed and read books or I drew, or I just stared into space like I was dead, too."

"But that's sort of normal. My mother and I stayed in, too."

"The only thing was...you see, I didn't feel like it was really me staying alone or getting on the bus to go to school. It was more like I was floating above it all, like when my mother and I used to swim in the shoals, in the shallow part of the bay where you could see right to the bottom. We would wear goggles or masks and float over this world, look down and see the crabs clinging to rocks, the killies darting in and out of weeds, the plants. We saw it all, yet we weren't any part of it." Andrew sat very still as I spoke. "So for the last year or so, I've felt like I've been watching myself, as though I'm part of a world that exists, but not like it did before, when my mother was alive."

"I think I know what you mean. You're not as connected to anything anymore because your mind is so far away."

"I don't really know why, but maybe that's it." A cart rolled by Andrew's room and I waited for the sound of its wheels to stop before continuing. "So I started taking walks in the woods around the neighborhood. Then I began going into the woods and experimenting with leaves, with dried sticks, and small pieces of wood."

"Experimenting?" Andrew's eyes ignited slightly.

"Yeah, seeing how long it took for each one of them to go up in flames."

"With your Dad working in the fire dispatch office you did this?"

"I did. None of it seemed real at first."

"You ever set anything major?"

"Once or twice. Only when I set the fires, it was as though I watched someone else setting the fires, like I was watching it all happen on the floor of the bay."

"Have you told anyone else this?"

A girl about my age walked into the room, her face moon-pale, her eyes open with a startled expression.

"Hey, Patty," Andrew said.

The girl looked at me and turned away. It occurred to me that Andrew went to groups, talked about things, about situations, about me.

"She's scared of everything right now," Andrew said after Patty left.

I smiled.

"So, about the fires—did you tell anyone else?"

"I tried to tell Dad, and he told your mother. She came to talk to me and neither one of them believes I set any fires; they think I'm saying this just to get attention. But if I hadn't stopped setting those fires, I might have ended up here in the next bed."

"But you stopped."

"Yes." I shifted in my chair, considering whether or not to tell Andrew about the fish.

"Do you know why you started going into the woods?"

"It just seemed to happen and I couldn't stop it from happening. At the time, the fires seemed like the right thing to do, like the only thing to do. I didn't make the choice: they just felt…necessary."

"But you never wanted to die."

"Not that I recall, though some days I had to remind myself I was alive. The fires made me feel alive, that I could create things." As I said this sentence, something inside me shifted, grew lighter and more weightless: I could see the perforation in my life between the time after my mother died and now. The divide was clear and separate, night and day with no dusk. I decided not to mention the fish.

"It's strange, Andrew, how we were both doing destructive things and they made us feel better." I sighed. "The problem is, that feeling passes."

He turned to me, his eyes wide and unblinking. "In here, nothing passes."

I had begun visiting Andrew every other day, driven to the hospital by my father and Dorothy. They waited in the lounge while Andrew and I talked for an hour. Then they came in the room. My father and I watched Dorothy fuss over her son, taking clothes from his bureau drawers and folding each article, rearranging his comb and brush on the top.

"Listen, Andrew, I want to ask you one thing about your wrists."

"My wrists." He looked down at the tight bandaging on his wrists. Rain slipped against the windows and the two of us sat in the silvery light, speaking in whispers inside his room.

"What were you thinking when you tried to do that? Were you thinking of anyone, of anything?"

"I don't remember all the details, not clearly. But no. I wasn't thinking of anyone, of any one person or anything like that. I just wanted to be done, to leave."

"And never come back?"

"I just wanted to feel peaceful. That's all I remember. I wanted all the noise and all the light to go. It's like when you want anything to end, that feeling that you'll do anything for it to end, just to end."

"You didn't see anyone's face or think of anyone, not even of your mom?"

"No. I just wanted the noise and the lights to go, to stop."

The noise and the lights. I wondered what my mother thought, at that moment as she sank into the bay. I wondered if she thought of me, if she saw my face or if she saw anyone, wanting only the noise and the lights to end. Like going underwater, I reasoned, reaching over to Andrew. I quietly embraced him before I went to get the adults.

That evening, right before dinner, I secretly took the bus back to my old house and stood on the windy beach, my head turned toward the pier where my mother had ended her life. "We're leaving," I whispered. "I just came to say goodbye if any part of you is still here in this bay. And Mom, I'm sorry. I never thought I would be standing here saying I was sorry to you, but I am. I never recognized anything you went through, but I think I do now. Hannah, of all people, Mom, Hannah…"

My cheeks grew wet and stung in the wind. The beach,

the water, the cattails, for a moment seemed perfectly still, stiller than I had ever remembered seeing them. No birds circled overhead, and the wind stopped for a few seconds as if my mother were answering me.

"Mom, it was Hannah who showed me that not everything is as simple as I once thought. She told me we're all just doing the best we can. And I think she's right: we are. I could never imagine leaving here. Ever. But now I see I have to leave here; I can't stay here with you any longer. I have to go, just like you did. You know I have to go because there's only one way staying here can end. And that's not what anybody wants."

I waited for a few seconds inside the stillness. The wind started again, birds cawed overhead. I turned from the beach, my eyes still stinging.

Mrs. Fish woke me up that night. She was lying in a coffin made of stars, the structure's interior eerily glowing light. She sat up in the coffin, and the long gown she wore rustled like leaves. When I looked closer, I saw her gown was made of fish fins, fins carefully strung together to make one piece of continuous fabric.

"What are you doing in that?" I asked.

She smiled, her needle teeth glowing in the starlight. "You mean in this dress?"

"No, I mean in that coffin."

"Oh, this old thing? I thought I was going to do good-bye, but it looks like I'm doing death. Just death."

"Oh. I see."

"Did I scare you, old Magda-bones?"

"Not too much. Hey, Mrs. Fish, you know what?"

"Surprise me," she said, opening her two fins in a submissive gesture.

"You're moving out."

"Really. Now that *is* news. And who, exactly, Magdalena my darling, do you have in mind to occupy this space?" She drummed her fin on her gown. "I do know a lovely octopus family that's growing a bit restless in Katria's head...or there's that lonesome sea bass who has no one's brain to occupy... nobody's at all..."

"Actually, Mrs. Fish, it's me who's moving. You can stay, but I'm taking you back to the beach in the morning and I'm letting you go."

"I don't think so, Magdalena. I'm here to stay. I'm settin' up shop, baby, I'm settin' up shop."

"It's time," I said firmly.

"You're breaking my heart," Mrs. Fish replied, climbing back inside the casket. "But you're such a liar, Magdalena, that I believe nothing you say, nothing at all. I fully plan to hatch in your brain while you're in college. Can't wait, in fact."

My father and I drove back to our house to meet Linn Pear. I went down to the beach while they spoke in the house. Mrs. Fish had been sitting glumly on an old suitcase, taking out pictures of Mr. Fish and Baby Fish.

"Here you go," I said to her. "Back into the bay with the rest of your friends."

"You know, I never asked to move in here. You were the one who summoned us from the comfort of our watery lives."

"Maybe." The beach was colder than the street had been, so I pulled my hood over my head. "It's just that I don't really believe in you anymore. I'm giving you up. Like a bad habit. That's what Dorothy said about donuts."

"Fine. As long as you understand this is it, this is really it and we don't come back after we've been let go. Ever."

"Gotcha. Hey, Mrs. Fish?"

"Yes?" She stood and carefully slipped the pictures of her husband and child into the suitcase.

"Thanks. You were a great distraction."

"Oh. Like that's something to be proud of. Alice Fish's life's work: distraction for a weirdo girl. Just brilliant. Now if I had helped you pass geometry, that would have been something to write the folks back home about. But a distraction..."

"It is something to be proud of, actually."

"Well, here's to." She moved her tartar cup hat very slightly, opened her mouth all the way so both her upper and lower needle teeth were exposed, then jumped into the air and disappeared.

"Goodbye," I said silently. I waited a few minutes to see if I had succeeded, or if the fish would manifest again. But my mind remained blankly still as marble. I decided to walk over to the shady section of the beach where Spring Robinson had lived with her mother. Only October, but already salt wind bit my cheeks; none of the small scuttling creatures could be seen stirring the sand; the beach had begun closing down in its own subtle way.

As I neared Spring's property, the foul odor rose toward me. The house gave off its fetid, salty smell, as though it had been constructed of fish carcasses. The structure of the house lay exposed to the elements now, one side caved in and the beams exposed and full of rot. Seaweed slogged at the foundation; gulls swaggered on the roof. I could see the water already claiming this house, and I knew that this winter, Spring Robinson's house would probably break apart and fall, element by element, back into the sea.

Even the inside had taken on the translucent quality of water. I walked to the doorway, and it took me several seconds to differentiate between the wall and where the wind had torn holes in the sides of the house; the introduction of the outside into the interior made the house seem like an object beneath the water: it seemed part of a dream, not quite real or connected to the day outside. I touched the counter. None of the items I had seen there were gone, but the cabinets had been taken from the walls. The house was only a skeleton. I stayed in the greenish light for a few minutes, my hand on the counter where she had eaten and spoken with her mother. The greenish light inside that house shone exactly as the light emitting from Mrs. Fish's coffin had. Then I heard her speak.

"Find anything interesting?"

I closed my eyes, but Mrs. Fish did not appear.

"I come here, too." Turning quickly, I saw a woman standing behind me with a camera strapped around her neck. She was around my mother's age, or the age my mother would have been, with windswept blonde hair and ruddy cheeks. Her eyes were soft and gray. But she had surprised me; the scrutiny of her gaze panicked me and I waited for her to turn into an animal, but she did not. She remained a woman standing before me, her face human and stable.

"I don't really come here," I said quickly. "I just remember the girl who used to live here."

"That's interesting. A girl used to live here. I'm doing a

photographic study on old bungalows between Raritan Bay and Sandy Hook before they all disappear. On this one, I put a girl's silhouette, just for my own purposes, sort of this ghostly image." She smiled. "You probably think I'm one of those roving wackos you meet on the beach sometimes. Well, maybe I am." The woman laughed. "I'm Jean Ackers," she said, holding out her hand. "I teach photography at the community college and I just wanted to finish up this theme before the weather gets too cold."

"I'm Maggie Sorrin," I said, taking her hand. "I used to live up the street from this beach. Actually, the house just sold a few days ago and my dad is up there now talking to the real estate agent."

"That must have been fun, as a kid. Having a beach down the street. I would have loved that."

"I liked it."

"I just bought that old bungalow on the beach. It's tiny, but I'm going to use it as a studio, maybe a guest house. Did I tell you I'm going to do a gallery show just before Christmas?"

"No. Where is your show going to be?"

"At the Staten Island Gallery of Art. The show is called 'Bungalows of Raritan'—you like that title?"

"That's a good title." The woman moved over to the window. Jagged teeth of glass held twigs and bits of cattails.

"I think it's perfectly boring, but the gallery owner insists on simplicity in the titles. He says he wants all our creativity in the art." She moved closer to the window. "See that," she said, pointing to the twigs and grass. "Doesn't it remind you of Asian calligraphy, the way those characters always look like branches?" She turned her camera vertically and shot several frames in succession.

"The bungalow you bought," I began, "is it the one right by the marshes with the garden fence?"

"It is. It's the only one on this beach, on most of the beach area around here, that isn't completely dilapidated. One wall is badly damaged by fire, and a good portion of the interior has scorch marks, but the frame and the other three walls are still stable. The owner supported the structure pretty well."

"You bought Chito's house?"

"I think the deed came from somewhere out...Michigan, no Ohio, I think."

"His sister," I murmured. "She must have owned it."

"You can come see it when it's done. I've got contractors coming in a couple of weeks to redo the interior. Your friend Chito wasn't too big on windows I take it."

"He wasn't..."

"I know," she laughed. "I saw those burnt mannequins he had in that garden." Her laugh bounced through the darkness of Spring Robinson's house.

"No one's really sure if he set them on fire or if someone else did, but he was a bit different," I said quietly. "Most of the people who live around here are a bit different."

"Aren't all the interesting ones," the woman said matter-of-factly. "Look at that beam up there." She pointed to the ceiling of the bungalow. "See those carvings, right into the wood?" Standing on a flimsy piece of flooring, she pointed her camera up at the beam. "Just great stuff in these old places. You never see exposed beams like this in the new houses, you know, in these developments they build all around the island. They all look the same, those houses, like there's one or two designs and they make the same house only bigger or smaller, move a few windows around. To me, a house should have some kind of idiosyncrasy, some spirit of the owner. Bungalows do."

I watched her for a few minutes, moving around the house. "You know, I never saw anything in here that I would have thought of as nice," I offered.

"Well, this place, like most of the beach bungalows, is on its way out, but in their day, they had something to offer. I've always been fascinated by water, by the buildings people put by water. Did you ever go to Coney Island?"

"To the amusement park, once or twice," I answered.

"As a kid, I grew up near Coney Island, and I wanted to live in a clam house, in one of those old places where the clammers came in and dumped all their catch and got paid by the pound, one of those stinking, fishy places. My dad took me there once, and I just got hooked on the whole idea of living next to water. We lived in this tiny walk-up in Brooklyn, so maybe that explains it."

"You wanted to live in a clam house?"

"Close to the water. I was a kid. I thought the water was like this magical place, that if I could live there, I would be able to figure stuff out. Then I grew up and moved to Dyker Heights. Not exactly near water."

"But now you have your house by the water."

"I do. And I'll have pictures of all these before they go extinct." She kicked a beam in the center of the room and we both looked at the soft heel of wood that let go from the post. "We should probably get out of here before this place falls down. Maybe," she laughed, "I should change the title of my show to 'Bungalow Death Knell.'"

"Not simple enough for the gallery owner." I smiled.

"Right." She blew on the glass eye of the camera lens.

"I have to get back anyway," I said. "My father is probably wondering where I am."

"Sure. I'm just going to poke around a bit in here, get a few more shots of these beams. Come down when the weather gets nice," she said, "when the place gets restored a little. I'd like to hear more about this Chito."

"Nice meeting you." I turned to leave. Wind knuckled through the gaps and holes in the house, making a forlorn sound. I wondered, briefly, if Mrs. Fish had anything to do with the sound, but I dismissed the thought before an image of her could form in my mind's eye.

"You too. And I mean it, stop by sometime. Tell me about the souls of these people who came to the beach before I did."

"I'm not sure I know much about their souls."

"You probably know more than you think, having grown up here, right by the water, right alongside them."

"Maybe." I looked at the woman for a few seconds before turning to leave. She had to have lived in the standard; otherwise, she would not be a college teacher. And she had longed for the drift, for the random, shaping forces that had been the watery boundaries of my life. She saw beauty in them; she talked about souls the way my mother had. Not many people I knew used the word "souls" so casually.

I walked back to the house the long way, going

through the field I had once set aflame. The ground shimmered with a dry sheen perfect for igniting. A few months past, I had called this sheen "fish-scale perfect." Sometimes the field grass in autumn and spring reflected sun in the same way fish scales do, splintering its colors into hundreds of shades. Leaning down, I touched the long, eviscerated strands, knowing one match would incinerate the field. Instead, I sat down, taking the sea grass between my hands, then letting go to watch the wheaty strands echo back into place. The woods that had held the mattress bordered the field, so I walked into the dusky scent that made the woods seem such a far place from the beach and the field. The mattress was gone, completely. Not a thread or a splinter of its wooden frame could be seen on the floor of the woods, as empty of any hint of human presence as Spring Robinson's house had been.

I could still see the field from the woods. A few husks of cars lay useless and rusting. In the underbrush, rabbits and squirrels skittered. Walking slowly back to our old house, I paused to listen. Where I had once heard only silence, I now heard the motions of animals and plants, a dry scrape of wind stirring the leaves, and the voices of people on the street.

The fish were gone. My mother was gone. Julia was gone. And not one of them would ever return. I turned to look at the woods for the last time, then I stepped out of their ferny, filtered light and walked toward the place where my father waited.

A Chinese family had bought our house. A few days before my father's wedding, the new owner called Linn Pear to tell her we had left boxes in the attic. My father and I went over one afternoon to retrieve them, and the woman met us at the door saying she had just put tea on.

The trees surrounding the house had been cut down. I could see clearly into the house, where light flooded the rooms. I had always thought of our house as dark, its darkness a permanent feature of the dwelling.

"It's so much brighter," I commented.

"I cut the trees down," Mrs. Mei said. "That's all it needed."

So she had gone outside and with a few swings of an ax, changed both the interior and the exterior of the house. I mentioned this to her, saying I had always thought of our house's dimness as an unalterable characteristic, along with its smallness and its age.

"You think I am a wizard?" she said, coming outside. The day was cold and bright.

"It's just...so different," I said, noticing too that she had trimmed back my mother's wisteria to nubs.

"Every owner brings part of themself to the home they inhabit. Come in when you are ready. Take your things." My father and I could see the boxes waiting by the door of the sun porch. He stood near the garden my mother had planted in order to catch fairies.

"You remember when she did that?" I asked.

"She did it for you," he said. "She did it because you liked to go on fairy hunts around the yard."

"I don't remember that it was for me."

"Most of what she did was for you."

"Let's go inside," I suggested, my eyes moistening. "Mrs. Mei just went in."

She put out tea and small cookies that tasted of oranges. Her furniture was low to the ground and simple; sheer panels hung from the windows, paintings of fish and conch shells laddered the walls in size order. I had never thought our house capable of such order.

"It's good that we met," my father said. "We lived here for so long, all of Magda's life."

"We will take good care of the house," Mrs. Mei told us. Then she turned to me. "I am going to have a baby in the spring."

"That's wonderful," my father said. "It's a great place for a kid to grow up, with the beach and all."

The beach. He says this calmly, quietly, as though he did not take her there right after the hospital and you walked behind them, scared to breathe. If your mother heard you, she would turn and look at you with those eyes she had worn ever since returning from the hospital, eyes that you had seen before only on a fluke, lying dead in the sun, the eyes still connected to life, but only by their openness, by the fact that they still had moisture.

And your lungs ached. They began to balloon, swell until finally you exhaled and your mother turned to look that day in early summer. Sailboats behind her, the day azure with islands of cloud floating behind her and you saw her face, heard her whisper, "Don't you see? This is where I belong now." Only it was her eyes whispering, not her mouth, and she did not speak in words.

"Yes, we like it, we like the way you can smell the fragrance of the ocean here. We've heard they are planning to build some new houses right on the beach, so we feel grateful that we got this place so close to the water."

"Get a boat," my father advised, and I looked at him. My mother and I had always wanted a motorized craft. Repeatedly, my father protested, saying boats created too much work, took too much time. "It's the one thing I regret about having lived so close to the water. We never had a boat; we just had this little dinghy…"

"Well, let's get the baby first," Mrs. Mei said softly, "then we'll take on a boat. But you are right. It only makes sense."

"Yes. Thank you again for telling us about the boxes." My father stood up. We shook hands and Mrs. Mei apologized that her husband was not able to meet us, but he worked on Wall Street and was rarely home during the day. We put the boxes in the car and drove back to the new house, waving to Mrs. Mei until we could no longer see her or any part of the house.

"What's in those boxes anyway?" my father asked.

"I have no idea." Lifting the flap of the box beneath my feet, I saw old magazines, a woman with viciously styled hair and a flippy little sweater. She had a pink-painted mouth that reminded me of the way Mrs. Fish had worn her lipstick.

"Probably something your mother thought was important. I've never seen those boxes before."

"Looks like magazines, old ones."

He nodded. "That was decent of Mrs. Mei to call us though."

"Yup."

He turned off the boulevard and up Julia's street. I knew the route was a shortcut, and I was safely ensconced in a car, but still, I did not want to see Julia or any of her family.

As we neared her house, my heart began to pound. Julia's house looked older than I remembered, its shingles tattered on the corners, the yard full of sharp-looking leaves, the shutters covered with a milky spatter. Darkness had begun gathering in the crotches of trees so the branches looked enchanted, as though they had been spun with webs. Marigold light combed from the windows, and I could see inside to the families sitting on sofas, televisions on, people moving inside kitchens and reading newspapers. I lived in a house like this too now. I thought of going up to Julia's door and ringing the doorbell, telling her mother that I lived in the same world now that they did. Only I knew what she would say: I would never belong to that world.

Holding my breath, I glanced at the windows of Julia's house. Her mother had already pulled the shades down; curtains were firmly together at the bedroom windows. Their position reminded me of a pursed mouth in front of clenched teeth. Nothing moved in Julia's yard or house. Her house passed and when I turned, I could no longer see even the outline of its roof. Craning my head around,

I could not see any hint of her street, as though the entire neighborhood had dissolved. I saw only the boulevard with its long seam of separation.

"That bra I bought you, Magda, the one that didn't fit, did you get a chance to return it yet? I would hate to see you look so bosomy in the church," Dorothy explained. "It's my fault, really, though I didn't think the dress would emphasize on the top the way it does."

I was learning Dorothy's language: by saying the fullness of my breasts was her fault, she meant it was my fault.

"I'll take it back right now," I offered.

I took the bus to the mall that afternoon. It was Saturday; in one week, they would be married. Taking a seat in the back of the bus, I gazed out the window at the boulevard. The air already spun early winter tones of gray and brown; the sky was obscured in scrapes of cloud. We traveled past my old street and when I glanced down, I saw the water at the bottom of the road, gunmetal and choppy, the way it had always looked in the cold months. Then the woman I had met months ago, the one who applied makeup to the dead, boarded.

I had forgotten about her, and when I saw her again a mild flash of panic wheeled through my abdomen. But she had not forgotten me; I sat perfectly still while she made her slow, deliberate way toward me, a boat coming to dock. She looked like a ghost, like a person haunted, with her hair now dyed a brash shade of red and her flesh white, her eyes heavily made up with kohl liner and shadow. She had a look similar to a Japanese Kabuki performer.

Her sag-and-crease style had not changed, only now she held several pocketbooks, three or four in her hands, and she had on multiple watches. My head was averted from her gaze as she settled in next to me. I did not turn to greet her.

Silently, I cursed Dorothy for choosing the Sears store on the other side of the island; my stop was not for another twenty minutes.

For a few minutes, she said nothing. I feigned absorption in the cars to the left of the bus.

Then she spoke softly. "I never forget a face."

The words chilled me and I turned to face her.

"No one forgets me neither," she continued, "and I'm always on these buses. You've been busy doing other things. No more buses for you."

"Yes," I agreed. I sat between the window and the woman's bags; there was no escape until my stop. "I've been busy."

"You're different, now," she said. "Not as easy to see."

"I beg your pardon."

"I read people," she explained. "Read them like some people read books. I know their stories from their faces. And you aren't as open as you were…it was a few months ago, I first saw you. You have to understand, people are my passion, my hobby, so I don't forget faces or their stories."

She pulled a sketchbook from her bag. "See this?" I nodded. "These are some of the more interesting people who ride the Staten Island buses. Go ahead, take it, have a look."

The faces were spectral, without lines or edges, just shadings and areas of light, and each of them had a floating quality as if the portraits had been rendered in bad light, the kind of light that would surround a city after a bombing. I stopped at one sketch. The girl's face looked similar to mine, but I did not recognize it as my own.

"You paused," the woman said. "Now, you knew that was your face, didn't you?"

"I thought…maybe…" I looked dead in the depiction, as though I had died and my face were floating underwater.

"You don't recognize yourself because I put a soul in your face. I remembered you because you were one of the few young people I've seen with an undissolved soul right there by you. Strangest thing. The soul was right there, plain as day."

"You told me that." Another passenger in front of us turned his head around sharply to look at the woman. Then the man looked at me.

I handed her back the sketchbook.

"I would draw you differently now."

"Do you think so?"

"Absolutely. You're more solid. I should have told you back then that you would become more solid, but you would never have believed me. You thought you would be water forever. You're starting to get the knowledge."

"The knowledge?"

"Yes. But you're just beginning to get it. I can tell you things now that I couldn't tell you then. You can't talk to someone who is sitting there with an undissolved soul right next to her."

"No. I wouldn't think so." I smiled. "So now the soul is gone?"

"I didn't say that. You've absorbed it."

I nodded. I understood what she meant, but I couldn't explain how I understood it.

The woman stood up and took a seat in the middle of the bus. As I was getting off, I walked past her. She had closed her eyes. "Bye," I called.

"Goodbye," she called without opening her eyes, and for a moment I had the urge to touch her, to pat her hand before I left. I knew I would never see her again.

Whatever work she had with me was done.

My father put the boxes Mrs. Mei had recovered from the attic into my room. The message was clear: he wanted nothing from our house on Raritan Bay. The separation between the two halves of his life would be clean and uncluttered; he did not want merging of any sort. I would be the caretaker of remnants from his first marriage, the curator of my mother's world. The first box contained magazines and a few photographs of my parents when they were just married. The photos had yellowed and the faces in them, although they were clearly my parents, had the same haunted and murky qualities about them that the bus woman's portraits had. This place, this time where my parents had abided had passed. I put the pictures in my desk and lifted the boxes outside my door to take to the garage later. As I moved the last box, one slim packet fell.

At first, I assumed the crenelated envelope would be filled with old letters or receipts, but when I opened the flap, several drawings of an infant fell out, drifting soundlessly to the ground. I knew at once these were my mother's drawings; she had a distinctive style of feathery strokes. The infant's face was strikingly similar to my own baby pictures; in fact, at first glance I thought these might be sketches she had done of me in my sleep. But the eyebrows were different, the chin larger, and my mother would have placed any drawings she had done of me into my baby book. I had the sense these portraits were culled from memory; they had to be drawings my mother had done of my brother. I put the drawings in with Brian Michael's birth and death certificates, in the bottom of my desk drawer where I had begun to gather all the things I would take with me when I moved. Mrs. Mei had found the boxes for that reason; the memory of my brother was meant to stay with me.

The morning of the wedding, frost sparked the ground and a thin enamel of ice ferned the windows. I sat up and looked around, jumping at the sight of a strange woman coming toward me.

Then I realized that Dorothy had hung my dress carefully over the door. It was the swagger of the dress, the flounce and flash of the fish-scale material, that had made the material seem animated. A pair of matching pumps waited beneath the dress. Voices filtered up the stairs where only Dorothy should be, and then I remembered.

Andrew had come home this morning with his day pass. I went downstairs to meet him, and he looked as disembodied as the dress and shoes had—he stood there, in his mother's kitchen, thinner and shakier, an outline of himself. I had seen him only days before, but he looked like a different person that morning, a deflated, subdued version of his former self, as though the hospital had pressed all the air out of him, flattening him until he had the dimension of shadow. It must have been the setting: Andrew had lost weight in the hospital, but the change was not noticeable until he stood in his mother's kitchen again.

"Hey," I said, "how have you been?"

"I'm better." He smiled. "I have to go back to the hospital tonight."

"But you're here," Dorothy said, turning from the stove. "You're here, and that's the important part." She placed an enormous stack of waffles in front of her son as though she could feed him back to happiness.

"Will you be able to come to the restaurant?" I asked. The reception was going to be a dinner party at Schroeder's, a crystal-and-linen-tablecloth place not far from the church.

"So long as your dad takes me back before eight o'clock."

He reached for a waffle. "Not exactly what he wants to do on his wedding night."

"I'm sure he doesn't mind," I assured him. "He's just happy you can make it."

Dorothy turned away from us to wipe out the empty sink. "The trick to second marriages, in my opinion," she began, "is that people come as a package deal. You have to know what you're getting into, and we are both going into this with our eyes wide open." I looked at Dorothy, trying to see her face. She did not look up from the sink, but I knew she meant I was as much trouble as Andrew. "But that decision is past us now, long past us in fact, and we are just happy that our family, all the members of our family, can be here."

She said this last sentence briskly, a yellow sentence rinsing out the gray tones of her "package deal" comment. She turned to me. "We have to be at the church before one o'clock, and we have to be completely done, hair, makeup, the whole thing."

"I'll get ready now," I told her.

"Take these waffles with you," Dorothy called, extending a platter of her waffles. "The last thing we need is for you to faint dead away at the wedding. The last thing…"

"Thanks. I'll eat these upstairs." I patted Andrew's shoulder on my way out.

"He's a little thin," Dorothy said, noticing my brief touch to her son's shoulder. "But that's easy enough to fix."

"Yes, but otherwise he looks great."

"You think?"

"I think." I did not want to tell her that he had the same cast to his eyes that my mother's eyes once held, that bleakness all lost people have, as though they are trying to remember the details and the routine of the ordinary life they once had, trying to find the familiar path.

But Andrew would be all right, I thought, turning to see his mother bringing him orange juice. He had her, and he had this house so immune to mood and so far from the changeable spirits of wind and water. And he was young.

"Let me know if you need anything," Dorothy called to me up the stairs.

But of course I needed nothing. Dorothy had left a new pair of pantyhose on my bureau and a demure band of flowers that matched the dress. I sat in front of the vanity, pinning my hair into a reluctant chignon and applying eye shadow. When I was done, the result was startling: I looked like one of the early photographs of my mother I had found in the box.

Even my father, when he came into my room, stopped his hurry to stare at me.

"I know," I said, turning to him. "Mom's back."

"I never noticed before how strongly you resemble her."

He never noticed.

"We better go," I said, seeing Dorothy come up behind him. But he did not hear her.

"I really never..." My father had not stopped gazing at me, and in that moment, I knew in that moment that my father still loved my mother. Regardless of how impossible a wife she may have been, he still loved her. Poor Dorothy was the default wife, the wife he would stay with in his declining years, as he slowed down, as his passion ebbed, as things mattered less.

"Dad," I interrupted, "are you breaking the rule by seeing the bride?"

I complimented Dorothy on her dress, a spangled pale mauve with fringe on the hem that brought flappers and thigh flasks to mind. She had her hair done up again like the wintry North Atlantic, and when my father looked at her his face went through a series of slow contortions, as though he had briefly lost his way and could not figure out who this heavily sequined, swirling woman was or why she stood before him beaming like a moveable, mauve lighthouse. I could see that after thinking of my mother, Dorothy, even doing her best in the cosmetic department, paled. "We should probably get going," Dorothy suggested.

"Yes, yes, we should," my father agreed. Then he held his arm out, still wearing a baffled expression. I wanted to tell him, there is no going back now, this is an irretrievable process. But he seemed to get his bearings as we drove to the church.

I sat in the back of the car with Andrew. All the way over, the fish kept peering around the corners of my brain, tiptoeing in the space behind my eyes. I ignored them.

"We're not going to stay," they said chorally. "We just want one final visit. A tiny peekaboo then a so-long kind of chat, that's all." Both of them were dressed in evening wear, Mrs. Fish in a strappy glimmer of a slip dress, Mr. Fish in a tuxedo with a derby.

"I would have thought, since we've been so good about staying away," Mrs. Fish said softly. "I mean, an invitation to the wedding would have been nice. After all this time. I told Preston, any day now, she'll come down to the beach and summon us to the wedding. But did you come? How long were we supposed to wait? I mean, exactly how long, my old Magda-bones?"

"I never had to go to the beach to get you before," I said silently.

"It would have been nice," Mr. Fish said. "That's all Alice is saying. By the way, Magda, sweetheart, you'll be happy to know we've patched things up. That's why we thought a wedding might be an appropriate note to end this quibble on. So, if you don't mind, for old time's sake, we'd like to attend the wedding with you."

"We already said goodbye. Seriously, go. You have no place here."

"Just a peek-a-boo at the wedding. We've been with you for so long." Mrs. Fish put her arm around Mr. Fish. "And we've put up with Dorothy just as much as you have. Imagine what she would say about us. So just the tiniest of peek-a-boos, old Magda-bones."

"You can watch," I agreed, "but I have an idea. Why don't you watch from Dorothy's mind?"

"We could never get in there," Mr. Fish laughed.

Mrs. Fish rolled her eyes. "Are you kidding? Her brain is an absolute cube, impossible to swim into, way scarier than the channel."

"Don't mind us," Mr. Fish said politely. "In fact, we'll be quiet as dolls. In fact, we were hoping you could just call us Barbie and Ken. Okay? We won't be any trouble, honestly."

"After all this time," Mrs. Fish said, coming closer into my vision. "After all this time, you would think old Magda-bones would treat us like family." She batted her eyelashes, which were long and false and had a metallic glitter. "It's not like you have such a huge family that you don't have room for three more, you know. And it's not like we require visits or gifts or any of that. We just want to be with you. And we have all the rules, remember that. We have the rules. Remember that, Magda. We hold all the rules."

"I don't believe you do have the rules," I said to Mrs. Fish. "In fact, I don't believe there is any book of rules."

"Oh, that doesn't matter now, anyway," Mrs. Fish said sweetly, glossing over her lack of any hold on me. "It's just that we've grown so attached."

"Yes, Magda, we have grown so fond of you. Why, Baby Fish was just saying the other day that you seem like an aunt to him."

"Only I happen to be human, is all," I replied. "And real. That's another detail. I might miss you guys too, but for right now, I want you to watch this." I closed my eyes for a moment and pulled down a shade on my brain, one that I installed on the spot. "You two stay back there. Not another word."

"Oh, just one last visit," they said again.

"You can peek from behind the curtain," I told them softly. "Peek all you want. But no talking and no more appearances in my brain. Goodbye." I made the shade disappear and looked out the window. I saw Hannah standing on the steps with Gabriel, a dark-haired boy with Hannah's mouth, tall and broad-shouldered.

We exchanged names with Gabriel and embraced.

"Congratulations," Gabriel said to me. "You must be excited about your father's wedding."

"Yes," I said just as Mrs. Fish flashed in front of my eyes, dressed in a wedding dress, translucent orchids trailing from her fins. I willed her away and she vanished. "I am excited for him. But I'm even more excited about meeting a brand new cousin."

Gabriel smiled, then flushed. "It's like a whole new family for me. It's sort of neat." He had the same facial expressions as Hannah, who stood next to him the whole time, her eyes trained on her son; clearly, Hannah never intended to lose this child again.

"You should be very proud," I said to Hannah.

"It's like being given a new life," she said, her eyes open very wide, her mouth softening into a bow-shape. "It's like living an epiphany. I always read about epiphanies," she said rapidly, "and I envied the people who had them. I thought they had better souls than me, that they were more sincere. Epiphanies are gifts, sudden, unexpected gifts."

"That's great," I said. Gabriel dusted phantom lint from his shoulder. "Maybe we should go inside."

"Ready?" Hannah said to Gabriel. They linked arms, and I followed behind them. In the long silence of the church, my father's brother, Paul, stood next to me with his wife, a dainty, nervous woman with a thin stem-like body and a dress scalloped so sharply at the bottom that she bore a remarkable likeness to an inverted tulip.

"We're going to be visiting more, Adele and I," Uncle Paul said, cupping me on the cheek. "It's been too long. The last time I saw you, you were a mite. Now look at you, the picture of your mother, my God...well, it is so good to see you."

Andrew stood on the other side of me during the ceremony. He seemed to be having a difficult time focusing on the words our parents were exchanging. We watched my father put the ring on Dorothy's finger, we watched the short dry brush of embarrassed kiss, we heard the organ bloom, bells chiming the steeple, then we walked back outside into the brisk sun of the day as though nothing had changed.

"That seemed fast," I whispered to Andrew as my father drove in the front and Dorothy fussed with her hair in the mirror. Uncle Paul and his wife, Hannah and Gabriel followed us in another car.

"Second wedding, hardly any guests. They go faster."

"Um. Nothing seems different now. That's the only thing."

"I never thought anything would," he replied. "What would be different?"

I shrugged my shoulders: I could not name what would be different, but I had hoped for some kind of mystical transformation—Dorothy's face to soften or my father's words to be more exacting, but everything remained exactly as it had been left: the car still had a vaguely medicinal odor from Dorothy's hair spray, the wind still carried chill, Andrew still looked bony and scared.

"Now your father can stay with us in the new house," Andrew said. "Even at night, but that's all that has changed, really."

"I guess. So you don't believe in borders between the married and the unmarried, that they are different states?"

"No. I don't believe in borders at all really. I think

people just go along pretty much in life and try to keep from screwing up too much. But that's just me."

I smiled at Andrew. He had a point.

"Right now I just want to get through this," Andrew said, gesturing to the restaurant. I followed his gaze as we drove into the crescent-shaped parking lot of the restaurant. In the front, fountains ordered water into spirals and plumes; statues, each of them cherubic and muscular enough to pass for the children of Mount Olympus, spewed water from their pursed lips. A few of the statues had wings.

"I want to get through this without getting my mother all upset," Andrew said as we got out of the car. "I don't want to say anything that gets her mad or upset, and I don't want to act foolish in any way. That's all I hope for."

We walked inside, where the same grandiose motif continued. A gigantic chandelier mushroomed from the vaulted ceiling of the lobby, and the ceiling had taken its artistic direction from the Sistine Chapel. A pinch of a man appeared and without smiling or speaking, led us into a room that was done in dusty gold tones. Our table was long and elegant, the chairs richly padded. Hannah sat to one side of me. "This isn't Peggy Noonan's," I said.

"I'll say. I feel like the Duchess of Devonshire in this chair."

I liked her then, her attempt at lipstick, her attempt at a joke. I liked the faint hint of powder that clung to her pale cheeks. She was trying. I could see how she kept her eyes on her son, how she watched the silently nervous boy with such admiration. Andrew was probably right: there were no borders, people just tried.

"Would you like an appetizer?"

I looked up to see a boy around my own age holding a pad. He had soft brown eyes and the roundly perfect face of a Medieval saint.

"What would you suggest?" I asked, wondering where I had ever heard that phrase. I felt a bit like I had heard it from a swashbuckling character in one of Hannah's old movies.

"The braised endive is a favorite here." He smiled. I saw him looking at the grapefruit-sized poufs on my shoulders.

"Oh. Now what would Heidi have?" I said in a low voice.

"That dress," the boy said quickly.

"Yes, I know." I looked around the table, but no one was paying any attention to us. "This dress. I'll have something Alpine."

"Fine. But promise not to yodel."

"A salad might be nice," I said. "No goat cheese though. You understand."

"Yes, goats are your peers, more or less."

"That's right. Just a green salad, thank you."

He moved on to Andrew and I watched him. He met my eyes. I knew I would see the boy again before the dinner was over, I knew I would see him outside of this restaurant. The thought made my heart beat rapidly.

"Is everything all right, Magda?" Dorothy called over. "She looks a little flushed, don't you think?"

This question caused every adult at the table to gaze into my face as though I were an entrée.

"I'm fine," I protested. "Just…hungry."

"Ahh," I heard collectively, then the conversations around me resumed in their separate spheres.

Picking up my water glass, I knew I no longer believed in borders, or at least not as I once had. The standard and the drift were not actual places. I had given them names, separated them in my mind, but they were not real or habitable. I would never be like Julia, never be like Dorothy, no matter what I did, no matter what knowledge I was granted.

Watching Dorothy lean over to my father's brother, a glazed, spurious expression on her face, I thought of conversations I had had with Julia, how she would look at me and not listen, but she would never reveal her preoccupation, not even when I asked her directly if she was thinking about something else.

"I'm listening," she would protest, "this is how I look when I listen."

I learned to immediately sense when Julia was drifting off and I would shorten my conversation. Dorothy was behaving in the same way now, a practitioner of the art of sitting in front of someone and pretending to care about what was being said, but actually drifting away into a different tide. I had given people who practiced that behavior a name: I called them placebo people, people who sat in front of you, real as a chair, but whose souls were not actually present.

My mother was the opposite of a placebo person. She took you inside her soul. Perhaps she did not show me how to iron a blouse or how to make soup, did not mop the floor often enough, and never gave me vitamins or worried about matters like bedtimes or age-appropriate films or conversation, but she had shown me how to listen to people, how to see what people meant even when they could not say what they meant. She would have wanted me to find enlargement inside loss. Even inside the most unimaginable of losses, she would want me to find enlargement in the diminishment. She had shown me how these two could be connected. That is what I needed to remember: what she had shown me, not what she had not shown me.

Once we had watched a gold coin at the bottom of a shallow pool in the bay. It was low tide and we were examining the ocean floor. Her intent was to find a clam moving; she said there was a slow grace and beauty to clams that no one respected. But, of course, it being my mother, we were enchanted by several other creatures and rocks that same morning. Then I called her over, convinced I had found pirates' gold. For a few moments we watched the solid coin flash from beneath the water, the sun hitting the golden sphere as though it were made entirely of light, spirit beneath a flesh of water. As wind shifted the water, the coin took on fluid magnitudes: we could not tell if the coin was huge or tiny, if it was firmly embedded in the sand or if it rested on its surface.

"Is it in the sand or not?" I had finally asked her, after she pointed out to me how the water and the wind changed the way it looked.

"It's both," she had answered. "Since we can't be certain."

"Is it pirates' gold?"

"It may have been, but now it belongs to the ocean."

We left the coin for someone else to find, though I did not want to leave it there.

"You should be happy enough to have found it. Think

how many people walk through life never once spotting pirates' treasure." My mother smiled at me and shook her head. "A gold coin is a brief moment," she told me. "The pleasure is in finding it, not in keeping it."

I left, though reluctantly, unconvinced of my mother's philosophy. Many times during low tide I returned to that spot, to see if someone had found the coin or if it was still there. But I never saw the coin again. Tides had captured it, moving it far out to sea. Even if I had found the coin again, the place I inhabited on that day with my mother was now gone; any pleasure in finding the coin would never be as great.

I had known my mother. I had been entwined with her for years. Now that she was gone I understood that as we inhabit a place, we are leaving it at the same time. I could hear her voice whispering the words, how we are always in motion, how we are constantly leaving and entering at the same time, how life has no map or borders; that the best knowledge is learning how to translate the dream of water onto land. And I heard these sentences in my mother's voice, not in the voice of Mrs. Fish or any other imagining.

It was time for me to leave this place of silence and aloneness as well. I did not know what I would find, but I knew my mother had given me the tools to understand what is not always spoken or obvious. And because she did, I had an advantage: I could go on. And I would go on; I saw that now.

She had given me all that I needed.

About the Author

Anne Spollen is the mother of three children. Her fiction and poetry have appeared in numerous anthologies and journals and have been nominated for the Pushcart Prize. *The Shape of Water* is her first novel for teenagers. It began as a short story in *Orchid: A Literary Review*.